DARKEST ENGLAND

Christopher Hope was born in Johannesburg in 1944. He is
the author of nine novels and one collection of short stories, including *Kruger's Alp*, which won the Whitbread
Prize for Fiction, *Serenity House*, which was shortlisted for
the 1992 Booker Prize, and *My Mother's Lovers*, published
by Atlantic Books in 2006 to great acclaim. He is also a poet
and playwright and author of the celebrated memoir
White Boy Running.

DARKEST ENGLAND

Christopher Hope

Atlantic Books
LONDON

First published in Great Britain in 1996 by Macmillan Publishers Ltd.

This paperback edition published in Great Britain in 2009 by Atlantic Books, an imprint of Grove Atlantic Ltd.

9 8 7 6 5 4 3 2 1

A CIP catalogue record for this book is available from the British Library.

ISBN: 978 1 84887 165 6

Printed in Great Britain by Clays Ltd, St Ives plc

Atlantic Books
An imprint of Grove Atlantic Ltd
Ormond House
26–27 Boswell Street
London WC1N 3JZ

www.atlantic-books.co.uk

For Ingrid

Acknowledgements

In seeking to understand better the traditions and culture of the Khoisan people, so insistently recalled in the notebooks of David Mungo Booi, I learnt a great deal from Alan Barnard's elegant study: *Hunters and Herders of Southern Africa*, Cambridge 1992.

I am grateful to Cambridge University Press for permission to reproduce Alan Barnard's explanation of the five basic click sounds found in Khoisan languages (see page 282).

An account of my discovery of the English notebooks of David Mungo Booi first appeared in the *Daily Telegraph* in October 1994.

The fragment of verse on page 166, translated from the original /Xam by Stephen Watson, is reproduced with the permission of the author.

Remember,
we are dealing with barbarians . . .

Tacitus (*writing about the first Britons*)

Foreword

I found them camped for the night somewhere between the little towns of Lutherburg and Zwingli. Pieces of corrugated iron propped against their cart made a night shelter. A couple of donkeys gnawed at the scrubby plants on the roadside verge. The wine was going around the fire in a silvery plastic sack, shaped rather like a hot-water bottle with a teat; five litres of rough white, known as a 'five-man-can', an udder of intoxication. Theirs was a solitary light on the dusty road that arrows between somewhere and nowhere in the immense darkness of the desert.

Although it was only about seven in the evening, the temperature was already below freezing, and falling swiftly. Even in autumn, on the high plains of the Great Karoo, nights can kill. The moon had barely risen and the stars were yet to show their blazing fury. The Southern Cross hung in the sky with a heavy, established look; important but a little silly, like a Boer among his minions.

The nomads of the Karoo, in the far Northern Cape, do not drink to forget. In order to forget you must have something to remember. They drink to dream. So when the father of the family, Old Adam Blitzerlik, tossed something in a dangerous arc through the flames I knew as it landed beside me, with the smell of scorched string, that he was at the cross-over point where one dream ends and another waits to begin.

I had received their message on election day, over at the Hunter's Arms in Lutherburg. The hotel was unusually packed. Trouble was expected, shoot-outs, sabotage. A dozen cops, drawn from distant stations, crowded the dining-room in hourly relays and munched through huge T-bone steaks before buckling on their weapons and setting off to guard the polling booths, and to patrol the town for bombs.

The hotel bar was thick with election officials, foreign monitors and United Nations observers, in the persons of Jean-Paul from Geneva and Matthias from Vienna. They put on their baseball caps when we got news of gunplay among the white extremists boycotting the election. When we had bomb threats they pulled on their loose blue waist-coats and walked up and down in front of the hotel: showing the flag.

Clara, the owner of the Hunter's Arms, was proud of the UN presence. 'Those guys phone Geneva,' she said. 'I feel I'm back in the world.'

To celebrate she went out and bought a pair of blue bell-bottomed trousers, a gold blouse and a hairpiece that she wore on top of her thinning blonde curls in a towering beehive. She put in a formal request to Jean-Paul and Matthias to declare the Hunter's Arms a UN safe haven. The UN promised to consider its position.

The message that the Blitzerliks wanted to see me came to Clara in the way of messages in those parts. Someone turned up in the backyard of the Hunter's Arms, stared at the sky, offered the usual compliments regarding her health, expressed the hope that hunting would be good in the springbuck season, and then abruptly told her that the travelling family had something 'to give the Englishman'.

Clara rolled her eyes and laughed in her wild barking way when she relayed the message. The Blitzerlik family had so few possessions that everything they owned was strapped to the back of their cart, pulled by two emaciated donkeys. A tin kettle, a black three-legged pot and a 'roaster', an iron grill for cooking over the fire. The Blitzerliks were not in the giving business, said Clara. They were the sorts of people you gave things to. And when you did, they boozed it away. She had watched the nomads straggling into town to vote for the first time in their lives and it made her heart bleed: 'What must they *think*? For crying in a bucket!'

Around the campfire I found Old Adam Blitzerlik, no more than thirty, too young to warrant his venerable title; his wife, Mina, looked about fifteen, and she fed the fire with handfuls of wiry ashbush. Ma and Pa Blitzerlik, Adam's parents, drew heavily on their pipes, their tiny, wrinkled, walnut faces wrapped in heavy woollen scarves. Old Adam rolled a cigarette from a scrap of newspaper and struck a match to the bitter, black tobacco. The winebag went around again, accompanied by a single cup. Each measure judged precisely. Half a cup, left to right around the circle, taken at a gulp, and passed on. Stringing a necklace of cheap dreams.

Now Grandfather Blitzerlik invited me to examine the gift. And Mina fed the fire with candlebush, which made it flare as brightly as if she had doused it with paraffin. I saw the parcel was wrapped in thick brown paper, tied with coarse string, which showed what at first I thought was sealing wax on the knots. Butcher's paper, I realized later. The sealing wax was, in fact, dried blood. The parcel was ripped in places where Old Adam had helped himself to cigarette paper. Through the holes I glimpsed the red-and-black bindings of two notebooks. Cheap and serviceable notebooks you will find at any stationer's.

Grandfather Blitzerlik, after shaking his pipe to clear the stem and spitting into the fire, began to speak in his melodious Afrikaans. I was from England, and so I would understand his story. It did not strike him as odd that he was speaking Afrikaans to an Englishman. The English were magical beings, capable of anything. Long ago had they not come to the Karoo, at the behest of their Queen, the 'Old Auntie with Diamonds in Her Hair'? And had not her soldiers, in their red dresses, 'kicked the Boer to Kingdom Come?' Such was the power of the Empire.

Well, then, some years ago a white farmer had found a child in the scorched ruins of a camp. A common enough accident; a family had slept too close to their fire one cold night, and only the little boy survived. Poor thing! The farmer, an Englishman from the Zwingli district, had taken the boy home and raised him to read and write and speak English, the only person within a hundred miles to possess such talents. His name was Booi – David Booi.

It happened, a few years later, that the travelling people of the Karoo fell on hard times. There were beatings, several murders, hunger and hardship; everyone was suffering badly – 'crying' – at the hands of the farmers. So they had come up with a plan. Money had been collected among sheep-shearers and jackal-hunters and fence-builders. It had been decided to send David Booi to England, to ask the Queen to send the soldiers in red dresses back again to kick the Boer to Kingdom Come! Was it not a very good plan?

A good plan, I said. But what had become of their messenger?

Opinions differed. Old Adam declared firmly that the English Queen had liked David Booi so much, she had begged him to stay in England. No, his father piped up, she had given him a thousand sheep and he lived like a lord. Wrong, said Mina, he was dead. He had perished at the hands of savages, somewhere on his travels; everyone in the Karoo knew it.

About one thing they had no doubt; the notebooks in the ragged parcel had belonged to this man Booi. And this was known because of the manner in which they had been acquired. Grandfather Blitzerlik had been waiting in the queue at the Scorpion Point Post Office when he had been presented with the notebooks by a white woman.

Wearing a blue hat, Mina added.

And the books were in a brown suitcase, said old Adam – long disposed of. Being far too good for books.

A very beautiful woman, Grandfather Blitzerlik dreamily repeated. She had asked if he remembered David Mungo Booi, and when he told her that everyone remembered David, she gave him the books and vanished. And here the old man turned, as he must have done when the mysterious donor walked out of the post office. He made a curious curving, or scooping, motion with his hand, carving an arc in the firelight, as if in his mind's eye he watched her leave once again: the white woman in the blue hat.

It did not matter what had happened to David Mungo Booi; the old grandmother spoke for the first time. For people said now that his mission had not been necessary.

But I was an Englishman. Perhaps I had not heard of the voting? Well, a new world had begun, and the wandering people did not need the help of the old Queen of the Red Frocks – now they were going to kick the Boer to Kingdom Come themselves.

Best of all, added Mina, in the new world everyone would be given houses, and in the houses there would be free telephones. No more would the travelling people, the People of the Ashbush, the Trek Folk of the Karoo, suffer at the hands of the Boer. The red dresses of the English soldiers were needed no longer. From now on the wandering beggars would be kings of the Karoo. Therefore it had been decided that I should take possession of the notebooks that Booi had written on his journey through England. I would be returning to that country, would I not? Should I meet him, I could restore the notebooks to him. Or to the Queen, if I preferred.

I said I did not understand about the free phones.

Old Adam gave me a pitying look. He pointed to the stars, blazing beaches of light now, in the black oceans above our heads. People would talk to each other, without wires, through the help of the stars. And there were more stars in the Karoo than anywhere in the world. He hoped the star phones reached England soon.

When I got back to the Hunter's Arms, Clara took one look at my parcel and begged me to leave it outside in the backyard until the 'ceremony' was over. The ballot boxes were about to be locked away for the night. I stood the parcel on the kitchen step and she advised gloves before I opened it.

I told her about the phones. 'For crying in a bucket!' Clara said. 'Don't they know that Lutherburg is on a party line – one line between thirty farms?'

Her beehive had listed to the left, a little like the Leaning

Tower of Pisa. 'Who will they call on these star phones?' she demanded. 'Each other?'

We all went into the bar. Although the UN had declined to declare the Hunter's Arms a safe haven, after negotiation it had been decided that while the ballot boxes were being transferred to a place of safety, Jean-Paul would assume a prominent position in the window wearing his cap and his blue waistcoat. Any mad right-wing farmer who thought of shooting up the place would know that the UN had taken the hotel under its auspices.

The ceremony began. Election monitors, members of peace committees and various foreign observers assembled in the street. What Clara called 'our official UN party' gathered in the bar and watched through the windows, as the officials began transferring the ballot boxes into wheel-barrows, to be transported to the post office, where they were to be solemnly locked up overnight before being taken the next morning under guard to the counting station. When it was discovered that the official sealing-wax had vanished, Clara saved the day by giving the observers – who had begun blaming each other – a bottle of her nail varnish. The ballot boxes were sealed with bright-orange paint called Namaqualand Blush, and the procession of barrows rolled rustily down the street, and everyone clap-ped. Clara said it made her proud to be South African.

When I returned to the hotel, I found a policeman, with an enormous belly held in check by his gunbelt, on guard outside the kitchen door. He demanded to know if I had left an unattended parcel on the hotel premises. Notebooks, I said. There was blood on the paper, he retorted. I was very lucky it had not been destroyed in a controlled explosion. I would have to wait now – for morn-ing. My parcel had been locked away.

There was enough starlight for me to peer through the barred windows of the post office. The ballot boxes were lined up like soldiers. Beside them, a sort of lesser relation – but sealed in blood, not nail varnish – was the parcel. Waiting for morning.

In the notebooks of David Mungo Booi, long passages in English frequently gave way to the vivid, earthy Afrikaans of the Karoo nomads, or 'Ashbush People', who travel on their donkey carts from farm to farm looking for work. In moments of excitement, Booi sometimes forgets himself and lapses into his mother tongue. He is unusual among the travelling people of the Karoo in speaking any English at all. There seems little doubt that he is largely self-taught and picked up the language in the library of the farmer who adopted him. The circumstances in which this man, 'the Boer Smith', as Booi calls him, found an orphaned child among the ashes of the fire that claimed the lives of his parents and the other members of his family are poignantly recalled.

It is from Smith that the young Booi's earliest ideas of England derive. It is always and only of 'England' that he writes. As if he is quite unaware of Scotland or Wales or Ireland. He never speaks of Britain. Of course, this sort of selective focus on England, to the exclusion of other parts of the United Kingdom, is not unknown, even in Britain today, and may reflect a similar prejudice on Smith's part. However, more likely still, is the possibility that although the old farmer was known to the local Afrikaner families as 'our Englishman', he had himself never in fact set foot in Britain. If his father or even his grandfather had come originally from Britain, this would have been enough for the locals to regard him as irredeemably 'English'.

Booi's first names are revealing. By calling him 'David Mungo' I suspect Smith was combining the names of two of his heroes: David

Livingstone and Mungo Park – the great explorers of the Dark Continent. By this evocative and effective device he dignified the little orphan boy he found among the ashes of the burnt-out camp.

As to Booi's true ethnic provenance, it is unlikely that we will ever know for sure. Certainly, he considers himself to be a descendant of the Bushmen or San hunter-gatherers. He talks lovingly of the 'Red People'; those truly indigenous South Africans – the Cape Bushmen. His references to particular religious practices suggest an affinity with the /Xam people who once inhabited the area around what is today Lutherburg and Zwingli. But the /Xam are extinct now. For Booi, however, they linger on in the Trek People to whom he belongs and in whose faces and restless spirits, he maintains, one can detect glimpses of his vanished ancestors. There are times, indeed, when he seems to argue that they never died out at all.

For a clue to the origins of Booi's prose style, and his subsequent career, we must imagine the sorts of book which the boy might have found in the library of the Englishman, Smith. Mostly, these would have been accounts of travels in Africa, for works by Burton, Speke, Livingstone, Stanley, among others, are frequently referred to in the journals, and Booi draws heavily on the experiences of the great explorers when planning his own expedition. That he had read Livingstone's Missionary Travels and Stanley's In Darkest Africa as well as the journals of his namesake, Mungo Park, and even Conrad's Heart of Darkness is plain. He was not only familiar with these explorers, but he felt that he was following, quite literally, in their footsteps, with the same mixture of courage, faith and at times – it must be said – crusading ignorance.

(For an explanation of the Khoisan click sounds which occur in the languages of the Bushmen people, and which give ex-Bishop Farebrother so much trouble, the reader is referred to the list given on page 282.)

The notebooks of David Mungo Booi are published as they stand, with occasional notes. The travels they document may be dated as having taken place, roughly, in the spring and summer of 1993.

Christopher Hope
March 1995

The Life and Strange,
Surprising Adventures
of David Mungo Booi
who lived among
the English.

As told in his own
Words and written
down by Himself.

Chapter One

The author tells something of himself,
his people and the great Promise made by the Old Auntie
with Diamonds in Her Hair; his expedition abroad
and arrival among the English

We are a little people. Light. Lone. Lithe. Scattered wide as the wind. Our names tell of our nowhereness: we call our children *Stukkie Ding* – 'Scrap-of-a-Thing', or 'Little Nothing', and 'Missing'. And we lose our children often. Sometimes to the flu. Sometimes to the farmer, who locks them away in the schoolhouse when they would be more useful to the family by tending the trek donkeys or fetching kindling. Sometimes we lose them to the campfire. (But in the end, as all know, everything falls in the fire.) Some call us Ashbush People, or Trek Folk, or Nomads, or Nowhere Men. Some call us nothing at all but 'Who goes there?' and 'Away with you!'

Once there were other names, names the visitors gave us. Visitors, black and white, who came to our country. And stayed.

These early visitors rose from the sea, crept up the beaches like waves and, looking into our slanting eyes, pronounced us to be 'Chinese Hottentots'. The longer the visitors stayed, the more names they gave us: we became 'Egyptian gypsies', or 'wild' Bushmen, as well as vagabonds, foxes, vermin, devils. The visitors stayed to steal our country. They were brave with their horses and guns. But they cried out in terror in their dreams – forced to sleep under the stars, sweating in the open air, fearing our attacks. Any part of the body even grazed by our arrows must be sliced off. Or it died. For our sweet, slow poisons never failed. Driven from our fountains, robbed of our honey, we took their cattle and ran for the hills. Then our enemies hunted us down like rock-rabbits. Crushed us like fleas in an old blanket. Until we were next to nothing at all. Reduced to scraps. Missing.

Or so our foolish visitors liked to imagine. But does the springbuck die when the knife slits its throat and blood pours down? Does its spirit not enter the hunter? Just so have our souls entered the visitors: yellow and brown and black and white. And mingled. So that today when you look into the faces of Baster and Boer, black and white, farmer and mayor and shepherd – ours are the faces looking out at you. We went away – but we did not travel far.

Before the visitors came was our First Best Time. Long behind us now. No roads, and no fences. No police vans, patrolling like yellow cobras, to catch people carrying meat or firewood. We followed giant herds of springbuck, spreading as far as the horizon; the land was fat and all the fountains flowing, loved by the she-rain falling softly from heaven. In our First Best Time we roamed as wide as the wind.

Then came the Boers in their wagons and hunted us, stole our honey and our children. We cried and the god !Kwha heard our cries. For one day there came tall soldiers in red frocks, from across the ocean, servants of the Sovereign of all the English, she who was called the 'Old Auntie with Diamonds in Her Hair'. These were our Redneck years. When the Red Frocks kicked the arses of the Boer all the way from the Snow Mountains to Murderer's Karoo. That was our Second Best Time.

The Old Auntie with Diamonds in Her Hair long ago passed into the veld where a thousand eland run each day into the hunters' arrows and the wine goes around in bags as big as the rhino's gut. But her going brought her son in her place. (So it is among the English.) And then his son, good King George, who came to see us, to thank us for fighting in his wars, and renewed his promise to kick the Boer to hell and gone whenever we should ask. Our people showed him the old Queen's Great Promise. And the king said to them, 'Yes, that is great-granny's sign. Believe you me!' So they put the paper back in its hiding place until the day when they would send a messenger to the Queen of England to remind her of her Promise. Believe you me!

Almost alone among the People of the Road, People of the Eland, Men of Men, I can read books. And I can speak the Redneck language. Almost alone among the nomads of the Karoo, I had the luck as a baby to be saved by a kind man, the Boer named Smith. In the white light before dawn he found me crying among the smouldering ruins of my parents' camp. The fire beside which my family slept had fed itself so fat upon the paraffin with which they watered the flames that it got up and devoured their wooden night shelter, as well as the wiry screen of ashbush that keeps the bitter wind at bay, as well as the family within, father, mother, brothers, sisters. Ashbush is our friend; ashbush is the only roadside plant the wandering people may gather freely. If the ashbush wanderers take anything else along the way, then the police in the cobra-yellow vans will throw them into jail. So we gather ashbush, and sometimes it warms us, and sometimes it burns us.

All my family burned, even the blanket under which we slept, the cart which was our house and on which kettles and whips and bottles were lashed for the daily trek across the endless Karoo flats, from Lutherburg to Zwingli, from Eros to Compromise, from Mouton Fountain to Abraham's Grave. Even the blackened kettle burned to a blacker nothing in the hungry fire. And the donkeys stampeded far into the veld and were never found again.

The Boer Smith was the only Englishman for two hundred miles. 'Our Redneck', the Boers of the Karoo called him, as if he was their pet. Maybe that's why he saved me. Because a pet needs a pet. He told his grand-father's stories of the wild Bushmen of the Karoo. Who lived and loved like the animals. Who were impossible to tame. Unless you caught your baby Bushman young. Barbarian monkey men who used a poison on their arrow-heads for which there was no cure. But he had caught me young: so I became his 'tame Bushman'.

My master had a fondness for apricot brandy which sometimes drove him into horrible unhappiness. 'Kissing the Devil', he called it and there were times when the Devil made him very angry. At no other time did he beat me. It was all very well, said he, while I was young, to answer to the name 'Scrap-of-a-Thing'. But it would not do later when strangers wished to know what to call me, and to know that I was a man and not a monkey.

Because he was generous, he gave me no fewer than three names, the first two being what he called 'good English names'. The last was a name that many people in these plains have come to use. He was sure no one would say I'd stolen it. No more was I to be known as a 'Scrap-of-a-Thing'; now I was called David Mungo Booi.★

From his old, rich books he taught me to say my letters, and told wonderful stories of horrible darkness and violent death, heathen tribes and disgusting savagery, as related by the great English explorers on their travels through darkest Africa from Bushmanland to Stanleypool, from Bonga's country to the Mountains of the Moon.

Their names became my hymn; I still mutter them to myself when I wish to sleep: Baines, Baker, Bruce, Burton, Grant, Kingsley, Livingstone, Speke and Stanley . . . Even now they make, when strung together like beads, a little Anglican necklace.

The Boer Smith faced great trouble from the other farmers when they heard he was teaching me to read. His neighbours sat in his front room and watched me with my book and warned that no good would come of it. It was like teaching a sheep to fly, and while a flying sheep was at least a way of transporting mutton cheaply, a reading Bushman was unseemly and an affront to decent people everywhere. As to my name – a man needed a name, said the neighbours, but a monkey did not. If you gave a Karoo gypsy a name, he would only lose it. Or abuse it. They very much doubted it was legal. And they foresaw a bad end to this foolishness.

Of an evening, when the shearing had gone well, and my master was happy with the great bags of wool stacked in the ceiling of his barn, he would call on his shearers to sit with him, after they had been paid, after they had feasted

---

★   The name 'Booi', and its variants, 'Witbooi' or 'Whitebooi', is well known among the so-called Basters, or 'Bastard' people, of Little Namaqualand, a remote territory in the North-West Cape Province.

on his gift of two freshly slaughtered goats with bellies fat
as pockets of sweet potatoes. A fire was lit under the stars
that powder the face of our father the moon,* and all
would be invited to bring whatever drink they could find:
Little John brought sweet white wine, and Pietman his
prickly-pear liquor; Old Flip and Sampie the Blacksmith
brought along their home-made brews that bite the eyes.
Pietman would unscrew his wooden leg. Boer Smith produced his favourite apricot brandy, and they would mix the
lot in a zinc basin and stir it with Pietman's wooden leg.
They gathered around the basin like geese at a garden tap
in a thirsty month. Little John and Sampie and Pietman
and Old Flip would send the white enamel cup with the
chipped blue rim around the circle. A little singing, and a
little gunplay. Boer Smith loved to practise his target-shoot-
ing under the light of a hunting moon. That was how
Pietman had lost his leg, having to mark a target for my
master; and my master, having dipped the cup into the
basin once too often, put a slug through Pietman's right
leg at three hundred metres, and it had to be cut off above
the knee. Pietman never blamed him, for this was the sort
of thing that happened when the cup went around the fire.
Besides, Boer Smith cut him a handsome new leg of the best
yellow wood he could find, which Sampie the blacksmith
shod with a lively steel tip that flashed like a hare's eyes in
the moonlight. When Pietman took his leave of us, after the
shearing season, feeling happy to have passed the cup around
the fire, stretched flat on his back in his donkey cart, all
you saw was his fine yellow-wood leg waving goodbye.

After the drinking – peach brandy, white lightning,

---

* Booi is very free with the moon's gender. Sometimes the moon
is 'our mother'.

Advocaat, swirling in the enamel basin – after the shooting, then the stories began. My master, being a man of great understanding, loved to tell tales of his own people and to teach us something of their glory and their genius. His learning at these fireside lessons deepened with each scoop of the chipped cup in the old basin. The Boers of the Karoo would have been astonished to know how much their workers knew of the history of England:

England, or *Britannia Prima*, as it was known formerly, is divided into three parts. These are known as the South-end, the Midland and the savage, uncharted wastes they call simply the 'North'.

In the very earliest times the first people sailed to England from lands across the sea. These were the Beaker people. They failed in their heartfelt attempt to civilize the aboriginals and died in despair, taking their drinking cups with them to the grave to be buried beside them. Later there arose in the island wild and savage tribes who dressed in animal skins, painted themselves blue and lived principally on milk and meat. They were slow to learn to till the land.

When the Romans came they wept to see the foolish-ness of the natives, who shared wives among ten or twelve men, worshipped the moon, oaks and mistletoe, and measured out their lives in fortnights. To this day, said my master, the English have great difficulty in thinking in periods of longer than fourteen days. If asked to think a few months into the future, they grow confused and resentful. If asked to think a year or two ahead, they grow mute and wan and retire to their beds or their alehouses.

The Romans took pity on the savages and built for them roads and baths. The natives refused to bath, since it would disturb the blue paint with which they adorned themselves and of which they were so proud, and preferred to scratch their furry parts in sacred groves, worshipping the moon, the oak and the mistletoe. And since they seldom went anywhere, what possible use did they have for roads?

Once upon a time hunting was good in England. There were woolly elephants, hyenas, wolves and even our common and beloved hippopotamus to be found in great abundance. Now there are none at all, said the Boer Smith, and his tears fell into his apricot brandy. Let this be a warning, he used to tell me – we in Africa, with our immeasurable richness of wild creatures, must know that unless we take care to preserve them, we shall go the way of the English.

These and other things I learnt from the Boer Smith. And they were to serve me in good stead.

My master left without warning. He was kissing the Devil one night when the Devil decided to keep him. So the Boer Smith passed to his rest in that land where the fountains flow for ever, and the good live on locusts and honey, where the rains are always on time and hartebeest run into the hunter's arrows. And he left a bequest to David Mungo Booi: the gift of a dozen sheep.

It was a great day. For who before, amongst the Trek People, had owned twelve sheep? All the Ashbush families came from miles across the Karoo to see for themselves the man who owned twelve sheep. The family Lottering came. And the Pienaars. The Blitzerliks, old Adam and Mina. And the clan of Witziesbek. And we held a great party and sent round a five-man-can of sweet wine and danced until the dust leaped to its feet and danced with us. The stars began singing. On and on we danced into the white light that comes before sunrise.

Old Adam Blitzerlik spoke for all when he rejoiced in

my good fortune. I would have to be very careful: I had had good luck, but for the travelling people good luck usually brought trouble. Twelve sheep. Yes – well and good. But what profit are twelve sheep to a man who cannot graze them? Did I own grazing land? The wandering people owned nothing of the land. Everything belonged to others. Blacks from the north and the east took our land. Whites from the south and the west took our land. The fences kept us out. Yellow police vans patrolled all day long so that we might neither stop, nor collect wood for the fires, nor graze our donkeys on an inch of farmer's land. Or pluck any roadside plant or shrub but for the harsh and bitter ashbush.

Therefore it was time to make a plan. He was calling a gathering of the travelling people from across the Karoo. The time had come for action. The time had come to read the Great Paper.

A meeting was arranged in the hall of the Dutch Reformed church in the coloured township outside Zwingli, though there was a lot of opposition from the township dwellers who hate us even worse than they hate whites. We would steal the light fittings and tear up the floorboards for our fire, they said. Our donkeys would soon be eating all the fodder in the outspan place provided by the municipality.

Our people travelled to Zwingli from all over the land. Gathered together for the reading were the Lottering family, the Pienaars, and the Ruyter clan who remembered losing a child to the English in the time of the old Queen (*Klein Seun* or 'Little Boy' Ruyter had been stolen one hundred years earlier); there gathered, too, the family Witziesbek; and also the Sea-Cow clan from Murraysburg and many Strandloopers* (though I'm sorry to say that some of them

---

* Literally, 'Beachwalkers'.

were deep in their cups): several of Harryslot, from Prince Albert Way, and the family /Xam,* from Victoria East direction; not forgetting old Adam and Mina Blitzerlik; as well as representatives of other travelling bands or their descendants, long ago scattered and dispersed: besides nomads of the Karoo, there were people of the Kalahari, Caprivi, Okavango and Angola; the People of the Soft Sand; People of the Eland; People of the East; River Bushmen and Remote-area Dwellers of Botswana, including also the =Haba, the G//ana, the !Kung, the G/wi, the !Xo – all true people of the First Time.

The Great Paper was being held by the Sea-Cow band, from beyond Murraysburg, safe in a leather quiver adorned with ostrich-shell beads. As the only reader, and the only English-speaker, I was asked to give out again the Promise to our people, then I was to translate the sacred words slowly into Afrikaans, so that those gathered could follow. But most of my listeners knew the Paper Promise by heart – even if they understood nothing of English – and nodded and applauded at certain key moments, as I declared the cherished words:

We, Victoria, by the Grace of God, of the United Kingdom of Great Britain and Ireland, Queen, Defender of the Faith, Empress of India, to Our Trusty and well-beloved San People, of the Cape Karoo, Greetings. We, reposing special Trust and Confidence in your Loyalty, Courage

---

* The /Xam were the original Bushmen of the area around Calvinia in the Northern Cape. The family claim to the name, rather like Booi's association of himself with this group of Bushmen, is rather tenuous. The /Xam have been extinct for nearly two centuries.

and Good Conduct, do by these Presents Constitute and
Appoint you to be a Favoured Nation and send you Our
Sign of Friendship — wherever you are. From the Snow
Mountains to the Sourveld. From the Cape even to the
Kalahari. Assuring you of Our Patronage and Protection
in Perpetuity. Like a Lioness her whelps, so do We,
Queen and Empress, draw Our Red People to Our Bosom.
Let no one Molest or Scatter them.

By Command of Her Majesty in Council, bearing
the date of Eighth Day of June 1877.

Some of the Ruyter clan could not resist reciting the
words along with me. The Strandloopers shouted, 'Hallel-
ujah!' every now and then. And when I had finished, several
members of the Sea-Cow clan called out, 'Amen!' as if we
were in church.

Then the meeting divided. Some of those present,
specifically the representatives of the !Kung, said the time
for talking had passed. Now it was time for war — we
would approach the Queen and request she make good her
Promise. Our lives were trampled like those of dung beetles
by black people and whites and browns. Let the Lioness
guard her whelps. Let the Great She-Elephant gallop to
rescue her children; let her send the Red Frocks to kill the
Boer; let her trample our enemies under her great feet, or
spear them with her tusks; and let her children sleep safely
in the shade of her generous ears.

Others, notably the Lotterings, said the time for war
was past. The only fate awaiting Red People, Real People,
Little People, was death. Better then to leave and live in
England if the place was suitable. England, they had heard,
was a rich paradise where there were many more sheep
than islanders; farmers could graze their flocks wherever

they liked, since it rained every day and grass grew even in the cities; in England – said Pa Lottering – the police carried no guns (this assertion was loudly mocked by the Strandloopers, who said only children believed in policemen without guns).

In either case, the assembly agreed, an explorer, or ambassador, must be sent to put our case to the Sovereign. And since I was the only man among them to speak the English tongue, I would be the natural choice to go on this expedition. I possessed two fine English names, and I had been raised an Englishman by the Boer Smith, and now I so resembled the genuine article that it was doubtful the English would realize I was, in fact, a foreigner.

The family Ruyter asked me especially to find out what had been the fate of the little boy, lost years before to the English when the Old Auntie with Diamonds in Her Hair was still in this world. The Red Frocks had stolen the boy and carried him to England as a gift to the Queen, from whence he had never returned. Since 'Little Boy' Ruyter had been a gift to the Old Queen, then surely her descendants would know what became of him? If he had been buried in England, then I was, please, to arrange to have his remains returned to the Karoo.

The Witziesbek band said that once the Queen heard my story she would ride to our aid. It was well known that the English were great protectors of weak people in the world and always kept their word. If, however, Her Majesty decided that her soldiers could not come and save us, because they were too busy saving others, then we should consider establishing a colony in England. In order to do so, we must know something of the climate, the terrain, the customs of the people. It was said, for example, that the English feasted on babies at special times of the year. Was this true? They had a special attachment to brass, mirrors, calico. This we knew from their early contact with our cousins, the people of the coast, to whom the English, when they first arrived from the sea, offered trinkets in exchange for sheep, honey and hides.

Now we would do likewise. For as the Dutch and the French and the English, whenever they propose to colonize a country, first send missionaries and explorers to prepare the way, so we would form a Society for Promoting the Discovery of the Interior Parts of England. It was as the agent of this Society that David Mungo Booi would be dispatched to visit the Queen of England, to remind her of the Promise made by her predecessor and/or to spy out the land with a view to future settlement.

While the chief object of our expedition was to ask the English Monarch to send her Red Frocks to our aid, there was a secondary objective, and this was broached by the Sea-Cow clan from Murraysburg who instructed me to ascertain the following: what was the likelihood of possible settlement in England, and the opportunities for commercial exploitation, if such a settlement took place?

The impression gained by the only man of our people to have visited the English (a certain abducted beachcomber named Coree) and who returned to tell the tale, was of a savage people who made constant war on their neighbours and frequently fell out amongst themselves.

Therefore, what protection could friendly native chiefs give to commercial enterprises? Were the rivers navigable? And were the tribes along the River Thames (said to be their sacred river, and to run through caverns measureless to man, down to a sunless sea) sufficiently intelligent to understand that it would be to their mutual advantage to maintain a friendly intercourse with the San settlers?

What tributes or taxes would be levied by the native tribes for right of way through their country? What was the nature of the produce and the employment opportunities which the natives might be able to exchange for the benefits of Bushman settlement amongst them?

Then Grandfather Harry, patriarch of the Harryslot clan, took from inside his coat the family's treasure – a beer mug on which appeared a picture of a young woman in a crown, and urged me to study it so I should recognize Her Majesty if ever I found myself in the Royal Presence.

We prepared to vote on the motion that the Society should appoint me as its official representative when Ouderling Basters from the local church, dressed in his toga, arrived to say that our time was up and we were to vacate the premises immediately. Ma Pienaar said he was probably there to count the lightbulbs. But we went away, as we were ordered, as we always do when our time is up.

We left the church hall and moved to the outspan place set aside by the municipality for the donkeys of travelling people, where we concluded the meeting, standing among our carts and beasts. On a show of hands it was agreed that the Society would raise funds for my journey and I was to leave for England as soon as possible.

Old Pa Lottering now objected that owning the Old Queen's Paper Promise was all very well, but how did we know it wasn't a lie and a fraud? The word of white people, in his opinion, was worth no more than sheepshit.

The Society resolved to ask Sergeant De Waal of the police station at Mouton Fountain. It was said that he had been to Cape Town, even. So he knew the ways of the world.

Sergeant De Waal, tearing his hair when he saw the Paper Promise from the great Queen, said, 'This is the sort of thing that made all the trouble in our land. This is the paper that robbed the Boers of their birthright. And will do again!' And he yelled at us to get out of the station before he kicked our arses to Timbuctoo.

We knew then that the Paper Promise must be true. We sold my twelve sheep and started a fund. Our people collected money together for the first time in their lives. The fence-menders who work all day in the white heat, lining fences against the jackals who steal the farmers' sheep; the hunters who bait their traps in the bush for the lynx; the shearing gangs who move from farm to farm: all gave to our fund, sure in their hearts that it was not too late to seek a newer world.

Very conscious of the honour conferred upon me, I gave to the Society this promise: I would describe those in England as they were, as I saw them, and as I judged them, free from prejudice . . . The journey might be long, the country savage, all may be wild and brutal, hard and unfeeling, devoid of that holy instinct instilled by nature into the heart of man. But I, David Mungo Booi, would say what I saw and heard – however dark – among the English.

For my travels I was equipped as follows: a great hat, its brim as wide as an ostrich feather, fashioned from finest buckskin; its cranial capacity very generous, measuring about the same volume as an ostrich egg, lined with three cunning pockets, sewn by Hippo-girl Lottering, with yarn made from the leaf fibres of the green rope bush, and strong enough to snare the wildest guinea fowl.

In the first of these pockets were placed two good strong notebooks, six green Venus pencils, well sharpened, and a small knife.

In the second of these pockets was hidden the flag of our people, which, until it was drawn by Stumpnose Du

Toit to show to the English Queen, had not existed. He was so old, this Stumpnose, that he dimly remembered something of the way our people had done these things once. On a good piece of linen, obtained from the General Dealer in Middlepost, Stumpnose painted our mother, the great moon. High in the right-hand corner, sailing golden and fat, as befits our mother. From the left-hand upper corner a swallow departs. The swallow is one of the rain's things, as we are; and so, as the swallow departs, so we too have vanished from the lands that were once ours. And under the honey-moon, our mother, in the foreground we see two teams of men holding a tug-of-war. The team below is made of white men; for it was from below, from the sea, that the first visitors came to us, those whom we took to be pale Sea-Bushmen. Above is shown a team of Red People. The contest to which this refers took place in the time of the early world, when animals were still people. When the men from Europe arrived in our country they said to us, let us pull the rope to decide who owns the cattle and sheep and goats. And we pulled the rope until it broke, leaving most of it in the hands of the Bushmen. And the white men said: there you are, you have most of the rope, take it and use it to snare game: duiker and eland and springbuck are yours. But we will have the cattle and sheep. You may have tsama melons and dress in the skins of wild animals. But we will wear clothes and sleep under roofs when it rains.

And watching this contest, in the right-hand lower corner, his hand to his eyes, is the praying mantis, the great Kaggen himself, who weeps for his lost Red People.

This flag I was to fly on ceremonial occasions, preferably when the Sovereign and I formally exchanged gifts.

Into the third pocket of my great hat there were placed

five thousand rand in old notes, this being the huge sum raised by our people for my expedition. With this money I would pay for guides and porters and provisions, as well as any taxes levied upon the traveller in England.

It was expected that I should be in the country of the English for no more than two months, as the kingdom was comparatively tiny and a man could walk from end to end in that time. Any monies remaining at the end of my safari, of course, should be returned to the Society. I was to outfit a caravan and endeavour to cut something of a figure. For it was only by a grand progress that I would convince my hosts-to-be that my mission deserved the highest attention.

In my baggage I carried gifts destined for the Queen of the Red Frocks, she being the kin-child of the Old Auntie with Diamonds in Her Hair: a little bush piano; the one-stringed fiddle; two ostrich shells, crosshatched in filigree engraving; a pair of the finest royal firesticks, cut from the oldest brandybush in the Kalahari, said to be the very bush from which, in the First Times, the High God made the Holy Fire from which all fires descend; also a fine digging stick with which she might search for tubers, roots, melons and grubs on her great estate, when the mood took her; a necklace of ostrich-eggshell beads, each bead carefully gnawed by expert crafstmen; a bow of *gharree* wood, strung with eland sinew; a set of twelve arrows, six tipped with flint, in the old manner, and six with iron; a supply of three choice poisons (the first was stored in an old ink bottle, a liquid clear as water, tinged with blue, which we pressed drop by drop from the jaws of the yellow cobra and edged with the dainty sting of the pretty black scorpion; the second, more potent still, was a matchbox which held the pinkish paste, squeezed from the belly of the poison-bulb; and, most effective of all, number three, fruit of the grubs who hide beneath the *marula* tree; a nest of deadly cocoons, stored for safekeeping in a container made from gemsbuck horn, plugged with grass). And, lastly, a parcel of 'star-stones', watery pebbles of great significance to the white man, collected from seashore and desert sand, where they lie scattered like gravel. A gift of the !Kung, who assured me that if ever I wished to seduce the aboriginals, I need only produce them; that they were more effective than fish-hooks, more lovely than calico and more lusted after than life itself.

And my people said to me, cross the ocean, David Mungo Booi. Show the Empress of the Rednecks, leader of the Red-frocked soldiers, the Great She-Elephant, child of the Old Auntie with Diamonds in Her Hair, this Great Promise. Say that her people are crying . . . Say that we have been molested and scattered. Say that we remember her; ask her – does she also remember us?

Now the question arose: who would transport me to Cape Town? Prettyman Lottering, his wife Niksie★ and their three children owned the youngest donkeys, and their cart had new wheels. And they were regarded as very reliable – so they were given the privilege. We left the same day for the aerodrome, and England.

It was a slow journey. Prettyman stopped at the farms Good Luck and Alles Verloren,† where he had shearing contracts; the last of the clipping was followed by the usual party when the five-man-can went around the fire. The parties lasted longer than the shearing and I began to despair of reaching our destination. When at last we glimpsed Table Mountain we had been on the road for a month.

★   Afrikaans: literally, 'Little Nothing'.
†   'All is lost'.

Cape Town was busier than a termites' nest. Everyone coming or going, always by motorcar, day and night; special roads ensured that the drivers all moved in straight lines without bumping into each other. Where they were going to, or coming from, no one knew or cared. But they were certainly very lively when they approached our donkey cart, sounding their hooters loudly, and waving, which Prettyman Lottering said was a sign they liked us.

I obtained my passport without difficulty after explaining to the clerk I was only the third person, amongst our people, to travel to England. The earlier travellers, Coree and 'Little Boy' Ruyter, having been stolen, could not be said to have made the journey freely.

This kindly official expressed his regret that so few of us had left the country, saying that, if he had his way, special funds would be available to ensure that more of my sort went to England.

Next we set off to purchase my aeroplane ticket. To my dismay, this consumed much of the money so painstakingly collected by the Society. When I showed Prettyman the paltry amount remaining, little more than one thousand rand, he advised me to think no more about it, giving as his reasons the following. My expedition was bound to be short, since for experienced travellers of our sort, moving through a country, which he was reliably informed was not much larger than several sheep farms joined, would be child's play; that the amount of money remaining represented the annual salary of his uncle, a farm labourer and considered well off because he slept in his own bed and was widely regarded as the luckiest man in Abraham's Grave: finally, I was carrying so choice a selection of gifts for barter and exchange with the English that he doubted I should ever need money at all, and he would be surprised if I did not return home with most of my funds intact. That being so, he asked, and I did not refuse, a small loan with which he purchased a good five-man-can, and we refreshed ourselves before continuing to the airport, and then set about equipping my expedition.

We bought a brown suitcase of the best cardboard to house the gifts assembled for the Sovereign. We earnestly discussed which clothes would be suitable, and in the end we chose a grey suit because it was known that the country was continuously grey and wet. Prettyman explained it thus: the rain is in love with England in much the way it was once in love with the life-saving fountains of the dry desert, in the days when the San ruled in Bushmanland. My suit, being of the sky's colour, signified our compliment to the heavens, by rendering to the rain the things that belong to the rain.

On the right-hand sleeve of this grand garment there was emblazoned the maker's name, picked out in golden letters on a green background: MAN ABOUT TOWN. I thought it a trifle ostentatious, and would have removed it, but Prettyman Lottering said it would show the English that I came of a people wealthy enough to equip a traveller in purest polyester. Wearing the name on my sleeve had other useful applications. I did not own a watch, but I could study the label on my wrist, now and again, thus drawing attention to the quality of the garment. Warmer clothing, Prettyman assured me, would be a waste of my limited funds, since the Queen of the English was bound to present me with woollen garments from her sheep, which were said to number more than the clouds in the sky.

I bought, as well, a pair of black rubber boots — for it is said that their country is one long field of mud, except for a few days in the dry season, and the house of the

Sovereign possesses carpets wall to wall. And an unknown number of indoor toilets. Its roof is as tall as the Dutch Reformed church in Lutherburg.

My suitcase should have been larger. There was only just room for my gifts for Her Majesty. A good selection of trinkets for the general native populace that I had intended for barter – several good clay pipes, a kilogram of copper wire and some bales of rather pretty calico – had to be left behind in the keeping of the Lottering family, who swore they would be returned to Ramgoolam's General Trading Store in Loxton, where they had been purchased, and the sum refunded to the Society. I must say that I had some doubts as to whether the goods would be returned but Prettyman swore that his wife would give birth to snakes if he failed to fulfil his promise.

My misgivings received an unfortunate reinforcement when, as the time came to pay for my modest purchases, my companions suddenly vanished. If there is a fault in our people, it is a certain love of trickery; the low cunning of a yellow cobra who sheds his skin in the veld and he who finds it, taking it for a golden belt, is stung as he touches it. At last I located the family Lottering in the bar of the airport, sipping sweet white wine, purchased, I am sad to record, with a bale of calico. Even so, courtesy required that I send the bottle around for a few last times, since, as Prettyman pointed out, weeping generously, there was every chance that they would never set eyes on me again, for I might be eaten by English wolves or drowned in some bog. As he was likely to be the last of our people to see me alive, some consolation was in order. It was my duty to provide at least another litre of consolation, for surely I did not wish to hate myself for leaving them to face my death alone.

And so I went for further refreshments.

As a result I was carried on to the plane with only moments remaining, and my last glimpse of my companions, which is with me still, is of the Lotterings dashing themselves fruitlessly against the barrier in an effort to accompany me to the door of the aircraft; weeping and waving, until chased away by the police, like naughty children. I have no doubt they then returned to the airport bar to fortify themselves for the long journey back to the Karoo.

I remember nothing of my journey except that I was provided with several plates of food, stored in a kind of plastic case, together with a collection of useful plastic tools, which I stowed beneath my seat. Thus it was that I arrived in London, England, in the gloomy hours of the early morning, consulting the label on the sleeve of my new grey suit, carrying my fine new suitcase and shivering a little, for this was springtime.

Chapter Two

He receives a right royal welcome to England;
is accommodated at Her Majesty's Pleasure;
learns why English wit is the best in the world;
the ingratitude of Humpty-Bloody-Dumpty

The aerodrome of the English is very big: at least twice the size of the landing field outside Lutherburg. It will seem that I say the twisted thing when I write that not since the last hunting season, when farmers from across the Cape descended on the Karoo for the annual springbuck hunt, landing like flocks of Egyptian geese on the gravel strip beside the Lutherburg municipal shooting range, have I seen so many aircraft.

Most amazingly, our craft did not make low passes over the field, as is the custom, but descended directly. This puzzled me until I reached the following conclusion. The machine need not first dive on the field, as is usual in my country, since there are no donkeys, grazing on the landing strip, that must be sent running before the plane can land.

During our descent I noticed what I took to be groups of pebbles scattered across the green landscape. Lying directly beneath the aircraft's path, they looked from the air for all the world like the sun-split rocks that crowd the slopes of the low hills in the Karoo. As we dropped lower I saw that they were, in fact, thousands upon thousands of human dwellings, glued closer to each other than the cells of the honeybee. Why should people live directly beneath such roaring engines? In a moment the answer came to me. The English probably reserved their best grazing land for animals. The proof was there to be seen below me. They preferred to let their own people endure the howling, noxious tumult of the great planes rather than inflict such suffering on pets or livestock.

Was there ever such a people! As the machine swam ever closer to the ground, I told myself that David Mungo Booi would rather be an Englishman's dog than a Boer's best friend!

Thick was the sky with other craft as a pepper tree is with sparrows; they fluttered to earth like feathers. Stepping from the door of the aeroplane, we were guided along a tunnel into a shed as big, at least, as the town hall in Compromise. Inside the shed were a number of holding pens where travellers waited, much as flocks must wait before shearing. Unsure which group to join, I hesitated until a man, waving his arms like a small windmill, in the manner that shepherds command vagrant sheep, directed me into the longest line.

And in the way that beasts are guided by the farmer towards the dipping trough, so the lines were kept moving forward, scrutinized by shepherding officials who prowled the ranks, sniffing and snapping at the loiterers and maintaining strict order. It was a long time before the object of our longer line came into view: *more* officials, at tables tall as pulpits, sat in judgement on each visitor.

We, patient supplicants of the longer line, were mostly

Children of the Sun, citizens of the Old World, dusky and dun or honeyed by our father in heaven. Whereas visitors from the New World, those lands where the sun barely showed his face, were directed into the shorter line. I realized these people were related by blood and tribe to the indigenous population and, as such, expected and received special treatment, as kinship demands. I found nothing surprising in this arrangement, since this has long been a custom in my land, where the Boer rulers long ago decreed that their families should receive the best game, land and milk. Such an unexpectedly familiar sight made me ache a little for my motherland.

As happens at hunting parties and shooting parties, one finds unlikely friends. I made the acquaintance of someone quite overcome with excitement. He was a little round man, just ahead of me in the line and shaped very much like an egg, who wept silently but copiously, his tears splashing on to the floor in such a profusion that those coming after us in the line frequently slipped in the spreading pools until at last one of the herders approached him and directed him to 'put a sock in it'. This was how I learnt his name; for the herder addressed him as 'Humpty-Bloody-Dumpty'.

As we drew nearer to the place of scrutiny, Humpty-Bloody-Dumpty began shaking, and his tears increased. Seated at a high table, rather as a cashier in the Jackal's Dance General Dealer is enthroned upon a tall stool, the guardian of the island was studying each applicant with terrible gravity, picking through his papers in the way a baboon will groom the fur of a mate, catching a tick here and a nit there. And holding it to the light before swallowing it.

Our herder now shook his head and said if Humpty-Bloody-Dumpty did not put a sock in it, he would have to leave the line. My companion, looking for all the world like a well-dressed ostrich egg, or a fat locust on legs, took our keeper at his word, for he immediately sat on the floor and removed one of his socks, poor affairs, holed and threadbare, and pushed it into his mouth. Then he removed the other and, with it, he began mopping up his tears.

The herder or shepherd or guardian who had occasioned this behaviour shook his head once again, and expelled the wind from his mouth in much the same sound as you will hear when the belly of the *kudu* is pierced with a hunting knife. Then he returned to his ceaseless patrolling of the line, muttering and mouthing to himself and giving every sign of his continuing displeasure. (Wind, I was to discover, is an obsession among these people. Its retention and explusion, through one or more orifices, is raised amongst the English to an art. And not only in their personal, private inspirations but, as I was to learn, also in their politics the movement of air is most important, especially in the winds of change that blow about their island kingdom and which chill and discomfit them, for they believe winds from elsewhere, the wider world, the Countries of the East, of the Sun, and of the European mainland, signify the end of all that is great. Thus do the English place enormous importance on flatulence – hot air, as they call it – used as a private recreation but also as a method of political analysis for diagnosing what is wrong with themselves.)

In the holding pens both lines, long and short, moved at their own pace towards the guardian at the high table. Looking at this fresh-faced judge I recalled that when I was a child and the Englishman rescued me from the fire and taught me to read, he showed me pictures of an angel carrying a fiery lance, sent to guard the gates of Eden after our first parents had been expelled from God's garden of happy delights. That angelic sentry did not seem anything like as fearsome as the guardian of the gates to our English Eden, seated at his high table, wearing a sports coat of grey wool, the colour of ostrich bile, and a tie as pink as a duiker's tongue.

Beside me, my round friend wept and mopped. Hoping to comfort him, I offered him a little refreshment from my small store of provisions in the plastic case I had been given on the aircraft. We shared an apple, Humpty-Bloody-Dumpty and I, though I had difficulty in persuading him to take the sock out of his mouth.

How pleased he was to eat, having been sick with fear since leaving his homeland, which lay beyond the edge of the ocean. He came from a people, he assured me (though I had to struggle to contain my disbelief that such oddity should exist in the world), who ate no meat and whose gods exceeded the stars in the sky. His face, though as richly coloured as mine, showed none of the lines of wisdom found among our people. He looked altogether like some tall infant. I felt him to be a simple soul, lost in the world, and gave thanks in my heart that he had landed in the land of the free, which welcomes to her bosom the lost and confused and protects them like a mother lion does her whelps.

All through our meal my companion wept. But if our herders noticed his continuing distress, they chose not to remark on it. As I was to come to realize, this was one of the most cunning hunting patterns among natives of Albion; when faced with some present or future event they find unpalatable, they lift their noses to give the most marvellous simulation of ignorance. So convincing is this feigned ignorance that it is scarcely to be distinguished from the real thing. I have noticed something similar in the behaviour of black bush pigs when faced by the ravening hyena. The pig affects ignorance even while it is being devoured. Thus it maintains its sense of superiority during its destruction. The hyena may murder the pig, but the victim never condescends to notice.

At last, my lunar friend and I stood before the high table of the recording angel. Humpty-Bloody-Dumpty, forgetting himself to be in a land where none of this was necessary, and probably imagining himself to be in his home country, faced by an official who had in his hands the power of life and death, flung himself on his knees and began kissing the guardian's hand. The young man blushed very red at this; the strolling herders in the holding pens smiled to see this expression of devotion, and called cheerily, asking if perhaps my poor moon friend had mistaken the guardian of England for the King of Bongo-Bongo-Land? (As I was to discover, they were fascinated by this distant country, to which they frequently referred in tones of astonishment and awe. I am of the opinion that since David Livingstone's travels through Bonga's country, west of the Zambesi, Bonga's name seemed to have stuck in English folk memory in its simplified or corrupted form of 'Bongo-Bongo'.)

We stood patiently before the official. Here was my first Englishman and I was determined to study him carefully. A young specimen, his skin was of the faintest pink, such as you may see in the last of the sun as it sets over the Snow Mountains. The surface of his face was pitted and somewhat pustular. Later I was to discover that his complexion is something that many of them strive to achieve from babyhood, often devoting themselves to a special diet of fat, sugar and fried potatoes, which, though we might find it nauseating, is highly popular. Clearly he must have shown great promise in the schools to have been put in this position of authority so young. One had only to see how expertly he extracted his hands from the desperate lips of my terrified companion. It was evidently a custom among them that those employed by the Crown should wield considerable power with very little or, better still, no experience whatsoever. This undoubtedly instils modesty and reminds them of their debt to their Sovereign. His face was soft and long, and much of it appeared to have slipped beneath his chin, where, you might say, it waited on developments. He wore, through his left nostril, three small gold rings, which I took to be a sign of his Royal Service.

When I showed him my Paper Promise with the great Royal Seal, and read sections of it to him, his eyes grew large, and an expression of tender pain crossed his face. He sctratched his hair in the way a child will do when it searches for lice. And when he spoke, his voice was high and trembling, like the cry of the *kiewiet*.

He agreed that my promise had indeed been signed by the Queen Empress and sent to her beloved San of the Karoo. The old She-Elephant had made many such promises. That was a Royal Tradition. And her children, kings and queens in their turn, had given similar promises to many people in colonies, dominions and protectorates on which the sun did not set. But that had been in distant lands in olden times. For, like a true mother of mountains, the Queen Empress had gathered half the world at her feet and looked out over oceans. But she had never intended that her distant children would all come to visit her one day. In ancient English Royal Tradition, one might visit others, but others did not visit one.

But if people who did not know the rules suddenly turned up on one's doorstep, claiming kinship, then it became necessary to distinguish between sheep and goats, truth-tellers and liars, friends and frauds. Did I take his point? If one allowed into the country every Tom, Dick and Harry one could shake a stick at, then the indigenous natives, upon whom people of my sort relied for help, would feel themselves swamped. Even extinguished. And, instead of welcoming us, would hate us and reject us and injure us. And we did not want that, now did we?

I saw his point. How very different the history of our people would have been if we had done the same. Once we hunted and roamed through all Bushmanland where the rains loved the earth and game crowded the veld. Then the visitors came, black and Boer and English; and where we had hunted the springbuck, now they hunted us. After the Boers came the Red Frocks of the Old Auntie with Diamonds in Her Hair – many of whom went by the names of Tom, Dick and Harry – and they hunted the springbuck and the Boer. And us. But today the Bushmen, like the running game, have dwindled to little bits of nothing. If only we had behaved as wisely as they had done!

Now Humpty-Bloody-Dumpty and I were requested to show him our passports. My egg-shaped companion began again to weep. To calm the poor man, I told the guardian we had come in peace. He welcomed this. He seemed to mean it, for no sooner had he glanced at our papers than he ceremonially delivered us into the hands of an official welcoming party who wore distinctive black caps, shaped like elands' udders, which meant, said my first Englishman, that they were officers of the Crown dedicated to keeping the Queen's Peace. My heart leaped. We had come in peace and we were received in peace. What better evidence could there be that our arrival had been foreseen by Her Majesty? This happy thought was further confirmed when my first Englishman told us that we were to be lodged in special accommodation pending Her Majesty's Pleasure.

Humpty-Bloody-Dumpty did not grasp the good news. Was his mind too limited by the barbarism of his upbringing? Or, perhaps, he was so badly frightened by the sight of the welcoming party in their fine nippled hats that he failed entirely to understand the honour we were being paid. All I can say is that his hair stood up on his head like the bottle-brush flower. He flung himself on the ground and began kicking and screaming. It was then that our welcoming party were forced to take measures to protect the poor deluded soul from injuring himself, and to prevent him from lashing out at other applicants in the queue behind him, some of whom were visibly distressed by his childlike tantrum, and began wailing themselves, giving out sobs and groans until all that great receiving shed was awash and the air filled with lamentations.

The soothing of Humpty-Bloody-Dumpty by the peace-keepers was swift and gentle. A leather belt snapped fast around the waist, a pair of steel bracelets about his wrists. Blind to the fact that they intended him nothing but kindness, he cried on the great Queen to save him, not realizing that her agents were already endeavouring to do so. This further distressed those who heard it, and so the welcoming committee had no choice but to close his mouth by giving him, to chew upon, a leather pad about the size and colour of a mare's tongue and, mercifully, his cries subsided. And, in this pacified condition, we were chauffeured in a large van to the place of Her Majesty's Pleasure.

We were, in the courtesy vehicle taking us to our Royal Guest-house, twelve in all: apart from us there were a family of five Bengalis, two elderly Pathans, three young women from Istria who had fled the tribal wars in that country.

Their good fortune at our right royal welcome cannot have
dawned on them, poor souls, for their faces were as white
as the petals of the Chinkernichee, and their teeth chattered
loudly. My friend, his head bandaged where he had dashed
it into the wall at the aerodrome, was weeping again, the
tears coursing down his eggy face. Luckily he could not be
heard, or my companions in the van might have been even
more greatly disturbed.

The generous arrangements for our comfort at Her Majesty's Apartments showed everywhere. Humpty-Bloody-
Dumpty and I were placed in a room together, and our
hosts removed his restraining belts with great good humour,
intimating with many a wink and a nod that they intended
him no harm. A wonderful portrait of Her Majesty graced
the wall of our room, and it was most humbling to know
that she watched over us and would no doubt summon us
to her Palace when she felt so disposed. I was given, for
my own use, a table and a chair which, I was astonished to
learn, would be left in my room overnight, even though
they must have feared I might have yielded to habit and
chopped up my furniture to make a cooking fire.
    Thrice daily we were escorted to a room where we
were handed a steel tray, scooped like a tortoise shell into
a series of craters, and into these metal depressions were
deposited a most alarming selection of materials which our
hosts regarded as very desirable.
    But when I looked down at my tray what I saw was a
mound of wet, grey leaves, beside a pool of semi-stiffened
porridge, below a hill of dry leather. Food, said my guardians, you lucky people! And I learnt that the leaves were
greens and the porridge whipped potato, and the hill of
dry leather had once been part of a pig.

For a short time I believed this meal also contained something even less to my taste, since our people place great store by donkeys and our guardians kept encouraging us not to look a gift horse in the mouth. But I was relieved to learn that this was one of their proverbs and not an allusion to an equestrian element in our diet.

I found, however, that I could not eat this food, free as it was. My eggy friend did no better, saying he preferred death by starvation to being sent back home. I sympathized, but I had no intention of starving to death on the verge of a royal summons.

Luckily, I discovered, on our daily walks around the private walled courtyard of Her Majesty's Lodgings, a garden well stocked with tubers and even a useful supply of ants' eggs, the English variety being a little saltier than our beloved Bushman's rice but tolerable if eaten fresh.

Our attendants were amazed but tolerant. If guests of Her Majesty preferred to dine off ants, or starve themselves to death, then that was their privilege. This I took to be a 'fine instance' of their forbearance, their desire to live and let live.

I was also given a small, free-standing lavatory. Our host was proud of his accommodation and fittings. Was there ever such a place, where I came from, where everyone was given his own WC and an endless supply of paper? I had to agree. If similar accommodation were offered in the Karoo, every police station between Zwingli and Pumpkin-ville, from Eros to Jackal's Dance, would be crammed with Ashbush People fighting to get in. Then, too, in our country, the supply of running water is so jealously guarded that our people are lucky if the farmer offers a waterpipe once in twenty miles. In England you may flush the toilet as many times as you wish. I imagined it had something to do with the rain, which, we are reliably informed, 'raineth every day'. They study the weather even more carefully than we do. It holds a sacred significance for them. If the rain fell for more than a week, our attendants declared a flood, and feared for their huts. If no rain fell for a fortnight, they declared a drought, and stopped washing themselves.

Our attendants, or hosts, as I learnt to address them, were ever attentive, and very concerned for our well-being. Twice daily, their chief, Mr Geoff, or 'Minehost' as he liked us to call him, encouraged us to walk in the walled gardens of the Royal Guest-house, though he protested cheerfully that taking meals from his garden presented problems. Ants were all very well. But he begged me to stop eating his daffodils.

My oval friend refused to join us on these pleasant walks. Turned his face to the wall, saying that exercise was not useful to a condemned man, and turned his back on the generous face of the Monarch. This invitation, said he, was simply a means of ensuring that when the time came to expel him from England, he would be fit enough to walk to the aircraft. He rained down protests on Queen and Country. He had come to England believing that a man persecuted in his own country might fine protection in the land of the free. What a delusion!

I must say I was shocked by his cynicism, and his lack of faith.

Minehost contented himself with the gentle observation that Mr Humpty was not 'playing the game'. He had eyes of the faded blue of the peacock flower; his hair was honey gold; and he wore a black peaked cap, his badge of office as a servant of the Crown. Mr Humpty's failure to 'play the game' was a source of sadness. It was not merely impolite, it was not sporting, he remarked, as he locked us safely away at night.

Mr Geoff was aided by a number of sub-hosts, all of whom wore the same black cap of Royal Office and carried at their waists a silver bush of keys, for it was a house rule that doors were always to be locked behind us – so great was their devotion to our privacy – and windows were to be bolted at all times, where they were not already barred. I remonstrated with my eggy friend, pointing to the locks and bars. Could anyone be better protected, I demanded?

Mr Geoff was great good fun and a natural mimic. Within hours of our arrival he was imitating each guest who had travelled in the special transport from the aerodrome. He was, by turns, Bengali, Pathan, Sanjaki and Istrian, using as props a headscarf, a limp, a tear and a faithful though unintelligible parody of each guest's language – or, as he called it, 'mumbo-jumbo'. (They are convinced that most foreigners speak this tongue as naturally as they speak English.)

Clearly, they have as much difficulty speaking foreign languages as they do with foreigners who speak English. But where another tribe might have shown embarrassment or vexation at this disability, not being able even to pronounce our names, the English, an inventive race, simply gave us new ones: 'Sooties', 'Spear-Carriers', 'Parkies'* and other nicknames too numerous to recall, for they vied with each other to invent new and better ones every day.

I knew from the history lessons of my master, the Boer Smith, that the English sense of humour exceeds those of all other nations; that they enjoyed nothing better than laughing at themselves. However, as with many of these legends, the truth is more complicated. In my experience

---

*   Pakkies(?)

they laugh at themselves all the harder when they pretend to be other people.

I would say that, when analysing the nature of the humour displayed by my keeper in the Royal House, it was by the degree to which strangers can be shown to be unlike them that the native wit of the English is manifested. Our distinguishing marks – the way we walked, for instance, or our shapes and colours, our costumes, our accents and, in my case, my naturally curled hair – had them absolutely hooting; my buttocks, being pronounced, were a source of such hilarity that at times they could barely speak and had to content themselves, between guffaws, with curving movements of the hands to indicate my slight steatopygia.

They fix instantly on some detail, so small, perhaps, no one else would notice it, but which confirms the comic distance between themselves and all others. Much as a group of children will seize with delight on some physical defect in one of their chums, a cleft palate, a stammer, a missing limb, a shrivelled arm, and, stuttering or limping, began mimicking beautifully the odd or clumsy defect, so the natives dote on differences. Nothing sets them laughing more quickly, except perhaps a robust appreciation of the bodily functions: to which they allude often but never mention directly, considering directness in these matters close to vulgarity, a trait I was to observe often, and which has led some critics to contend that they are very great hypocrites. It is not hypocrisy at all – but a special kind of delicacy.

Try as I might, I could not hope to match their natural sense of humour, yet politeness required that I should at least make the attempt, and so I took to laughing at their pink faces, so comical beneath their black caps – so like monkeys playing at men – and alluding to their very powerful body odour, for, besides their interest in rain, which

I have mentioned, their interest in water for washing is theoretical. When I told Minehost that we seldom bathed, he was impressed. But when I told him that the common method of washing among Karoo travellers was to strip naked and wash at a stand tap, using sand to scour the body, which has been treated with a good layer of sheep's fat, he was appalled. Why should we go to all that trouble? he demanded. To which I replied, in true English fashion, so as to smell a little sweeter than you, Minehost – whose dung signature, a mixture of cheese and ashes, would scare a *kudu* at fifty paces. But his brow clouded and he was not amused. The English do indeed like laughing at themselves, but only because they hate others doing so.

In my commodious quarters I was also given a bed, entirely to myself, with two blankets of the finest grey wool. But years on the solid earth gives a man a taste for a plainer couch. I pulled the mattress off the bunk and leaned it against the steel edge of the bed and crept by night into this shelter. Just as we lean our strips of corrugated iron against the wheel of the donkey cart when we outspan by the roadside for the night, and pack the gaps with the rough ashbush to keep out the bitter wind.

Fixed to one wall of my apartment was a wonderful engine, all curling pipes about the thickness of a man's wrist, painted white and very lovely. Around and around an ingenious thicket of metal branches hot water travelled. The heat was about the same as you would feel if you were to warm your hands over the intestines of a freshly killed goat, of which, in their tangled beauty, these water pipes were a distant reminder. By night they would rumble; the belly music of the goat.

This engine made me long for home. It was very quiet in my room. My friend on his bed said nothing, though he wept from time to time. I was happy enough as I awaited Her Majesty's pleasure, but I could not see the stars. So I crept out of my shelter and lay close to the water heater by the wall, and felt its belly music carrying me back to my childhood on the road, when after the day's shearing, on the farm of Jan De Waal out near Compromise, we were given two goats. My father would tether them beside our shelter overnight and when the fire burnt low, and the frost formed like a thick white rind on our blankets, our hair and the donkeys' ears, in that intense cold that comes just before the dawn, I would slip quietly from under the blanket, where my mother and father and sisters and brothers lay sleeping, and go and lie with the goats, pressed close to their bellies, which were silky and warm and rumbled through the night beneath the great fields of stars, the million eyes of God.

Through the bars of my window I noted the paltriness of stars in England. They are still in the skies, I know, but the natives no longer look up. They have made the lights of their cities so bright, the stars fade. They do not worship them. Or steer by them. So advanced are they that they live lives unconnected with the universe. They have only to switch on their street lamps and the million eyes of God go blind.

Arriving with our evening meal, Minehost was considerably surprised to find me on the floor. What on earth was I doing? he demanded. What was the reason I lay on the floor, beneath a blanket, backing my rear end into the radiator?

I explained to him the importance of goats. I described the great feast that takes place at the end of the shearing. When the goats are led into a circle, and their throats are slit. How the blood is carefully collected in plastic bowls, unless people are too drunk to hold the things steady, which, I am sorry to say, is often the case. Then the headless carcasses must be skinned, while the children often, in their innocent way, take the goats' heads with their gentle, cooling eyes and place them on sticks and stand them to watch over the preparations. The children will fight for the bladders and take them and blow them into footballs and play for hours while the meat cooks. And the women sit and gossip and smoke. The men send off for a five-man-can of white wine from the nearest bottle store, and when the feast is ready, they drink until the sun goes down and the million eyes of God shine in the skies.

Minehost begged me to stop.

My description of this blood-stained country sport, played by filthy urchins before a dinner of goat's meat, distressed him. Even more, that the bladders were used in this way repulsed my second Englishman. In hushed tones that spoke feelingly for the butchered goats far away in the Karoo, he explained that what might have been just a 'game' to my kind was something so sacred it united England from one end of the island to the other.

Did he not eat meat? I asked.

He bridled. They were the greatest nation of beef-eaters in the world! Had I not heard of the roast beef of Old England? It developed their brains. The present state of the nation's intelligence testified to the superiority of their beef. If ever I was told that English beef caused brains to soften and fail, I should reject it utterly. Lies spread by foreigners across the water jealous of bigger, beef-bred English brains.

I had to tell him at this point that the brain is not the seat of intelligence. It simply gives you a headache. It is the intelligent life of the heart that teaches us to know good from evil.

Such beliefs might be fine in distant places where they kicked around goats' bladders, replied Mr Geoff. But if I went through England talking of the life of the heart, I would not get very far. He begged me to say no more of goat feasts. He deplored what we did to these animals. It was as bad as the cruelty of the French towards veal calves, or the Spanish to donkeys. It was one thing, Mr Booi, said Minehost, to enjoy a good bit of meat and quite another to approve of killing. If such things were necessary, then so be it. But they should be done under adequate supervision, quickly, painlessly and preferably silently. Above all, one preferred not to be told about it.

I realized then that in England entire generations had never seen a freshly slaughtered animal. Never set eyes on the great wash of its blood which sprays like a crimson sea, or seen the steaming offal lifted from the slit the knife makes in its belly. In this way they have arrived at such a pitch of delicacy that we can only wonder at.

Imagine, then, my feelings when I awoke in the morning to see upon the wall a shadow of something swinging, very like the great pendulum of the clock in the Dutch Reformed church at Abraham's Grave. As my eyes grew accustomed to the dawn light, I saw that Humpty-Bloody-Dumpty had hanged himself from the top bunk by his belt, and swung to and fro beneath the very eyes of the Queen of England.

I grieved for the deluded man. Yet, if I am honest, I felt a touch of anger. Just as when I am hunting in the veld and the game flies before me, that instead of waiting to take in the neck or flank the little poisoned arrow that will soothe it to death, the foolish buck runs madly into the road and is killed by a passing farmer in his truck. What waste. What foolishness!

I looked up at my departed friend, his trouser legs tied to his ankles, his sock protruding from his mouth, in what looked like the cheeky gesture our children make with their tongues when the Boer sails past in his insolence. Slowly swinging in the white light of dawn. And I felt sad for my own people. The Children of the Sun who flocked to England in the hope of better things. Was this how we responded to native hospitality? To the tolerance of our hosts? Following the kindly eyes of the Monarch, which seemed to watch very closely the swinging figure of Humpty-Bloody-Dumpty, I felt that something in her look seemed to say: 'What, have you left so suddenly, poor fellow? If only you had waited!' Truly, I had to agree. If this was the way we behaved when accommodated at Her Majesty's Pleasure, one had to ask whether we deserved the privilege.

Chapter Three

He learns something of modern military strategy;
the stirring history of Dicky the Donkey and the war
for Tiny Alma; the creatures who cried in the night;
a Royal Summons that goes sadly wrong

I knew my hosts were most distressed by Humpty-Bloody-
Dumpty's sudden departure, for they never mentioned it
again, except to ask me not to allude to it before the other
guests, as some were simple souls, very easily led. And one
would not like to encourage similar behaviour, now, would
one? Respecting this request was rather difficult, since my
fellow guests, when they met me walking in the garden,
would contrive to find ways of referring to my friend's
disappearance, and when I replied, as I had been urged,
that he had returned unexpectedly to Bongo-Bongo-Land,
I am afraid they expressed their scepticism very crudely, by
a variety of devices, such as raising their eyes to Heaven or
drawing their fingers across their throats. When our hosts,
who accompanied us up the garden paths, forbade further
questions, the other guests took childish revenge by confer-
ring on innocent flowers in the garden new and terrible
aliases, calling the scarlet rose climbing the high walls 'prisoner's blood', or asking our attendants whether the creamy

clematis was cultivated for wreaths to adorn our unmarked graves.

I brooded often on my late friend's tragic end. How unfortunate an impression he had made. Yet I missed him. Although my attendants were never far away, I lacked company. Humpty-Bloody-Dumpty came, like me, from a short people. Now I found myself alone in a world where meals were too large, beds too wide, chairs too high and men too tall. When Minehost inquired kindly into the state of affairs among the starving whom he took to be very many 'down my way', it was never clear whether he was referring to my country or my height, as if the air ten inches below his nose held worlds he would never visit, though from time to time he caught glimpses of them from on high.

Time passed, and my name changed. For my attendants found Booi too difficult for their tongues, too round and rude, and so, much as the farmers do in my part of the world, they gave me a new name, and I became, amid much chaffing, the Boy David.

Mr Geoff, he of the honeyed hair, the bush of keys and the distinctive dung signature, a mingling of cheese, ashes and whisky, watched me fondly, and promised a Royal Summons 'at any moment'. Its timing depended on a decision 'on my case'. When I replied that this sounded horribly legal – at home we were always awaiting decisions on our cases by the police into whose hands we had been abandoned – Mr Geoff reminded me that this was England, and Palace procedures proceeded at their own pace, and he could guarantee that some day soon I was in for a Right Royal Surprise, believe you me.

And I did believe him. Because he gave many signs of his regal connections, telling me that the paperwork for my transport was 'in train', and that punctuality was the

45

politeness of kings and uneasy lay the head that wore the crown and many other moving testimonies of his closeness to the Royal Household.

Besides, I realized, if Her Majesty had not intended to receive me, she would hardly have gone to the trouble of detaining me at her Pleasure.

Perhaps my friend's disappearance would have caused less suspicion among other guests awaiting Her Majesty's Pleasure had our hosts not continued to insist that he had been called away to live in that mythical land, somewhere at the world's edge, where dwell all Children of the Sun.

Among the English, I discovered to my surprise, there is an almost complete ignorance of the fact that they dwelt for many lifetimes in such places. Minehost denied all knowledge of this. He knew nothing of Africa. I must be mistaken. He knew nothing of the great explorers, nothing of Livingstone. And when I told him that his people had been in Africa, in large numbers, for many years, that they had fought and died and dug for gold and diamonds, shot lions and ruled over the tribes, from the Cape to Cairo, he looked at me as a child does at a storyteller, or as if I had drawn for him in the air a land as fabulous as Monomatapa, peopled by giants. All this might have occurred, long ago and far away, he conceded, but that had nothing to do with him.

I was tempted to ask whether this ignorance was not related to their excessively shrunken world view. Their notions of the world have contracted like a leather cloak left out in the rain. And rain is, perhaps, the key. During my stay in the Royal Guest-house it rained almost every day. And this excessive moisture, damp or liquidity has probably affected their sense of distance, shrinking the world to the size of a miniature toy no bigger than the wooden tortoise a boy carves and keeps in his pocket.

Yet, paradoxically, what is closest to them they consider very large indeed. Although the island, by our standards, is pitifully small, they talk about it as if it were twice the size of Africa. They can imagine nothing beyond it. Yet if you probe patiently, you will discover faint racial memories of the role they once played in the world, 'long ago and far away', sometimes stirring in their hearts.

If they have forgotten past dreams of glory, except when racked by spasms of involuntary race memory, they have managed to increase their emotional purchase on three things: animals, gardens and the starving. Mr Geoff was always asking after the starving, of whom he had seen many pictures. He appointed me official spokesman. Were there many starving where I came from? Would they always be starving? And if they would be starving always, what possible good was there in feeding them?

Questions flowed from this amiable man. He was, he said, ever interested in the other man's point of view. But, personally, he preferred plants. Gardens were his true love. Had it not been his duty to wrestle daily with ungrateful Children of the Sun, he would happily have cultivated his garden. A lovesome thing, God wot!

As we walked around the garden on our evening promenade, amid foxgloves and columbines, he spoke of his yearning for a time he believed to have been golden, when Englishmen lived better, sweeter, rural lives. Before their trees died, when they inhabited a land unenclosed by hedges, when their noble forebears ran with the rabbit, and talked to the robin, and wandered on a carpet of greensward thick with elms and thronged with hosts of golden daffodils.

I could grieve with him for this vanished time, since it recalled our own – which had lasted longer, and ended more recently, with the arrival of the white visitors and the Queen's soldiers.

In Bushmanland it had been the farmers who had destroyed our game. In England who had destroyed their trees? I asked.

Enemies from the Netherlands, or Low Countries, had unleashed a plague, came the bitter reply. A doubled-edged destruction. Trees which survived the plague were destroyed in a great wind conjured up by evil forces, somewhere 'over there', which had cracked its cheeks and huffed and puffed until all the rest fell down.

Knowing how tenderly he felt towards the slaughtered goats of my childhood, I was very surprised, as I walked alone one evening in the peace of this garden, to hear the long, keening sob of what I took to be a lynx trapped in the hunter's wire snare. His cry echoes across the rocky desert, interrupted only for brief moments when, demented by pain, he pauses to try and chew through his own leg . . .

Although I heard these cries of pain most distinctly, I saw no sign of the victim. But for me the scent became overpowering. I knew its ingredients: fear, helplessness and the hot breath of death.

No wonder then that I stepped carefully around the columbines. For the fiercest thing in the world is a heavy steel trap. It takes the leg and holds it until the hunter returns, be that a day or a week.

I begged Minehost to allow me to end the suffering of the lynx who cried in the night.

He said, wonderingly, that he knew nothing of the lynx.

If not the lynx, it must be several jackals, I said, though

I had not known that this animal was found on the island, a clever, sly, greedy person, who runs as if he has burnt his feet in the campfire, and takes new-born lambs and pregnant ewes and sends the farmers crazy. Then we must send for John Jacobs, the jackal-hunter, who comes with his windhounds, Napoleon and Caesar, and sets his traps for the jackal; a little jackal piss makes his potion, skullbone of rock-rabbit and a perfumed leaf, scattered on the layer of earth that hides the newspaper under which waits the steel trap. Surely nothing so cruel lay buried in this peaceful garden?

Pressing a finger to his lips and giving a fierce look to signify that what he was about to show me was, as they say, 'strictly confidential', Minehost led me deep into the cellars beneath the Royal Palace of Detention. The cries of the trapped creatures grew louder at every step until at last we stood before an iron door. Lifting a flap of metal that snapped snugly against the door, as an eyelash upon a cheek, my guide invited me to press my eye to a cunningly concealed spy-hole.

I saw three men lying on their beds. I call them 'men', in a manner of speaking. Three twisted and damaged creatures were confined there; one had no legs; another was without arms; their faces reminded me of those rough sketches children scratch in the sand with their fingers: an eye here, a sort of nose, a hole where the mouth should be.

Minehost's revelation of the identity of these creatures was a further surprise; these were, he hissed, enemy soldiers. And his face turned red as the flower we call the 'cannot-kill-aloe': a sign of real anger in these pale natives.

Looking back, I cringe with embarrassment when I think of how naive I must have seemed in the early days of my expedition. How many of my first English must have felt sure that David Mungo Booi and his wandering brethren in the Karoo understood little of the subtle power and beauty of their customs!

Minehost was very patient. Although he could not bring himself to name the place from which these soldiers came, he managed to nod in that direction. Over there, said the nod. Across the water. Place of blood feuds, cruelty, killing, maiming. His country was out of it – thank God! As if to console himself, he broke into a snatch of 'God Save the Queen', explaining he would rather hum a single verse of the National Anthem than sing so much as a bar of that filthy foreign muck so prized by frightful Fritzes and Jesuitical Jacques across the water. Time and again his country had gone to the rescue of Gallic ingrates, Hunnish hordes, Iberian aboriginals, only to be repaid with malice and ingratitude. The flower of English youth lost in the weed-choked charnel-house 'over there'. And so nothing was more unpopular among them now than the notion of their soldiers fighting and killing in some foreign place – unless it was the notion of their soldiers dying in some foreign place.

My perplexity grew. At the risk of appearing obtuse, I asked what soldiers were supposed to do if they were not fighting. And if they were fighting, how could they be prevented from dying?

The answer was as beautiful as it was logical. You left the killing, wherever possible, to others, and, by this means, you left the dying to others. This was advanced military strategy.

But what would happen, I asked, if their enemies employed old-fashioned military strategy? And tried to kill his people? I had in mind our own experience in Bushmanland. First the black man and then the white man encroached on our game and murdered our women and children as if we were so many fleas ... We, the Red People, the Real People, the First People, found ourselves trapped between white and black in their hatred to destroy each other. While they, devils that they were, paused in their mutual destruction only when they turned their attention towards destroying us. We had spoken to them in tongues of peace, and they had replied with tongues of lead. What would happen if their enemies mistook civility for weakness?

My friendly host smiled serenely at the depravity of our history – far removed from anything they knew on his green and pleasant island. If anyone tried anything like that, they would be bloody well sorry. Just let them try. England would stand her ground, fight her corner, knock them for six. If Johnny Foreigner wanted to make trouble, and that was absolutely typical of him, well, he shouldn't be surprised if he got a bloody nose. And serve him right! As for those engaged in filthy little massacres across the water, they should understand that English soldiers would never again shed blood in tribal wars. And if anyone tried to inveigle them into a war, there would be trouble. Make no mistake. After all, they possessed the largest standing army in Europe.

That seemed all very well. But if they had given up the notion of fighting and dying, what did they keep soldiers for?

Doing good, came the reply. Taking up positions between people who wished, for their own private reasons, to kill each other. Observing them while they were fighting. Dropping food parcels on the combatants when they began starving. Burying them when they died. He was proud to say that not one of their European partners had a better record for burying the dead. The Germans could not hold a candle to them. Always dragging their feet. Slow to send troops to the cemeteries concerned. As for the French, well! They got bogged down in arguments about graveyard design and endless philosophical speculation about whether they should be doing more. Calling for subsidies. Demanding standardized coffins. Making speeches. Plotting to do the English down. While our chaps – said Minehost – just got on with the job, the alleviation of suffering, where necessary. Animal as well as human. Soldiers and victims agreed why British burials were simply the best! Commonsensical procedures. Measurable results. I had heard, he was sure, the tale of Dicky the Donkey.

And so we sat down outside the metal door, behind which the broken men groaned horribly, and told sad stories of the death of donkeys.

Somewhere in the Iberian Peninsula, not long ago, Minehost recalled, there lived a little donkey called Dicky, whose fate it was to be beaten and kicked and starved by hoodlums. Their customs, said Minehost, required the torture of animals, a talent learnt in infancy when babies were taught to drown kittens. Youths threw chickens from cliffs, in play. Adults were encouraged to murder bulls. Dicky was abused by all the generations – he was kicked, beaten and driven through the mire. Simply because he was a donkey. Soon he lay dying in some filthy foreign byre.

Alerted by travellers' tales, England mobilized to save Dicky. Children gave their pennies; candle-lit vigils filled the streets. Protests were made to the ambassadors of the foreign sadists concerned. One dark night, after the celebration of some pagan feast, when the sadists lay sleeping off a drunken orgy, highly trained soldiers snatched Dicky from his Iberian hell and delivered him safely to a hospital in the south of England, where a special ward had been set aside to receive him. Universal rejoicing rang out across the land. But the danger was not yet past, and people were asked to pray.

Teams of surgeons, refusing payment, worked through the night. Outside the hospital crowds wept and watched through the hours of darkness. Progress bulletins were posted by the doctors. And when, the next morning, it was announced that little Dicky had pulled through, the entire nation celebrated, churches offered prayers of thanksgiving and several Celtic natives from a neighbouring island, dark-haired and strangely accented, were beaten up by crowds under the impression that they were Iberian sadists. Unfortunate for the victims perhaps, said Minehost, but useful in serving notice to other tribes that if they abused their donkeys, they would suffer a similar punishment.

Even as we sat on the ground the memory of the struggle for little Dicky's life so overwhelmed Minehost that his sorrow broke in a flood.

Following on the successful salvation of Dicky, it was felt by the general public that soldiers might also be used for the occasional relief of human suffering, always providing they operated within strict rules of engagement which would protect troops on the ground.

So it was that when yet another beastly war broke out 'over there', memories of the glorious victory of Dicky the Donkey stirred the nation to a frenzy of compassion.

As it happened, at about this time it was reported in the newspapers that a girl in some distant city suffering in that beastly war, a pretty, innocent little ten-year-old, had been shopping with her family when an incoming shell exploded, killing all but the child. Her name was hard to pronounce, her injuries complicated but of her bereavement there could be no doubt. She became known to the whole nation as Alma, that being as close as English tongues came to wrestling with the extraordinary sounds of her real name. Alma lay unconscious in hospital. And although many unconscious children lay alongside her in hospital, they lacked something extra, something special, that made the public take Tiny Alma to their hearts. It was a horrible fact that children had been dying each day beneath the rain of shells exploding in that city, but only Alma prevailed. Only Alma was chosen.

Why Alma alone? I asked.

Native pragmatism, came the reply. Concentrating in a single victim rather than dissipating one's compassion on the dozens about whom one could do nothing.

Just as they had taken the donkey to their hearts, now it was Alma, Our Alma, Tiny Alma, who moved the country to tears. Alma, unconscious in a primitive hospital in a city on the verge of collapse, where people were eating grass. Tiny Alma, dying by degrees. And it was agreed by press and political leaders and people everywhere that *Something Must be Done!*

A great debate began across the kingdom. The question was as follows: if it is right to save suffering animals, could one not argue that military assistance should be offered to help Tiny Alma? After intense debate there followed the rough and tumble for which the country is renowned – with some saying, 'Yes!' and others saying, 'No! – and people displaying yet again their genius for compromise by arriving at a position with which almost everyone agreed, namely, that children probably had as much right to national compassion as did suffering animals.

Thereafter action followed swiftly. Tiny Alma was declared 'an orphan of opportunity' and other nations were warned that if they attempted to interfere with plans to rescue her, they would be severely dealt with. If others wished to find their own deserving cases, that was their privilege. But Tiny Alma was spoken for.

Though ignorant officials in her own country tried to thwart the rescue, Tiny Alma was plucked from her hospital bed and evacuated to the very hospital where Dicky had been saved. When she arrived, children cried in the streets and people queued for hours with gifts and flowers, hoping for a glimpse of her. The nation took her to its heart, vowing that England would do her duty by the Tiny Almas of this world, wherever they suffered, and solemnly condemned butchers in God-forsaken places for being unable, or unwilling, to put an end to their unspeakable bloodshed. They were urged, said Mr Geoff, to take a leaf from our book.

As so often happens, when we have shown the way – he nodded, quiet, modest, as always – others have followed. For a brief while, at least, those across the water forgot their politicking and their beastliness and flocked to follow the example which they had been given, ashamed now of their tardiness.

As we sat on the ground I clapped my hands and cried out that this was surely good for the world!

Alas! What was good for the world, Minehost shook his head and sighed, was seldom much good for England. Once again, they had pioneered an original idea and the world took it over. After jeering at the rescue of Dicky, and condemning the rescue of Tiny Alma, suddenly *everyone* wanted orphans of opportunity.

Gallic ingrates, Hunnish hordes, Iberian aboriginals, Eytie half-breeds, Greasers, Wops, Frogs, and Fritzes began competing for orphans from this savage little war which no one had even noticed until the rescuing of Tiny Alma.

All over the war-zone children now became targets for competitive benevolence. This new battle was fought with special offers of French dolls, German dresses, Belgian chocolates. In some cases competing nations were even offering free education for life, where target victims survived.

But an even nastier element now crept into the war for Tiny Alma. The appearance of the victim began to tell, for or against survival. Plainer children were increasingly unpopular. The cry went out for the pretty ones.

It was then, said Minehost, that his country had put forward the idea of equal access. Wounded children must be properly displayed, in a decent light, so that the clients might see, clearly, what they were getting. For some hospitals, anxious to attract attention from rich consumer nations, were passing off children with little chance of survival as suitable cases for treatment. Often these children died before one got them home. It was a bad business. Since consumer nations measured success by live showings, losing children meant losing face. Monstrous, was it not? Well, they put forward a plan, explained Minehost, in terms of which foreign hospitals in war-zones were asked to sign a code of conduct. Those wishing to place less popular children – say, the blind or the paraplegic – were obliged to indicate the life expectancy of each child; those past this date could be offered at a discount or given away in batches, thereby allowing poorer countries, anxious to upgrade their compassion ratings, to take, for example, three somewhat plain meningitis victims for the price of one pretty, less severely wounded, child. We enhanced market opportunities by letting poorer players take a share of the action, Minehost explained. Levelled the playing field. Was that not an achievement of which the nation could be proud?

I said it was a solution of sheer genius.

Not so much genius as groceries, said Mr Geoff modestly. They had been playing to their strengths. Like good grocers, they applied the idea of loss-leaders to the compassionate market-place. As a result they hoped – indeed, they had insisted – that many more Tiny Almas stood a chance of survival.

Yet once again the English fell victim to their own generosity and the cruelty of alien cultures. They had believed that their invitation to send us 'lots and lots more Tiny Almas' would be understood and honoured. Alas, the innocence of the island race! When planes began arriving from the war-zone, several young men were found hiding among the wounded children. Some were blind. Others could not walk. What on earth was to be done with them? People disguised their disappointment as well as they could and made, as they say, 'the best of a bad job'. Hospital beds were found, and cigarettes, pyjamas, books and the finest medical attention in the world.

This state of affairs might have gone on indefinitely had not one of the wounded young men – in an unguarded moment – told his doctor that he had half his face blown away while defending his town against an enemy attack. Then a second young man admitted he had lost a leg while on patrol in a minefield which the attackers had sown around his town. Suddenly the shabby secret was out. Alerted by an ever-vigilant press – fiercer, finer, freer than any in the world – across the country the dismal recognition dawned: 'They've sent us soldiers!'

Naturally, the surgeons, who had been the first to discover the deception, refused to operate on the charlatans. There was no point, said the physicians, in treating combatants who, once they were fit, would be eager to return to fight for their country and all too unlikely to survive.

As so often in English history, honest compassion had been abused. A hundred Tiny Almas lay dying in makeshift hospitals in the war-zone, yet English hospitals were expected to treat young men with no faces. It was not fair, it was not cricket; it was just not on.

There began another heated nation-wide debate in alehouses and newspapers. The question was this: should the overstretched medical services of the island be squandered on itinerant foreign males when there were so many more pressing cases for treatment among the indigenous population? Soon enough, and quite rightly, the answer given was a gentle but resounding 'No'.

But what would happen to these men? I asked.

Deceivers, replied Minehost, who had passed themselves off as victims. Naturally they would be expelled, as soon as they succumbed to their wounds, unless collected by their governments before then. England having spent a fortune bringing these impostors to safety, they should not expect free tickets home.

I could not help pitying the creatures in the locked rooms, impostors though they may have been. We shared this in common, that we all awaited Her Majesty's Pleasure. But whereas I was sure of the Royal Summons, these poor souls were virtual prisoners. Emerging from their rooms after dark, for exercise, when their wounds were hidden and would not distress the other guests. Sometimes keening to themselves, a sound I last heard when a lynx tried to gnaw through its leg after being caught in John Jacobs the Jackal-hunter's steel trap, in the far-away Karoo.

I shall never forget the day the call came. One fine morning, without warning, Minehost – of the tender heart for Dicky

the Donkey, champion in the war for Tiny Alma, honest
yeoman of what they call the 'old school', meaning, by this
endearing title, one who knows his place within the tribal
order and does not deviate from it – asked me to step into
his office.

Several large, reserved men stood guard before the windows and doors, ensuring, Mr Geoff explained, that our
meeting remained top-secret and he whispered that these
husky fellows were special servants of the Crown, responsible for the Care and Consolation of Foreign Visitors. Was
he not a man of his word? Minehost inquired, with a wink
at his silent colleagues.

Certain decisions, the honey-haired royal hotelier murmured, had been taken. Plans had been laid in the highest
circles which, he felt sure, would benefit not only me,
but the wider community. He spoke now in the strictest
confidence. I was to pack my possessions and say nothing
to my fellow guests. Their envy would lead to unruly
behaviour. Some might even try to prevent me leaving by
spreading lies and slanders about my royal appointment. I
should rather put my trust in the chaps who would escort
me to my date with destiny.

I saw at a glance why these men had been chosen as
Consolers of Foreign Visitors. They were immensely jolly,
calling me a fine little chappie and asking if I had my
boomerang. Was I ready to go walkabout? And reminding
me to pack my blowpipe. And my shrunken heads. And
asking me repeatedly to tell them the time, and laughing
hugely when I consulted the MAN ABOUT TOWN label on
the sleeve of my good grey suit. Mr Geoff, then, for old
times' sake, as he put it, joined in the good fun by giving
a last impersonation of me. He painted his cheeks yellow,
stuffed a pillow down the back of his trousers to increase

his posterior and, tugging at the corners of his eyes with his fingers to give them a slant like mine, he announced that the Great She-Elephant awaited the presence of Boy David in the Royal Kraal.

So I went whistling back to my room to pack my gifts, overjoyed by this clear assurance that matters were in train, and that my meeting with Her Majesty would not be long delayed. I gathered together the bow of the finest *gharree* wood, strung with sinew from the eland's hide; my reed arrows, in their honey-bear's quiver, with their beautiful flint and iron heads bound with grass; my necklace of ostrich shell; two dozen of the finest copper leg bangles, and, of course, the Promise of the Old Auntie with Diamonds in Her Hair, written and sealed by herself, to gallop to the rescue of her San people, whenever they called upon her. And I rehearsed the request of the family Ruyter, that the bones of their lost relative, stolen by the English, should be returned to rest in peace. Then, planting my fine hat firmly on my curls, I took my cardboard suitcase and set off for my Royal Audience.

Minehost was waiting for me, keys in hand, to let me pass through the great doors which kept a clamorous public from the knowledge of the delights that guests of Her Majesty enjoyed at state expense. I should hurry, Mr Geoff urged, for events were in train and the train was leaving the station. With the devout wish, as they say, that all my landings should be happy, and a wink and a nod, the good fellow gave me into the safekeeping of the two silent fellows I had first seen in his office, the Crown Consolers.

My feet barely touched the ground as they helped me down the corridor and out of the guest-house. They held me by the elbows, and, with the ease that comes of years of practice, they handed me into a large van, something

like the transports used to move sheep between the abattoirs
in Eros and Zwingli, only much grander, of course, and
cleaner, and splendidly spacious, and commodiously fur-
nished with long leather benches running the full length of
the internal metal walls; with a very thoughtful touch, the
windows had been darkened to keep out the glances of
the curious and the envious.

Having settled me securely in the great van and turned
the key in the door, the Consolers gave two loud bangs
on the metal doors, a double drumbeat of flesh on iron, an
echo of my jubilant heartbeats as I prepared to set off on
my Royal Progress, still unable to believe my good luck.

With the same heart-stopping double beat, some time
later, I was alerted to the glad news that we had arrived at
our destination. I gathered about me my gifts; I doffed my
hat. I practised a few low bows. Then, the steel doors
swung open; I straightened my back, and lifted my chin
and, holding out my hand to greet Her Royal Majesty, I
stepped towards the light.

As I did so my breath froze in my windpipe. I found
myself far from the Royal Palace of my fond imaginings.
No smiling Sovereign held out to me the hand of friendship. No pages ran to receive me. Instead I confronted a
dismaying, weary, stale, flat and unprofitable terrain. I did
not fail to recognize my surroundings. I knew them all too
well. I was back in the aerodrome at which I had landed
some weeks earlier. Except that this time we were not in
the huge sorting sheds where the young guardian at the
high table distinguishes between foreign sheep and alien
goats in their holding pens. Now we stood on the even, grey
field where the planes waited to receive their passengers.

I turned to my jolly friends, the Consolers, and asked
for an explanation. They responded by taking hold of my

arms and carrying me towards the steps of the waiting aircraft.

I am sorry to say that I felt I had no option but to protest, even though I knew the natives generally feel horror at a noisy scene. But it seemed to me, as my toes bumped on the steel steps leading up into the aircraft, that I was suffering, quite literally, a miscarriage of justice. In the course of expressing my protests, I managed to direct my elbow into the eye of one of my companions and to sink my teeth deeply into the fingers of the other. This delayed, for a moment, our onward rush. And I heard one of the Consolers express the odd opinion that 'Sooty' was getting restless.

In vain I looked around for this so-called 'Sooty'. Innocent that I was! For I failed to see, until it was too late, one of the Consolers producing from his pocket the same belt that had been used so effectively on Humpty-Bloody-Dumpty. They snapped the belt around my waist and the manacles around my wrists, and inside a moment my hands were chained at my sides. I had just begun to ask whether their Queen would be pleased to receive me in this condition when they slipped into my mouth the wad of leather, the size and colour of a mare's tongue, and words failed me.

When we hunt the ant-bear, as everyone will know, we first pluck him from his sandy hole and then bind his snout with grass and then strap his powerful limbs with sinew. When this agile person is thus subdued, we sling him from our spears and hoist him over our shoulders for the long walk home across the veld. So it was that I was bundled towards the aircraft, tasting in my mouth the bitter bile of the captured prey.

Suddenly, a small man with a pink face and a white

collar which circled his throat as does the ruff the neck of the fish-eagle, waving a piece of paper, interposed himself between the officers determined to push me aboard the plane and my manacled, mute, despairing person, loudly proclaiming that he had an order demanding that the Consolers release me immediately into his custody.

Rescue had come at the last possible moment, but it had come. And, in my blind, bound, prostrate condition (my Consolers, when presented with my rescuer's piece of paper, had dropped me, and my head had struck the steel floor rather sharply), the last thought I remember before darkness fell was the joyful truth that there could be only one possible explanation for my rescue. Her Majesty, no doubt anxiously awaiting my visit, had got wind of my imminent departure and sent one of her servants to prevent it. Justice and fair play had prevailed! God had stood up for Bushmen!

Chapter Four

Travels with a flying Bishop; stiff upper lips
and dental traditions; love among the English;
Beth, the Bishop's dark-eyed daughter; he discovers
an ingenious method of preserving one's modesty

I awoke to find myself still imprisoned, but now far more
comfortably, by a single belt across my midriff. And I was
bowling along, in a superior vehicle which smelt exuber-
antly of high-class cow-hide (a suppleness achieved, in my
experience, only when the leather is softened by being
chewed by a dozen elderly women for several weeks), glid-
ing through England's green and pleasant land, all set about
with trees of oak and ash and the occasional dying elm,
killed – my driver confirmed, following my glance – by
the Dutch.

He was a plump man, nervous as a porcupine, who
threw glances, like quills, left and right. His dark, spiky hair
reminded me of nothing so much as the serrated sword-
leaves the red aloes wear for heads, as they march across the
plains of the Karoo like lost soldiers fleeing some terrible
war.

He was somehow sharp and soft at the same time; like
a thorny desert plant, a rough stem covered with spiny

needles, but inside, the pith of him, was pale, light fluff. Even his words showed me this; my tormentors who had thrown me on to the plane, trussed like an anteater, were bastards, declared my rescuer, but all was well that ended well.

As one still recovering from the shock of discovering that the Queen of England had traitors in her service, I thought this last remark somewhat premature – all was far from well, and nothing had begun.

Such was my introduction to Edward Farebrother – who had been, he explained to me in his rounded, brown tones, 'shot out of the sky'. He wore a long black frock, with a little white bib tied beneath his chin. It was a uniform of his own making, something 'as close as possible to the real thing, while still being different'. That definition, I was to realize, was also as good a description of his religious beliefs as I was likely to get. His dung signature was a mixture of nuts and brandy.

He apologized for his gloomy appearance, so oppressive, he knew, to an African eye, with its love of bright colours. His costume had been once a lovely figgy purple, but he had been diminished to this plain garb upon the loss of his faith. He was not permitted to wear his customary frock. But as no one else wore full fig of the traditional old sort any longer, so he had adopted a form of that costume to show that he lived proudly in the past. After all, the present was closed for repairs. The future was up for auction. Where else was there to live? As a living relic myself, he felt sure I would understand.

Until recently he had been flying, as he put it, a bishop airborne in a godly squadron of the Church of England. He flew missions of mercy to groups of troubled priests, terrorized by the sudden influx of women into the ministry.

I understood from this that in his Church there was no idea of female healers, as we know them, the profession being confined to males. Ex-flying Bishop Farebrother's flock reported that they were being bewitched by the new priestesses. Women who thought nothing of breast-feeding in public, or stroking the statues of long deceased clergy with the intention of raising the dead, or weeping in the pulpit at the drop of a hat.

His crime, Edward Farebrother declared, if crime it was, had been to give succour to these priests. To point out that, traditionally, women had been burned at the stake for such offences.

He was a bridge, he cried. A fleshly bridge, stretched between the little fellow and the grandees in Church government determined to ride roughshod over genuine fears among many of the lesser clergy that there would soon be a priestess in every pulpit, statues would be stroked as a matter of course, and only clergy prepared to weep or dance or breast-feed need apply for preferment: a link between the hierarchy and the roast beef of Old England.

He had gone into bat for the little fellow. He had gone aloft for his fellow clergy. He had preached to them, reminding them that they were not leaving the Church, the Church was leaving them. They were the roast beef of Old England.

For bearing witness in this fashion he had been stripped of his flying licence, shot down in flames, struck off the roll, exiled to the remote provinces, a tiny hamlet among the Black Mountains, known as Little Musing. And there he lived with his daughter Beth, his wife having died a few years before, spared, poor soul, the pain of seeing him blown out of the sky.

As I understood his explanation, this is the way of their

religion. They profess their faith openly, love their fellows freely, and obey the laws of their faith voluntarily. But those who fail to do so are dealt with.

First, he had been grounded. That is to say, he had been forbidden to fly between those distressed clergy who feared the arrival of female healers and whose testicles were now in imminent danger of dissolving and their brains of boiling like sheep's fat on a fire.

Then he had been defrocked. That is to say, he had been ordered to desist from going about in the distinctive dress of their holy men and barred from using his little church. And this for announcing his discovery that God was redundant.

As an atheist, I said, the removal of his frock must have come as a relief. The flying Bishop (grounded) threw me a perplexed glance. I had failed to grasp the complexity of their customs. He was *not* an atheist. True, he had ceased to believe in some God 'out there', some old man with a white beard who punished or pampered his errant children with brimstone or gifts. Instead, he now believed in the God within. He had rejected that dread phantom which so terrified deluded souls from one end of the earth to the other; chaps who worshipped cows – all well and good, of course – or fellows with a thing about the moon, or naked fakirs who adored little yellow idols on the road to Mandalay – nothing against them, if that's what they want. But he had given it up. And in return found a deity more modest, more in keeping with the pragmatic spirit of his people. Somebody who was – Heaven be praised – more like them.

And nothing, declared the good ex-Bishop, his sharp, dark hair springing dangerously about his head, could keep a good man down. He had a vocation to fly. I had the impression that he patrolled the heavens, from where he would descend, at regular intervals, among neglected, endangered souls.

Casting a fond glance at me, he said he had not seen anyone who more closely fitted the bill in a long time, as he watched me being carried, trussed like a turkey, to the waiting aircraft. He had been on my case for weeks. In this very vehicle he had followed the Royal Transport. When the Consolers produced the restraints and bundled me up the steps of the aircraft, he was not far behind. When the little chaps go down, promised Edward Farebrother, this bishop gets airborne! If I could have seen the look of horror on my face as I was bound and gagged; if I could have glimpsed the mute, beseeching glance I gave as I was lifted up the aircraft steps; if I could have heard the sound of skull on steel when the bastards dropped me on my head!

I now began to realize this was to be my destiny in England: to be little seen but much watched. I had been observed by a variety of individuals, beginning with my attendant, Mr Geoff, in the Palace of Detention, and extending to others more malign who chose to regard me, not for what I was, a traveller in an antique land, but as some creature from another world, a distant member of some semi-human species, where I was regarded as part of that species at all.

For the earthbound prelate, I was a living relic, a fugitive, a curiosity, an acquisition, an apprentice. More than all these, I was a 'little fellow' and the Right Reverend Mr Farebrother had devoted his life to the care and upliftment of the 'little fellow'. As he told me often. And, as I was to discover, this love of 'little fellows' had roots deep in his personal life.

He had watched, with mounting anger, as one by one

all my companions – Bengali and Pathan and Istrian – who had arrived in England with me, and joined me in the special transport on that high and hopeful day when we were conveyed together from this very aerodrome to the Royal Guest-house, were summarily expelled from the kingdom. He had pleaded and argued with the powers that be to allow these exiles sanctuary in England. Without success. But when it was my turn to take the transport, he had been ready. He had made a special case for me. Though he had been unable to help the other 'little fellows', they were not quite as little. And they were at least 'part of the world'. Their expulsion from the kingdom, while unjust, was not especially cruel and depraved, since they came from real countries; they were mature adults, literate and modern. They were not woolly little aboriginals, last of a dying breed, mere children adrift in a world of uncaring adults, living relics from the Stone Age, last in the line of hunter-gatherers, rare as the Great Pandas of China. Rarer even than the gorillas of Rwanda. And for whom expulsion from England spelt extinction!

I had to admit, I said, I found it hard to recognize myself in this portrait.

The Right Reverend Mr Farebrother replied that that was all the more reason why he had recognized me on my behalf.

The question I now asked myself was: had I been the victim of a conspiracy? Or had I unwittingly added to my own misfortune by missing some crucial cultural signal which should have alerted me to the fact that those responsible for taking me to the Palace intended to do something very different? Just as the foolish hare, hiding in its burrow, seeks to escape the long steel hook of the hunter by digging ever more deeply into the earth, thus ensuring that its capture becomes inevitable, had I trusted too much to their celebrated love of fair play? And, when confronted by the sharp truth, fought against it until skewered on its hook?*

The suspicion that the natives were not all of equal honesty began to take hold of me and spread through my yet disbelieving consciousness, like one of our own poisons making its slow but irresistible journey through every level of the body, until it settles in the seat of life and love, the heart itself, only to kill the creature to whom it brings this knowledge.

I began to suspect that there existed cunning lesser breeds, without the law, who would not hesitate to wreck my mission. I felt a stabbing sorrow for Her Majesty. Among her flunkeys there were those willing to thwart their Sovereign's wishes.

In answer to his question, I assured Mr Farebrother that I would alert the Monarch as soon as we met. And I planned an early meeting.

Alas, sighed my saviour, that would not be possible. Any movement, other than that envisaged in our agreement, was not permitted. I would be staying with him for the foreseeable future.

I remembered no agreement.

I had signed it, came the reply.

I had signed nothing, I cried.

If I could not recall doing so, said the priest, that was probably because I had been asleep at the time, on the floor of the plane, on which I had hit my head a fair crack when

---

* The hunting of hares with steel hooks is practised among the !Kung people of the Kalahari today. It was probably also prac-tised among the /Xam Bushmen of the Cape to whom Booi claims to belong. But it is worth remembering that the /Xam are extinct.

my captors dropped me. He had been obliged to improvise, by placing a pen in my hand and helping me to sign my name.

But how had he known my name?

Transportation papers and legal dockets gave me the name of 'Boy David'. He had assumed that this was a corruption of my true San name, probably because those who had first detained me in the remand centre could not pronounce it. At any rate, signing my name had not been a problem. It was a fair guess that I could neither read nor write. He had therefore made my mark: not some Eurocentric, mark mind you, but one from my own tongue one which would make me feel at home – the sign! – which he understood resembled the sound of whiplash.

Thus: ≠.

I did not bother to correct his pronunciation. I am sorry to record that I grew rather frosty at this juncture. No piece of paper was needed to save me, I declared. I possessed the most important guarantee of all – and here I retrieved from its sacred quiver my Paper Promise from the Old Auntie with Diamonds in Her Hair. What was more, he was wrong to think of me as a mere visitor. Unlike the other guests awaiting Her Majesty's Pleasure, I was not an exile but an emissary. The official representative of the Society for Promoting the Discovery of the Interior Parts of England. I was grateful for his intervention. Though I had felt sure that, in another minute, Her Majesty's representatives would have rushed to my aid. Yes, I would stay with him, as he had so kindly intimated – but only briefly, using the time to recruit guides and porters for my expedition to London, where I would remind the Sovereign of her solemn vow. And, clearing my throat, I began reading from the Great Promise.

He begged me to stop. It would do no good.

Rather dismayed, I now took from my brown suitcase samples of my special gifts; I showed him the three choice poisons and the ceremonial digging sticks included for the Great She-Elephant.

He waved them away with the weary gesture of a sick man scaring flies. I was not free. Certainly not. He had won me a temporary reprieve while my case for asylum was considered. But I should not place too much store by my good fortune. He patted my head and again called me his poor deluded son.

It seems there is a custom among their holy men of referring to all and sundry in familial terms: father, son, sister, mother – kinship terms often used by them in a very casual fashion. Yet I soon realized that they have a very vague idea of the patterns of kinship. Perhaps they understood something of them once, but the memory has faded like the duiker's urine in the desert. For instance, they know nothing of joking partners, as we do. Their system appears functional to the point of awkwardness: all foreigners are regarded as avoidance partners; all related natives are held to be joking partners, or kith and kin. Or, as they say, in their economical way, the world is divided into 'Them' and 'Us'. This is, in our terms, a crude distinction, but it seems they know no other.

Such gifts were worthless, came the implacable reply, either to buy my way among the tribes, or to sweeten the Royal Heart. And the only piece of paper worth a damn was the one to which we had signed my name and given my agreement.

But to what, I wondered with growing unease, had I agreed?

His answer astonished me. It seemed that I had sworn that were I to be sent back to my beloved Karoo, I would almost certainly be murdered by white farmers. As so many of my kind had been in the past. The thought of this crime now moved the grounded ex-Bishop so greatly he was obliged to stop the car and weep by the roadside for some minutes. If he could save *one* innocent wretch from massacre by white farmers, he would not have lived in vain.

I appreciated his concern. But, for the sake of accuracy, he should know it was as likely I would be murdered by black as by white farmers. Things were changing in the Karoo. In the past it had been customary to kill only members of other groups, but, under the new dispensation, people were free to kill members of their own group.

These were, agreed Edward Farebrother, undoubtedly small, significant advances in my country. But we should not give way to facile optimism. Certainly there were straws in the wind. But we should be careful not to run before we could walk. Or there would be tears before bedtime. Only that very morning news had reached him that gunmen had burst into a church service and sprayed worshippers with bullets. Feelings of horror, outrage, pain and grief overwhelmed him. For the first time in many years, since his faith in God had become as faint as the stars in the dawn sky, he had cried to the heavens to punish men so evil they would murder black people at prayer.

Later that day he had learnt that the dead were not black, after all, but white. More unexpected still: their killers were black.

For some hours, cried the good ex-Bishop, his joy blazed like a comet. Things truly were changing in my country. It seemed as if God (even if he did not truly exist), for so long deaf to his entreaties, had regained his hearing. Only his stiff knees, unaccustomed as he was to sustained prayer, together with unseasonably sharp weather, had prevented the grounded cleric from running into the streets to proclaim a miracle!

But a dozen dead whites did not mean the tide was on the turn. As the proverb said: 'One swallow does not make a summer.'

It would be foolhardy to risk my life in my own country when England offered me safe, civilized asylum. That was what we must fight for: the right to remain. Though he had saved me from deportation, my stay of execution was temporary. We must now convince the authorities that my application was genuine. And that was why we had given a sworn testimony that my life was forfeit should I be returned to my country.

In order to win my release into his safe-keeping, he had made further declarations: he promised to provide lodgings, to stand good for food and clothes and medicines while my application was being considered, to hold in a safe place my air ticket and my passport. He swore that, if injured, or ill, I would be treated at his expense. And should I outstay my welcome by a single day, he would hand me over to the authorities for immediate expulsion.

As to my dreams of calling on the Monarch, well, we must proceed cautiously. My mission had his full support. But it was a tough assignment. If I wished to approach the Palace, there were ways of doing so. When conditions were ripe. In the fullness of time. In the meantime, he advised me to listen and learn. To wait and see. To pause and reflect. To look and learn.

And so I did as he bade, sure that in the former flying Bishop I had found a friend. I told him I was prepared to wait. A hunter who finds the waterhole dry must be able to wait. Patience is the mother of rain.

★

In the next weeks, I discovered that to live in England requires a kind of resolution that people from older, freer cultures know little about. It is as if a man had to spend his life buried up to his neck in an ant-heap. The sky is lowered like a roof, grey and grooved, until it slopes across the top of your head in exactly the same way as do our strips of corrugated iron, which we lean against the side of the donkey cart at night, and then crawl into the crowded dark. But, fortunately, being accustomed to nothing better, they have adapted to conditions which would destroy people accustomed to freedom, light and air.

Their land is a world made of grass, monotonous, broken by trees or small woods with bulges here and there that pass for hills and a few mountains. I estimated that one cannot run in any direction for more than an hour without coming across a batch of little huts that seem to burrow into the cracks and creases of the green, grassy skin like fleas in an old springbuck pelt. The natives, on this island, are less occupants than infestations. It is clear that they breed like rock-rabbits, and have done so since the beginning of time. If you were to slice through the centre of a tall standing ant-heap in the Karoo and examine the writhing life inside, you might have some idea of their clustering, scurrying, teeming millions. So it is in England. There is hardly a place on the island they have not colonized, and what they call 'remote places' are to us as crowded as a termites' nest. Yet if, as some say, they are a violent, brutal race, how is it that they appear, despite these pressures of overcrowding, still to manage at least the semblance of civility? It is surely because they are at heart an amazingly tolerant people that they do not sting and poison each other like snakes in a sack.

As the former flying Bishop drove me through the scurf

of houses with which they like to adorn the edges of their cities, I noticed many small factories given over to the manufacture of false teeth. This intrigued me. Among the wanderers of the Karoo, when our teeth are gone and we are no longer strong enough to lift stones to shore up a fence against the jackal, or too rheumy-eyed to hold the shearing scissors, we are sometimes set to soften leather, sitting for hours gently gumming the springbuck hides until they take on a suppleness as elastic as the tongue of the rock leguaan. Thinking of the well-chewed, supple leather seats of his motorcar, I inquired of Mr Farebrother if they practised something similar.

He was perplexed by my question. Their teeth were no better or worse than those of other people.

Even as he spoke these words he opened his mouth and showed a line of pitted, ungainly dentures.

My saviour had never been beyond the European mainland and so could be said to have travelled scarcely at all. Or he would have known that the English are recognized everywhere by the challenges to their dentures. In many parts of Africa – where they are remembered at all – it is for red necks or black teeth. Which of these attributes sticks in the mind depends entirely upon whether the people in question saw them retreating (red necks) or advancing (black teeth).

The weakness of their dental equipment possibly explains why they have such difficulty in pronouncing even rudimentary sounds. Edward Farebrother was quite incapable of saying even the simple word '!Kung'. And between the clicks produced by tongue against the palate and the simple sound made from the side of the cheek, the sort boys use to encourage cows into the kraal, he heard no difference!

When I demonstrated that there could be sixty or seventy of these musical tongue-in-cheek tales to tell,* he turned the blushing pink of the desert aloe. Try as he might, he could not produce one of them. I suspected (though I did not say so to this kindly man) the reason hinged upon defective teeth. I also believe that somewhere in their heart of hearts they are ashamed of their disability and constantly hide it. Later I was to observe that the higher a native stands on the social scale in England, the less he moves his lips when he speaks, preferring a kind of clipped enunciation much prized by them as a sign that the speaker is from elevated circles. In part this is done to disguise the limits of his vocal range. It also has important and no less fascinating social consequences based on the following paradox: the less he moves his lips, the worse his teeth are likely to be. But the worse his teeth, the greater will be the social esteem in which he is held.

Here we approach the primitive origins of the famous 'stiff upper lip'. This may even be a form of penile substitution. Perhaps their peculiarly repressive sexual culture allows stiffening of the lip, where it frowns upon tumescence in other procreative organs? However, the dental basis of the social cachet must never be forgotten. For what is this phenomenon but a national defence, sanctioned by time and custom, against the derision that ensues when lips slacken and the weakness of their dental equipment is revealed to a scornful world?

Watching the grey-green watery fields, set about with ailing elm trees struck down by the Dutch, slip by my window, I was struck by the splendour and the savagery of

---

* For the five basic clicks of the Bushman languages, see the description on page 282.

these people. Their bravery and their kindness cannot disguise an air of melancholy. It is born of the knowledge that, although still without equal, they were once even more splendid. Surely they are less a people than a perfume? They rise to the nostrils in an aroma composed of a hundred subtle scents and sweetness, bound together (and this is what makes them so singularly interesting) with the acrid taste of anger, the sombre tincture of failure, the flat brown odour of blood. The English are like the tsama melons. They grow best when the earth is driest. They cannot be eaten for their flesh, being altogether too bitter. But their pips are palatable, if well pounded in a mortar, mixed with giraffe fat and toasted over a fire.

Nothing had prepared me for the sullen solitude of that sodden landscape in spring. Nor for the sense of regret, the air of defeat, that was everywhere apparent. It was as if some dragon had clawed her way across the country, blasting with her fiery breath all she found upstanding, leaving behind smoking sad ruins, where workers stood idle on street corners and waited for tomorrow.

I saw deserted factories and broken chimneys, I saw mills – not dark or satanic, as I had been promised, but eerily silent. What a miracle of determination it must have taken to decline from the greatest producer of riches and armies and ships and medals and feathered hats and explorers and horses and guns and tobacco into a bare shelf in an empty warehouse, where others deposited their goods. Once the kingdom had been a noisy engine, a god of power. Quick and wild as Kaggen, the mantis. Terrible as the god Khwai-hem, the All-Devourer. A furious demon with steel teeth and smoke curling out of its ears. Now it has been swept bare.

You know how it is in the veld when the children play?

They take stones and build cities in the dust: huts and storehouses and forts and churches. Suddenly the children are called home at the end of the day, and they forget their magic circle, their enormous city, and it lies there in the last light of the setting sun. The stones wonder what has happened to them. They wait for the children to come back. And they never realize, poor stones, that they are huts and storehouses and forts and churches no longer.

We began passing through fields of squalid dwellings, tall brick huts, joined as closely as the cells of the honeycomb, though nothing like as sweet. Here was one of his desolate places, ex-Bishop Farebrother (grounded) explained. Here we would pause briefly to give his flock of the 'little fellows' hope and comfort. I might leave the vehicle and accompany him, but I did so at my own risk. If the inhabitants got wind of me, they might stampede. They could be unpredictable. I would be reasonably safe if I followed certain precautionary rules.

If pursued, on no account was I to run. I would be taken for one of the detested visitors who descended on these reserves and frightened the inhabitants, a rent collector, journalist, doctor or midwife, individuals no longer welcome in this wilderness, since the estate dwellers believed they harried and extorted and enslaved the tribe.

If attacked, I should freeze. The authorities were forever donating toys and novelties to these people in the hope of diverting and calming their hearts: clowns, magicians, books and films and primitive curiosities from foreign places. If touched, I should stand very still and pretend to be a donation. The attention span of these creatures was very brief. If I did not move, they would lose interest after a few minutes and return to their browsing among the television channels.

So great was the distress and helplessness of these dis-
carded people that they saw any stranger as a threat,
assuming him to be at worst French, at best a native of the
mainland bent on looting and destruction and the theft of
their livelihoods. That they felt this painful, even though
they no longer had livelihoods to lose, showed the depth
of their dispossession. Worst of all, they might take me for
an alien. Such fear and loathing does the alien bestir in the
native mind that these people, who in their own way, he
assured me, were perfectly normal, really, kind to animals
and capable of great generosity, would think nothing of
turning on me and tearing me limb from limb. It was
nothing personal, I should understand. These same people
would be appalled to feel that I should think any less of
them if it happened. But he could never forgive himself.

With that we left the vehicle and moved cautiously on
to the reservation.

At first sight, the locals looked surprisingly normal;
what struck me forcibly was that many were nursing
mothers, their young clasped to their breasts, some
accompanied by toddlers. The young gamboled and frolicked, as the young of all species will do, in innocent, vivid
play. We were well downwind of them. They showed no
sign of catching our scent but went about their business,
which, so far as I could see, consisted of lounging on street
corners, or leaning over fences and calling to each other
with raucous little cries, or hurrying into their shelters
where the television flickered like a hearth fire.

Of men I saw not a single one. I assumed they would
be out hunting, or looking for work in the nearest town,
or sitting at a campfire somewhere, telling stories of better
days, when they were the finest warriors in all the world,
which quaked at their approach.

I asked the name of the place and he told me it was called Green Meadow. Nothing could be less green or further from any notion of a meadow. But muttering spells and incantations over the place, said the wingless cleric, made the horror of it, for the most part, endurable. People sprinkled charmed names over their despair: Beechwood Gardens, Pleasantlands, Happy Fields, Golden Grove, Oakcroft: names that looked over their shoulders to happier times when God was in his Heaven and all was well with the world.

Motioning me to remain where I was, ex-Bishop Farebrother walked cautiously towards a group of young women, calling in a low voice such pleasantries as he thought would soothe and reassure them. We do much the same when stalking birds like the bustard, which are very susceptible to the sounds of their own voices. The quarry seemed surprisingly tame, and their young, batches of filthy six-, seven- and eight-year olds, were obviously very easy in his presence; even the little ones in their prams, or clutching their mothers' skirts, screamed happily as their older siblings tried to attract the Bishop's attention, sometimes punching each other in the face, slashing at friends with pieces of glass, or throwing stones through nearby windows, all in a very natural, high-spirited way.

Encouraged by this show of friendliness and high spirits, I forgot his words of warning and I stepped forward to meet them.

With the shrill clarion call to arms you will hear when the she-elephant sees a hunter approaching her child, the females began trumpeting the alarm. Wheeling and pointing and gibbering, like a troop of baboons sensing the arrival of the ravening leopard. The young took this as an inducement to attack and came at me like hyenas. The ex-Bishop, keeping just in front of the pack, ran towards me, shouting to me to enter the vehicle or perish!

He ran well for a man more used to flying, and we reached the safety of our vehicle ahead of the mob, though their howls were so loud and so near they quite drowned the sound of the engine as the ex-Bishop raced the motorcar away.

We were almost clear of our pursuers when a rock flung by one of the most determined of them shattered our windscreen, and shards of milky glass rained on the two of us. Although somewhat cut about the face and bleeding from the eyebrows, Mr Farebrother clung to the wheel for dear life and, with a burst of speed of the sort you will see when the locust bounds over the head of the pursuing meerkat, we suddenly found ourselves among safer, quieter streets.

My hat protected me when our windscreen shattered. Mr Farebrother was not so lucky. My friend and protector drove gamely on, wiping blood from his face and expressing his deep sympathy with his little flock. I was further amazed when he suddenly pulled over to the side of the road, parked the car in what he called a 'lay-by', saying that this was a very old English custom and I could not really be said to have visited his country if I had never had tea in a lay-by. Whereupon he set up a table and chairs, cleverly assembled from the boot, covered with a fine red-and-white cloth, all the while apologizing for neglecting his hospitality towards me, blaming for his negligence his concern for his poor little flock, which made him forget how strange all this must seem to me.

He produced a flask of tea, and when I suggested we should rather treat his wounds, he said perhaps later, but first a cup of tea would do him the world of good. And so there we sat in our lay-by while enormous lorries raged by like charging rhinos.

I should understand, said my friend, that he would do all in his power to ensure that I achieved my ambition of seeing the Queen. If I were to achieve my goal, then I must first learn something of the temper of the people. When in Rome, one did as the Romans did. I would need to learn survival skills. Street-craft. Combat preparedness. Although, to the trained eye, England might seem peaceful by comparison with the hell I had escaped in my own land, where assassination and racial hatred and wild animals and poverty threatened little fellows such as myself, he would be less than candid if he did not admit that England too, had problems, as I might have noticed. Oh, yes, indeed. He apologized for the reception I had received. It was the children – and they could be deadly.

I begged him to say no more. Had I not been given the most vivid introduction to local conditions? How many foreigners had experienced the sight of native young roaming their natural habitat? It was a kind of bushwalking. How else did one encounter local fauna? I reminded him that I was, after all, a child of the veld, the son of hunters, and I was well aware that on a safari of this sort a traveller must expect a little discomfort.

Only after I had refused a second cup of tea did he allow me to clean his wounds with the remains of the tea and to bind them with strips torn from his little white bib, and all the time the good man apologized for the behaviour of his flock. Their lives, were mostly nasty, British (*sic*)* and short. Sadness had driven them quite mad. But I should remember that, however badly they may have felt

---

*   Br*u*tish?

when they attacked us, they would be feeling a lot worse when they realized they had come close to killing a fellow whose life was actually far worse than theirs. I need have no doubt that a handsome apology would follow. Just as soon as they had simmered down. And reason prevailed. And fairness returned.

Believe you me, said ex-Bishop Farebrother.

And, of course, I did. Since my arrival in England, I had been inspected, detained, dropped on my head, almost expelled and saved. Now I believed I was on the right track.

The village of Little Musing lies deep in the isolated western reaches of the kingdom. It is larger than, say, Scorpion's Hole, but a trifle smaller than Pumpkinville. It has about it nothing of the rough and dusty nature of a Karoo town, being situated in deliciously wet and beautiful country, where emerald fields divided by tall hedges run as far as the Black Mountains, beyond which, the locals say, there live savages. Worshippers of leeks and hut-burners.*

A cluster of ancient houses in a green hollow: a scene, I imagined, that was little changed from primeval times when the ancient English lived in wooden huts surrounded by a stockade to protect them from their warring neighbours, for even then they had been a turbulent people.

Lovingly held by its wooded hills (they call mountains), the way you might lay a child in the fork of a tree to protect it from the leopard's leap, in the early mornings it is hidden in a little mist. In the evenings it is bathed in the setting sun that sends great golden fingers across the brow of the

---

* Wales? The county is probably Shropshire or Herefordshire.

hills which cradle the village, as if stroking a favourite child to sleep.

Little Musing comprises roughly a hundred individuals, Remote-area Dwellers, we would call them. A single road and a stream wind through the heart of the village, passing close by the church door, where beloved ancestors rest beneath mossy headstones. A flock of ducks splash and squabble by the humped-back bridge which crosses the stream where it meets the road in the middle of town, opposite the single grocer's shop and the little butcher.

Little Musing, my guide and mentor felt sure, would soon warm to me. He pointed happily to the homes of his friends. Old Jed lived down Duck Lane, in the cottage with the broken roof tiles, and Miss Desdemona over there in Aga Close; she was cousin to the local Lord who dwelt in Goodlove Castle and was the good Lord's eyes and ears. And legs, he added rather mysteriously. His two very good neighbours were simply dying to meet me. Absolutely everyone was watching us go by.

But all I saw were rows of blank, heavily veiled windows; in a tantalizing hint of hidden watchers, from time to time I thought I saw a lacy veil twitch. Once a child wandered into the garden and stared at us silently as we passed, only to be reclaimed by its mother, dashing from her house at full gallop, who scooped up the infant and disappeared inside, slamming the door behind her.

People were bound to be a bit shy, at first, explained my friend. Only natural. Never seen someone quite like me before. If I saw what he meant?

I thought of the pink Sea-Bushmen heaved up on our shores, helpless as prawns. Yes, I saw what he meant.

Not that the good folk of Little Musing were ignorant of foreigners, said my guide. Their own butcher had married a person from Thailand. Forced to do so. Marriageable women being pretty thin on the ground in those parts. He'd ordered her by post. Blossoms of Siam Friendship Agency. But the woman had pined. It had been a terrible disappointment. After everyone had been so friendly. Waving when they caught sight of her behind her lace curtains. But she faded away. Which had left people sad and puzzled. There they were, taking to their bosoms a strange woman whom their butcher had decided to import – they might not have liked it, but it was a free country, wasn't it? They had made every effort – and it had not been easy – to adjust to the presence in their midst of someone with pretty odd habits, dietary, cultural, sexual and so on. And she went and popped off.

Little Musing had emerged from this experience sadder but wiser. One had to allow developing people to develop – at their own pace – and not expect them to behave as one did. If ever I thought he was in danger of forgetting this truth, I would do him a jolly special service if I reminded him. Everyone in Little Musing had learnt something jolly important when the butcher's wife did herself in. And everyone would remember what it was when they came to deal with me.

The former Bishop lived in an ancient house built from what looked to me like wattle and daub, with a crooked chimney and tiny leaded panes. He shared a courtyard of cobbles and a garden with his two neighbours. Peter the Birdman, lived on his left and Julia, the widow, on his right. Both neighbours came out of their houses to greet me.

Peter was a rumpled, sleepy, friendly man, his hair and beard and even his ears stuck with plumes, stray feathers, so that his head looked like a recently vacated nest. He welcomed me warmly and congratulated me on escaping from oppression in my own country, expressing the hope that I would settle happily among them. He believed fervently that men, like birds, should be free. But the world was imperfect, and men were not free. Birds, too, were oppressed. He made it his mission to find birds in the fields threatened with attack and brought them home. He had forty-two refugees in his house, victims of farmers, hunters, children, cats, and thought of them as his family.

But how did he allow his birds freedom inside a house which looked to me somewhat cramped, with its little windows and low roof?

With a sweet smile he explained that all internal doors were left open and he had broken through the floors and walls to encourage his friends to fly between rooms; he had removed all the furniture but for a small bed, and a stove, to increase the area of exercise available. He cleaned his windows frequently and used no curtains so these refugees and exiles might enjoy a clear view of the surrounding countryside. Of course, even among birds you got hoodlums and killers, and so he allowed no owls or hawks or other predators into the house. But then birds did not have exclusive rights to the butchery of their brothers and sisters. As he was sure I would know to my cost.

Julia wore a weatherproof coat and a dark-green scarf pulled tightly over fine grey hair. She had the stabbing manner of an ostrich, bobbing beak beneath exasperated eyes. She now addressed me as if her words had each been purchased at great expense and she was loath to give them up. She was, she told me, a serial widow. She had had several husbands, all deceased. I commiserated. She advised me to think no more of it. Much more interesting to her were my thoughts on black magic. She seemed delighted with her fortune, but appalled by the manner in which she had acquired it. Since I came from Africa, I would have a natural understanding of occult forces, in which she too took a scientific interest. Perhaps I might give her some advice? Was she occult? Certainly she seemed to have fatal effects on her husbands. What could be done to remedy this situation? Did my knowledge of the dark forces suggest some answer? She had consulted English witches but found them – like so much of modern English life – hopelessly ineffectual.

I explained that my people practised only the Trance Dance, and knew nothing of witches.

Well, then, would I throw the bones for her? Surely I knew how to throw the bones?

I said I was sorry, but we did not throw the bones either.

At this Julia's eyes became even larger, and her nose seemed to grow longer and sharper. In a voice in which were mixed honey and knives, she wondered aloud why Bishop Farebrother had gone to the trouble of bringing to Little Musing a person who appeared so inauthentic? And for that matter, if I did live in Africa, why did I not bother, if not to practise witchcraft, at least to throw the bones from time to time?

In the silence that followed these questions, she examined me from head to toe and pronounced me an odd little beast, adding that I would not have looked at all out of place in the menagerie at Goodlove Castle.

Then, growing even sharper, she demanded to know whether Mr Farebrother expected to accommodate me without paying extra rent. Everyone was taking in refugees. The Farebrothers had me. And there were nearly fifty in Peter's place. But she lived entirely alone. In a house of the same size she used one room, never turned on the heating, for it cost the earth, and she was not made of money, yet paid a whacking rent. It did not seem right. More bodies meant free heat. She intended to take up the matter with Miss Desdemona, when the landlady next called for the rent.

With that, she returned to her house, tossing over her shoulder the opinion that since I knew nothing of throwing the bones and zero about witchcraft, some activity to occupy my days in Little Musing would be welcome, and I might, if I liked, mow her lawn from time to time.

Which, the ex-Bishop said, was a sure sign she liked me.

Edward Farebrother threw open the door to his house, and announced that I was as welcome as an angel of the Lord. Small and humble though his home was, it was mine for as long as I wished to stay.

They have forgotten how rich they are. Humble! His home was as large as the church hall over Williston way. My bed would have slept a family of six.

Now there stepped forward a young woman, quick and graceful in her movements, very shy, with hair almost as dark as the ex-Bishop's, though she was not very much taller than myself; her eyes were of a blue we never see except in Heaven. I put her age at about thirty, though it is always difficult to tell with them. Being younger than they appear is one of their peculiarities; preferring to look back to how they were, to value the past over the future. And such sad clothes she wore: a dark and shapeless jumper, fraying grey trousers and heavy, ugly shoes.

She told me I was much younger than she had expected. Even though my face was so lined.

They associate the puckering of skin, so natural to us,

with excessive age. To them, a young person is always a smooth person. They like their skin to be wax-like, pink and grey and tightly stretched across the face through which the bones press in what to us is an eerie and somewhat repulsive fashion, like stones glimpsed through an inflated goat's bladder.

But then she turned. I felt my heart leap once, twice, in my breast, as a hare will when thrown into a hunter's sack, kicking at my ribs. For this woman, otherwise unexceptional by our standards, pale, of course, as one would expect in this sun-starved island, lifted my brown suitcase and preceded me to my room. Such a simple thing. But in doing so showed the truth of her, full of flesh; quivering tautly with each step she took, globular, generous, sweet as watermelons, round as the moon and sun. Or, like some otherwise nondescript village the passer-by would scarcely glance at which suddenly shows to its rear a glorious, generous dam filled to the banks with shining, shifting life, so did Beth now reveal her delectable hindquarters, a rump the equal of anything I have seen in the loveliest of our women; this English woman was, in a word – steatopygous.

She was very sensitive about it too. For she felt my eyes admiring the lovely rhythms of her haunches, and turned and began pulling at her shirt to hide her charms and I wanted to cry, stop! What a crime to hide such an adorable protuberance! I saw how she flushed, red as the flame lily, and saw that this was not, as it is for us, a source of great pride, but a bad and dismal saddle of flesh she deeply regretted, a hateful fundament she wished to hide.

Addressing me through her father, she begged me to stand beside the door jamb and produced a tape measure. Once my height had been marked off, she exclaimed with delight that I must be a pygmy.

Her pleasure at my arrival was rather touching. She

asked if she might take me into the garden and play with me. Or would I like a run? She was sure that we would be the very best of friends. And she lifted my hat and looked with amazement at my curls.

It is a moot point as to how much enlightenment the English native can understand or tolerate. Very gently I explained that the First People of Africa were not to be mistaken for the pygmies. We came from the south; the pygmies lived in the north, in forests so distant from us that if you travelled from one end of England to the other, repeating that journey once a month for an entire year, still you would not have covered the distance that separates the Red People from the pygmies. An even greater distance lies between our natures, origins and physical appearances.

Beth made an honest effort to follow my explanation. As I have noted, to them the entire world has shrunk to the size of their island. The primitive belief that their island land is so large it leaves room only for places which are very small (or very far or very filthy) has been useful to them, and has gone largely unchallenged through the centuries. Nothing will convince them that theirs is not an enormous land lying at the very navel of the known world. The wise visitor will not exhaust himself attempting to remedy this delusion. The configuration of their brains does not allow it.

The grounded Bishop's ungainly daughter took one look at me, the first English person I had met who did not peer down upon me as if from some lofty plane, and decided that here was the stalking companion of her dreams. It was a relief, she said, to meet someone as small as herself.

I replied that it was a joy to meet someone so perfectly formed. My eyes drawn irresistibly towards that wondrous fundament.

She blushed formidably. I presented her with a copper

bangle and beads of jasper and tiger's eye. Trinkets, but pretty enough.

The grounded Bishop said he knew we were going to get on.

Beth, in return, delivered me to the bathroom. If I was ever to meet the Queen, then a good scrub was in order. The bath measured the width of three donkey carts, silver taps the size of rams' horns; soap as white as bread; and from the silver taps poured a geyser of boiling water that soon filled the room with thick, rich steam. She placed a tall screen between us, on which was painted a magnificent tableau depicting a wild boar lanced by pursuing red-coated horsemen, and she instructed me to hand my clothes to her, over this painted wall, and she would see that they too had a good wash.

I was very happy to rid myself of these cumbersome clothes and to return to a natural state. I undressed, passing each item over the head of the dying boar who gazed up at his pursuers with a look both wild and strange, as if he wished to say something important to those who killed him.

I retained only my hat. It contained my journals and money and my flag, and I had resolved while in England never to let it out of my sight. Once decently naked, I stretched and yawned, as one does when released from some tedious task, and climbed into the bath where I stood a moment, enjoying the plenitude of liquid lapping at my knees; reminding myself that I was about to immerse my body in enough water to serve a family for a month.

My peace was ruined by a loud cry from the other side of the screen and I heard Beth run from the bathroom as if pursued by lions. I sat down in the water and asked myself if perhaps she suffered from religious fits, as some of our women do, when they believe a god has visited them. Even then, you see, I thought of Beth as one of us. And, as events were to show, I was not far wrong.

Beth's behaviour reminded me of the G/wi women, who live in the desert, and whose god G//amama sometimes shoots arrows at them. They scream and leap to avoid the sharp points because they wound more easily than men. Then they must be healed. So they dance by the fire and the medicine man, going into the sleep of Heaven, that healing dream, sucks the poison from their bodies, pulls the arrows of the god from their bodies and throws them away so that the women are cleansed. And we know all this good comes from that point in a man that points upwards.

The flying Bishop burst in on this reflection. He ripped from my hand my large tawny hat and, waving it like a flag to make the steam part much as the prophet Moses waved and the waters of the Red Sea parted, he opened the curtains of mist long enough to show a dark head rearing in that lovely room, in the inquiring way a mongoose will raise its head from its desert hidey-hole.

The Bishop seemed transfixed by that part of a man that keeps the world turning, that part of him which maidens anoint with *buchu*, that part that makes him a man on the night when the boy first first shoots milk at the heavens and informs his father, that part of him which is the power that can bring rain when he points it at the fire and rains a few drops on to the flames, that part of him which is a man's weapon so powerful that he believes he has an eland bull between his thighs and rides the great eland until it finds a mate. That part of a man without which the world would die of dryness.

Again he pointed. I felt a degree of amused perplexity. It is said in the outside world that the English male native is immensely fond of his own sex. Was I to understand my saviour saw me as more than a passing friend? Perhaps even as a joking relative? The Boers are of the opinion that English male natives, above a certain level of refinement, are almost entirely captivated by their own kind. This led to a variety of afflictions, including the inability to shoot straight. For there is no Boer on earth who will admit that the English can hit a buck on the hoof at anything over a hundred metres. Or that, when mounted, they can hit anything at all.

It stood on end, the good ex-Bishop thundered. Did I not see how it stood out, stiff, pointed, proud?

Well, what of it? Would I deny my member stood on end? It was my *qhwai-xkhwe*.* Among the Red People the phallus never slackens. We are born upright, pass through life erect, and go to our graves still bravely standing. It is the last thing to die. It points always before us, a sign to the richest game. It is the arrow of a man. It is a fact as old as our people and we are older than all the tribes in the world. Indeed, when we were already ancient, the English tribes were first putting their noses outside their caves. And even then the *qhwai-xkhwe*, in the smallest infant or the oldest man, pointed to the medicine moon and to the milk of the sky from which the rains come when she showers her blessings on those she loves.

Again the ex-Bishop pointed the finger. Imagine the effect upon an unsuspecting girl! That dread head aimed at her through the steam of her own bathroom. What did a man grow an erect member for if not an assault?

---

* Early travellers among the Cape Bushmen noted that males seemed to be in a state of permanent semi-erection. Many cave paintings of hunting Bushmen confirm the phenomenon.

Assault? Try as I might, I could not keep an entirely straight face. I reached for, and hid my face behind, my great hat. How wonderfully consistent they are. How foolish their consistency! Because their bodies bend to a certain line they imagine all other bodies will do likewise. Are all bowstrings bent to the same tension? Are all arrows cut to the same length?

When I had fought my features into some form of composure I asked ex-Bishop Farebrother why my stub of semi-erect tissue should cause such consternation.

Sitting on the edge of my bath, the defrocked aviator told me of a wave of hatred against women of all ages sweeping the country; of girl-children savaged in ditches; women murdered without compunction; old ladies raped on a regular basis, in flats and bedsitters across the land, robbed, battered, locked in their cupboards, and left to die.

But who would do such things? I asked. Barbarians?

He gave me an odd look. And this explanation. For centuries it had been the custom for Englishmen – being very often overseas – to take their rougher pleasures abroad. Rougher, only because foreign females failed to understand the civilities of gentle contact. Very often they did not even understand English. As a result, they very often said 'no' when they clearly meant 'yes'. What normal bloke wished to embark on a lengthy semantic discussion when in haste to answer an urgent call of nature? So chaps simply proceeded, in pragmatic fashion, without further argy-bargy. For centuries this had been perfectly satisfactory. However, when the empire dissolved, young males found themselves deprived of their traditional right of inspecting their foreign holdings. More and more they were thrown back on their own domestic resources. They approached women, meaning well. Alas, their inner moral core had been corrupted by exposure to foreign females. The sort of animal high spirits, all very well 'across the water', proved disastrous at home. Getting drunk and attacking some passing woman was all very well in the Countries of the Sun – but it did not look good in England. English women were not foreign females. Many otherwise decent Englishmen now quite openly hated women. Was it surprising, then, that women increasingly mistook men for thugs? Or that, in this season of rapine, poor Beth should mistake my honest, upright *qhwai-xkhwe* for something worse?

Given his stumbling pronunciation, these simple words, usually so full of the music of hoof and horn, emerged in hard little parcels from his lips, like the stubborn droppings of a costive goat. Once more my trusty hat provided welcome cover, behind which I composed my face.

I said I understood completely. But just as Beth could not hold back her fear of assault, no more could I undermine the natural rigidity of my member. Among the Red People it lasted from boyhood to old age, whether standing, sitting or sleeping. However, I promised I would do what I could to avoid frightening her in future.

And Beth, I realized, had been spying on me. I felt a twinge of sadness. Yet another who saw me as a specimen – one to be observed. Despite her wonderful outline, she was not of my people. More importantly, this episode taught me to put aside the understandable but futile desire, while in England, to find someone of my own sort. I decided then that the success of my expedition required that I become more like them.

Lying back in my bath, I considered my position. Once, when the springbuck were plentiful in our world, in the First Times, when we were alone and lords of all, when Kaggen made the eland out of a shoe and fed it on honey, and the gemsbok and the hippo and all animals were still people and lived happily beside us, in those great good times before the visitors came, a hunter would put on his becreeping hat, a house of springbuck skin still with its horns and nose and eyes and ears intact, and, hidden beneath it, he would set off after the game, knowing that the gods would be kind to his hunting because he heard in his heart the steady beat of the springbuck's heart, heard it crossing the veld, felt itches in his scalp where its horns grew; he was the springbuck he hunted.

Well, now, I would go hunting amongst the English. And if I was to succeed, I would have to hide my Bushman parts beneath my becreeping hat, for I saw they are more sensitive to an alien presence than is the rock-rabbit among the cliffs to the rank body fume of the stalking lynx.

And if I suspected I was being watched, I would take precautions. I did so now lest Beth felt tempted to repeat her frightening experience. I lay back in the bath, casting my eyes politely at the roof, where the light bulb hung in the steam like a weeping moon. And I did so henceforth whenever I took a bath in that house. As the placid body of the duck disguises its webbed feet in the water below, propelling it forward with invisible digital dexterity, I ensured that my great round hat at all times floated in the water, directly above my *qhwai-xkhwe*.

Chapter Five

Lessons in Little Musing; the charms of Beth and the miracle in the church; learns something of their custom of abusing their young, and how this has strengthened their democracy

Gratitude speckled by suspicion; mystery dotted by disbelief; temptation sharpened by nostalgia; these emotions struck me successively in showers, like stinging arrows, after I took up residence in the village of Little Musing.

Edward Farebrother's welcome alarmed me. It was so firm, so lengthy, so decided. He may have hung up his flying gloves, yes, but he flew freelance now. Third World cases were of very special concern to him. The rich North was building a living bridge between the developed world and the impoverished South. I was his very own aid programme. But between ourselves, given the extreme sensitivity of people to sexual harassment – and especially with the fears of disease coming out of Africa – it would be advisable to keep myself tucked away.

I could not respond with the gratitude politeness demanded, for I sensed that, far from wishing me well on my way, my friends foresaw a lengthy visit; and I dimly perceived that my saviour, in rescuing me from those about to expel me, only achieved this act of redemption by agreeing to become my keeper.

I suspected that my captivity was important to him, for it mirrored his own – and that relieved him. He warned constantly that should I venture out alone, or set off unguided, or, worse, if I 'ran off', I must surely come to a terrible end: 'Chop, bloody chop!' were the words he used to warn me against straying amongst the natives.

If anything, Beth's welcome alarmed me even more. She insisted on accompanying me wherever I went; a burly, watchful woman in her father's shoes. Yet her shapeless clothes could not disguise the naturally lovely lines of her astonishing body. She told me that a little corner of Africa had come to an English village and she had always loved Africa.

Beth said I would be happy if I settled with them. Which I took to mean that she would be happy if I settled with them. She explained that I was classified as a seeker by the authorities.

I seized joyfully on this. Yes, a seeker! What could be a better description? I was on a voyage of discovery. I was prepared for danger. My people who had sent me on my travels were very curious about the island of which they knew little beyond legends and myths. Its culture, dietary habits, and history were the source of so many childish stories. Therefore I had been given the responsibility of preparing a true and accurate portrait of this near-mythical island race.

Many were the questions to be answered. Would there always be an England? Did the Lord Mayors of all great English cities keep talking cats? Had Jerusalem been built in England's green and pleasant land, as legend insisted? At what precisely did the English aim their arrows of desire?

Were there corners of foreign fields that were for ever England?

Beth explained that the terms under which I had been released into her father's care forbade me to seek any of the aforementioned. For the record, I was not permitted to seek employment either. The only thing I was permitted to seek was asylum.

And, seeing the disappointment in my face, they offered the following items of encouragement:

(1)   Rome was not built in a day.
(2)   More haste, less speed.
(3)   Patience is a virtue.

To which I replied, in the words their ancestors, facing similar difficulties, had used to rally their courage: nothing ventured, nothing gained.

Speaking slowly, smiling to show my good intentions, I explained that, far from seeking employment, I intended to offer employment to others. I would need helpers and guides. I appealed to their own tradition of exploration. Did the brave adventurers, pressing deep into Africa, refuse to give employment to native porters and bearers? Did they ask first if the authorities found it acceptable? Imagine if they had stopped to ask permission! Or spent their time seeking asylum when they could have been seeking cities of gold. And ivory. And slaves. They would never have named a mountain, forded a river, shot a rapid, or left their names at some magnificent river falls. Or succeeded in bringing the light of civilization to great stretches of the continent. Very well, then – to retreat from my plan would be to shame the memory of those heroes whose books I had devoured as a child in the library of the good Boer

Smith: Stanley, Livingstone, Kingsley, Burton, Speke and Park.

They shook their heads and foresaw many difficulties; fatal obstacles as well as grave repercussions, lurking dangers, tears before bedtime. They warmed to their task of cataloguing impending disasters, and I began to see that, far from saddening or even worrying them, such muscular gloom is practised much as we practise the preparation of favourite poisons. They are, in fact, never happier than when sharing such black prophecies with each other.

After this little orgy of foreboding, the good Farebrother told me, frankly speaking, that a miracle had saved me and he had a duty to see that I jolly well stayed saved.

Beth, more gently, pointed out that if ever I mounted my expedition to London, I would need special training. To experiment first with the native villagers of Little Musing would be advisable. They were a slow and tolerant lot. Better to begin gently before facing the merciless citizens of the metropolis.

Together they reached this consensus: on balance, taking all things into consideration, erring on the side of caution, I was better off where I was. Better to do nothing. To go nowhere. To wait and see until the time was ripe to make a move.

Now, having spoken from their hearts, they looked happy and relieved. We all knew where we were, said Beth. We had cleared the air, said her father. And they felt sure, said both father and daughter, that we would be very happy together.

This movement between lack of expectation on the one hand and, on the other, the assertion that the little they have is better than the best anywhere else is something so natural, so calming, that it induces in them a state of tranquillity other natives derive from chewing narcotics – or smoking *dagga*,* as our people do. The difference being that when we take the weed, it is with the intention of inducing dreams, joy and dancing; but they drug themselves with dreams of glory that lead but to a kind of mutinous indolence, and a rancorous domesticity, and to a fatal immobility.

I tried to set their minds at rest. I had powerful protection against any who might wish me harm. From my bag I took a tin of strong medicine, a cunning potion of jackal's kidneys mixed with ashes. I had as well a mixture of dried gecko† and kidney fat. Making a cut in the wrist and rubbing in this medicine, one has protection against a variety of enemies, including snakes.

They waved aside my remedies, locked them in a cupboard and kept the key, saying they would be perfectly safe, and they suggested that the primitive potions from Bushmanland were of no use in the jungles of modern England. For there, said Mr Farebrother, an individual is judged not by what he does for himself, but by what others can be persuaded to do for him. Many people were instinctively well disposed to rank and wealth. Unfortunately, I possessed neither. Thus we were left with the alternative of making people wish to help me because they felt I was 'one of them'. Given my appearance, this was difficult, but not impossible. I had only to assume the demeanour of a real Englishman and people would soon forget how very odd I looked and take me for one of them.

I should learn, for a start, to be less headstrong. He noticed my unfortunate habit of blurting out what I felt.

---

*   Marijuana.
†   Lizard.

Nothing was more sure to make ordinary people feel very, very uneasy. Also, I must get out of the way of asking directly for things. Preface all such requests, Boy David, with an apologetic disclaimer, the good man suggested. Something like 'By the way . . .' or, better still, 'Would you very much mind if . . .?' And never, ever speak *frankly* without saying first, slowly, so there should be no mistaking your intention, 'Frankly speaking . . .', for this will reassure your listener that you are not making some emotional commitment to honesty or brevity but simply using a conversational convention.

That you mean nothing serious, or strange, Beth advised.

Or sudden, her father added.

In a word, nothing that was not 'nice', Beth explained. The importance of being nice was something about which I had lots to learn.

I made slow but steady progress with my lessons. I learnt not to be frank without apologizing and never to ask directly for what I wanted, but to get others to provide it, without asking. I still had trouble being nice. I saw how Beth suffered. Here, said I, was an opportunity for being nice.

It was clear to me that although Beth was the beloved daughter of the house, she endured the hours with a kind of ungainly simplicity of which her body spoke more eloquently than her lips. She was housekeeper, hunter-gatherer, gardener, laundress, companion and cook to an increasingly frail old man who, yes, called her his dearly beloved daughter, but behaved towards her as if she were his servant.

For that matter, he called me his dearest son. But treated

me as if I were his prize possession. Appreciated, yes; but imprisoned.

But I did not say so, for that would not have been nice.

Beth's magnificent equilibrium, the swing of her great posterior jutting out a foot or more, at right angles to the back of her spine, two pumpkins on springs, twin udders of elastic delight, I soon came to realize, far from being a source of pride to her, was something so shaming to the poor woman that she seldom ventured out of the house lest the villagers smile and point and mock.

She went out only in the very early morning, or in the evening when few were about, or darkness hid the magnificent mounds from the neighbours' eyes.

In my country every man from Eros to Mouton Fountain would have left donkeys and wives and firesides to stand cheering as she sailed by, but in her own land she hid from the eyes of men. Strange.

She saw the admiration in my eyes. My almost uncontrollable urge to cheer when she went bobbing by. Each step, as her heel struck the earth, sent a shiver dancing, as wind does on water, across the fleshy plateau of her majestic buttocks. So broad, that lovely shelf, you could have balanced a cooking pot on it. And so I told her how beautiful she was.

To which she answered that I was very kind.

Not kind, I corrected her false impression; positively wild with admiration. She had the most naturally perfect body I had ever seen in a woman.

Too late. I saw from her face that I had made the mistake of being frank when I thought I was being nice. And I began to realize that speaking English is no great advantage when one has to communicate with the English. In fact, the belief that we share a common language often only serves to worsen understanding.

So I told her instead that she looked very nice.

She replied that I was also 'very nice'. Meaning, I think, to compliment me.

But looking into her troubled, dark-brown eyes, I knew she had not believed a word I said. She called me 'Boy', assuming this to be my name, taking it from the promise to seek nothing but asylum which her father and I had signed shortly after I had been dropped on my head during the horrifying attempt to expel me from the kingdom. How long ago it all seemed!

Boy David, said Beth to me, if ever you are to meet Her Majesty, you must learn to bow – without scraping. And bowing lessons ensued, with Beth sitting in for the Sovereign. I would arrive at the Palace, carrying my suitcase, remove my hat with a flourish, advance into the Presence and bow easily from the waist, being sure to keep my nose in 'line' with Beth's knee, as she sat regally upon a green-upholstered chair – and tapped my chin with a plastic ruler whenever she felt it dipped below the crucial level where bowing became scraping.

It was while we were playing happily at bowing and not scraping that our neighbour, Julia, arrived to say that old Jed who lived at the bottom of Duck Lane had not appeared for some days. Next, Peter the Birdman arrived and said that if old Jed at the bottom of Duck Lane had not been seen for days, that was no bad thing and he for one would not weep. Old Jed was a hunter and hater of birds, shot them, ate them and kept them in cages.

Julia now suggested that a useful task for their little yellow friend would be to get him to climb inside the cottage and discover why old Jed had not shown his sharp red nose out of doors these past five days. Being a wiry and lithe sort of chap, she felt sure I could be inserted through some large crack in the roof or lowered down the chimney.

Peter proclaimed that he stood ready to rescue any robin, hawk, sparrow or starling that might seize its chance of freedom when Jed's house of horror, as he dubbed it, would be opened to the wholesome light of day.

And he ran to his house and shut it tightly so as to join us on our expedition to Duck Lane, and I saw the sparrows, doves and starlings dashing themselves helplessly against the windows and thought how strange it must seem to these creatures of the air to find themselves living in an English cottage – almost as strange as I found it myself.

Down the muddy length of Duck Lane we traipsed, a pathway not, as I had thought, remote and lonely, but packed with houses from which villagers emerged, drawn by promises Julia made to all and sundry that they would soon see the little yellow chap earning his keep.

After knocking at the door several times and receiving no answer, after trying the door and finding it locked, after walking about the little house and shaking the windows in their frames and finding them barred, Mr Farebrother pointed to the crumbling section on the roof where the tiles had slipped and which might be widened enough to allow entry.

To shouted directions from Peter to go gently so as not to scare the birds, I crept through the aperture and was soon inside the house. I found it to be dark and malodorous. The curtains were drawn against the light. I entered a small, airless room heavy with dust and neglect. I knew the scent well enough. Had I not picked it up a thousand times in the veld, where the lion has killed? Where the jackal-hunter had left his traps cunningly buried in the sand beneath a sheet of newspaper? Where the vultures gather?

When I climbed back through the hole in the roof I was met by a barrage of excited demands for information. What had I found inside old Jed's house?

Simply old Jed, I replied, stretched on the carpet, staring

at the ceiling with a gentle, quizzical look on his face, as if considering how very surprising it was to die, as one had lived, alone and unconsulted.

To my astonishment, considerable relief greeted my news. That was all right then. Not as bad as they had thought. Old Jed had had a good innings.

I knew, of course, that an Englishman's home was his castle, but was it also his grave? To die alone, among neighbours – was that not strange? I asked my saviour.

A very Afrocentric line of reasoning, came the reply. Old Jed's neighbours would not interfere with a person's right to privacy while alive and so were hardly likely to intervene in death. A few weeks of silence did not necessarily mean a fatality. How was one to know that one's neighbour was dead? And not simply living quietly? If people were forever calling on friends and neighbours, on the off-chance that one of them may have passed away, well, this would be seen as an outrageous invasion of privacy which no decent person would tolerate. And he had no doubt that Old Jed would have felt exactly the same.

Even as I stood on the roof, above old dead Jed, several locals came by and chaffed the grounded Bishop for this manner of forced entry, pretending to admire his talent for burglary, saying they had never expected it in a former man of the cloth. With many a wink and a nod they asked if they could hire the clever little monkey, as they had a bit of fetching and carrying he might usefully do for them.

Which showed, my wingless friend assured me, that they understood me to be not a bad little chap after all, and, amongst them, that was high praise indeed.

I was pleased. But I suspected that however the locals understood me, I was still some way from understanding them.

*

My lessons in learning to be more like them took another step forward when the terrestrial Bishop suggested that I find some method of integrating myself among the villagers. If they saw I had something to offer, the people of Little Musing would soon take me to their hearts.

Then there began an animated discussion between father and daughter as to what, if anything, I had to offer. After a good deal of discussion, during which all my suggestions – a love of England, a personal promise from a member of the Royal Family, and so on, were gently rejected – the Farebrothers concluded that my most useful attribute was my natural unspoiled innocence.

Might he know something of our marriage customs? the good Bishop inquired.

I replied that amongst our people marriage preceded the begetting of children and that children, when they came, were few and much loved.

Beth thought this very moving. I had seen for myself the difference in their culture, where the opposite prevailed – where young males believed that the insemination of as many women as early as possible to be among the chief rites of manhood. They then declined all further responsibility, and decamped to some other place, there to continue the tradition, often with violence. Her father and I had been lucky to escape alive from Green Meadow. From what she told me, the fact that our pursuers had been children had made them more and not less dangerous. For these tiny people, guns were fun, killing was a sport, and dying something unimaginable. Children, in some cities, now carried guns as a matter of course, and fought to the death for cash and drugs, to which even eight- and nine-years-olds were addicted.

Perhaps my disapproval showed on my face because she

asked, rather tartly, whether murder was not a popular pastime in Africa? Especially in my own country?

I agreed that it was. And my people knew it. We suffered at the hands of the visitors, hunting us, hating us worse than the lynx and the lion and the jackal. Cleansing the land of the Red People and shovelling them into unmarked mass graves where sometimes a shin bone or a skull will fight its way to the surface, to be found by some little Boer child who will play football with the skulls of the First People, whose hearts and homes once reached across the endless flat grass of Bushmanland. And where, today, only ghosts sing in the high places; their hair is to be glimpsed in the rain clouds, their tears fall in the rain. My ancestors can be faintly seen when you look into the faces of the wandering Ashbush People; then their ghostly faces peer out at you – much as the traveller, passing through a dying village, sees the thin faces of starving children staring from the doorways of darkened huts.

But, in England, I cried, it was surely quite different. The Queen loved *her* people. Her servants, the soldiers and the police, were on the side of the people. Yet from what I had seen, the average citizen was in danger of being killed by armed children.

That was the very reason why it would be very wonderful if the children of Little Musing could be brought face to face with unspoiled innocence, said Mr Farebrother. Something might rub off.

Heart to heart with a survivor of an earlier age, said Beth. Boy David from the Karoo, and the only Bushman in England. Face to face with a genuine hunter-gatherer in the late twentieth century. What a privilege it would be to meet me!

It would give the little children 'hands-on' experience, said the ex-Bishop. I might make a difference.

I might also be killed, I pointed out.

They nodded. But after talking about it they felt, very strongly, this was a risk worth taking. Among the adult male population such education was almost certainly too late. The ancient love of freedom was partly to blame. Freeborn Englishmen could not be forced to behave peacefully. Violence could not be confronted without creating more destruction. Containment was the only option among violent young males.

But with children, perhaps it was not too late. If there was any way I might help, then I would deserve the gratitude of generations to come.

The good Farebrother begged me not to write off all children merely because some wayward infants had tried to kill me. He appreciated my point, but I must not give up hope. After all, much of the misunderstanding between peoples arises when one nation makes unshakeable judgements about another. Sees it as less than human. Surely – the good man demanded – being human means we all make mistakes?

And indeed I had to agree. For I recalled how, in the old days, we had laughed at his people, the Sea-Bushmen, when they first dragged themselves ashore in our country. So pale, so blind, so soon pink in the sun, so incapable in the wild, so lost in the dark, so reliant on their guns, as needy as is the donkey in the Karoo bushes. So linguistically limited they could not get their tongues around a word, not even the name of our land, calling it Carrow and Camdeboo and other nonsenses. They looked at us and declared we must be gypsies from Egypt. Or the link by which animals were joined to the upper orders. Thus their sojourn in Africa influenced their religion and led to the belief that there were three orders of creatures: the animals, the others and the English.

We felt pity for these wretches who could not tell the difference between the spoor of a *kudu* and an eland; between the Men of Men and the Red People.

Oh, yes, how we laughed at this pallid infestation! Clumsy visitors who seemed no more noxious than flying ants, no more alarming than the white ants' eggs which they saw us eat by the fistful, and called 'Bushman rice'. Oh, yes, how we darkened with shame at their shameful incompetence.

But how wrong we were! For they proved to be more toxic than the greatest of our poisons, which kill surely, but singly. As it happened, these apparently weak, defective, cowardly, diseased creatures were to become a pink plague, a most deadly and obliterating invasion; wherever the pale Sea-Bushmen so much as appeared, we died.

Yet in the beginning, when they first fell on our land, they were received everywhere with great kindness; both by our cousins, the Men of Men, the Korana, the Strand-loopers, and by the Red People. We permitted them to buy a good ox and a fat sheep for one iron hoop apiece. In exchange for the brass cut from their ships' kettles, we gave many dozens of sheep and cattle. In truth, we had very little interest in their trinkets but took them out of politeness, not wishing to offend these pale Sea-Bushmen who evidently attached great importance to scrap metal.

Next they came with copper bangles. These pleased us for a time. When we tired of those, they brought glass beads, knives, mirrors, iron and copper wire, in exchange for which we gave cattle, sheep, ostrich eggs and honey.

When we tired of those, they came with bullets.

As the flying Bishop had rightly said: we all make mistakes. My people had taken the visitors to Bushmanland to be our friends. And they had proved lethal. Well, then, perhaps I was just as wrong about the little murderers of Green Meadow estate. And though I did not much care about the gratitude of generations to come, I was prepared to do anything that might win me wider acceptance among the natives. I agreed to visit the village school.

The children asked that I wear my traditional clothes. I was happy to oblige, dressing in a small leather apron that protected my *qhwai-xkhwe* from the world, took up my bow, a quiver of arrows and a drinking gourd made from an ostrich shell, and set off for the school.

From the Bishop's house to the little school beside the railway station was scarcely two minutes' walk; in that time most of the villagers were in their gardens, or leaning from their windows to see us pass.

There must be something in our appearance frightfully repulsive to the unsophisticated natives, for the infants took off like hares when they saw us, screaming for their mothers. Alarmed by the child's wild outcries, the mother rushes out of her hut, but darts back at the first sight of the apparition, crying to the good Bishop that he ought to be ashamed to bring such a thing to the village. Dogs turn tail, and vanish. And hens, abandoning their chicks, fly screaming to the tops of houses. And mothers, holding naughty children away from them, say: 'Be good or I shall call the Bushman to bite you.'*

None, of this, said my episcopal companion, was to be taken seriously but should be seen as rough, rustic, ready wit, and showed that the villagers had begun to warm to me.

---

*   This bears a surprisingly close resemblance to Livingstone's account of reactions to his appearance in a remote African village, given in his *Expedition to the Zambesi* (1865).

I said I thought they were casting slurs upon my person. I heard, most distinctly, someone ask whether the little bloke didn't catch cold, walking about in leather underpants.

Mr Farebrother corrected me these were not slurs, but real concerns, cloaked in broad good humour, and all part of the warming process.

In the schoolroom I was stood upon a chair and the children were invited to touch me as part of the warming process. It took a while before they conquered their fear of the strange and the wild, and many questions had to be answered by their teacher – a young woman pierced in ear and nostril with a splendid array of steel clips, not unlike the sort of thing the first English had bartered with us, for use as fish-hooks, when they washed up in Bushmanland. Ritual scarification appears to be a cultural phenomenon among the island youth.

Would I bite? Was my skin so wrinkled because I was very old? These were just some of the questions asked by the children who crowded around my chair.

Their teacher explained that I was a rare survivor of an ancient people who had been hunted and hounded by the colonialists and imperialists of the Western World. It was a miracle I had survived, and she, personally, wished to make a sincere apology to me and my people for the crimes committed against us by her ancestors.

I replied that, speaking very frankly, I welcomed her apology and would have passed it on to my people had they still existed; but I had no doubt that poor shadows of their ancestors though they were, the sponsors of my expedition to England would accept it gladly.

Whereupon she declared that I was really very nice – and I began to feel I had done a good thing in coming to the school.

Mr Farebrother now invited the children to get some 'hands-on' experience, and, after a little shuffling and giggling, curiosity got the better of them and they crowded around my chair, stroking my face, digging me in the ribs, and trying to lift my breech cloth so as to expose my lower regions. Soon, indeed, they were so enjoying themselves that several times they very nearly knocked over my chair – though I have no doubt this was quite accidental – and had to be ordered back by their teacher, and forbidden to lay more than one hand on me at a time. And to stop pinching. And poking. And peeping beneath my skirt. But the pandemonium continued until Edward Farebrother and the teacher were forced to call a halt, lift me off the chair and place me on top of the stationery cupboard for my own safety.

Now, standing on the chair I had so recently vacated, Mr Farebrother appealed to the children. There I was, a poor little fellow, without clothes, or money, or a home. My mummy and daddy were dead. But wicked men wished to send me back to where I had come from. All those who believed Boy David should stay in England where he would be safe, please put up their hands, he cried.

Like a field of prickly pears, little hands stabbed the air.

And would those who wanted the wicked men to leave David alone, please put up their hands? -

Such was the determination of the class that this should be so that some children now raised both hands. And several shouted that the wicked men should be killed!

And then my guide and mentor took me home, rejoicing in the success of the warming process. His people, the good man explained, were slow to anger. But, once aroused, they were lions in the fight against cruelty and oppression. He talked of the battle for Dicky the Donkey; of the war for Tiny Alma and of the many ordinary people who devoted their free time to saving calves, cruelly torn from their mothers, imprisoned in tiny wooden boxes in which they could not see, or turn, and sent to Europe, where they were eaten by Belgians who had disgusting tastes in meat; he himself had been several times to France, where he had stood between horses destined for the abattoir and angry Frenchmen addicted to horseflesh. By taking me to their hearts, the children of Little Musing had shown that English compassion for the underdog, or bitch, was alive and healthy in the rising generation, and he, for one, gave a cheer.

It was my custom to walk around the village each day, learning, as best I could, the ways of the Remote-area Dwellers of Little Musing, and considering whether this was a tolerable place in which to settle a colony of our people. Though I seldom saw a human face, I knew that behind the lace curtains in the little dwellings observers kept track of my every step.

They dwell in far-away times; much of their lives could be said to be lived in a damp dreamtime, and if you watch their faces closely, you will see them sometimes fix into that rapt introspection, like man at stool, straining for something to which they feel they remain attached, even as it is passing from them.

They dwell, too, in overcrowded conditions, at almost a thousand to the square mile. Perhaps this proximity to each other explains the extreme discomfort they feel at bodily functions and the exposure of the body, often resulting in a kind of cramped comedy which they use to disguise their embarrassment. Bodies and their functions are a source of public mirth and private horror among them. Individuals need to preserve private space; but they know they have to coexist. Yet any further forced intimacy would drive them mad. So the native genius had come up with a way of making the intense dislike they feel for one another almost bearable – coolness, diffidence, tolerance. Toleration is really just the acceptable face of hatred.

Nothing sustains the English in their present sad and shrunken circumstances (rather worse than those of many of the races who were once their servants) than the knowledge that once upon a time they lived better than anyone on earth. It is a distant race memory which many natives of the island retain, and it is a consolation, of almost religious importance.

Their religion, as I was to discover, is not a question of churches. The closest they come to a feeling of transcendence, and a sense of the sacred, is when they turn to the past. Their faith is a form of ancestor-worship. And the only spiritual experience which binds all orders of society – in fear, awe and loathing – is the blood-sacrifice.

This discovery took place rather unexpectedly. I had begun to hope that by allowing the children of the village to gain invaluable 'hands-on' experience of my unspoiled innocence I might have relaxed my passage into English life.

Indeed, it seemed to have done so, for no sooner had I returned from the school when Peter the Birdman and Julia invited me to an ancient ceremony on a nearby estate. They told me that from time to time all the villagers dressed in clothes which once marked their station in life, as peasants, or honest yeomen, archers, beaters, ploughmen, and then, said Peter, they made a pilgrimage to what they called the 'Big House', a great mansion, some miles away, where dwelt, they said, a magnificent Lord. And there these peasants and yeomen and matrons re-enacted an age-old ceremony for the benefit of foreign visitors who paid handsomely for the privilege of accompanying the Lord of the Big House upon an ancient English hunt; they chased birds and shot them out of the sky, and killed foxes and even deer, and by this traditional blood-letting they felt themselves to be, once again, part of a chosen race whose feet did, in ancient times, walk upon England's mountains green.

Even Peter the Birdman took part in the ceremony, explaining that although he was implacably opposed to the taking of aviary life, the ancient customs of the countryside deserved support, and he worked, not with guns, but with a bag, collecting game knocked out of the sky.

It seemed a wonderful idea, the villagers dressed up, pretending to be peasants, and the Lord of Goodlove Castle dressed up, pretending to be a nobleman.

And I was invited to join the festivities.

To my disappointment, Beth and her father were vehemently opposed to the idea. The Lord of Goodlove Castle, they muttered, might not quite see things my way; and if I ventured on to his estate, I might never leave it again.

I saw how fearful of this Lord the Farebrother family was when the monthly ritual of the collection of rent came round, and Miss Desdemona, cousin of the Lord of Goodlove Castle, would appear, carrying an old shopping bag and talking cheerfully of the garden and the weather and a host of unrelated subjects until at some precise, but undefined moment, a handful of notes were pushed into the shopping bag, apparently unnoticed by Miss Desdemona and unmissed by the Farebrother family, for neither party to the transaction said a word.

Miss Desdemona then moved to Peter the Birdman's cottage and called on him to come out. Peter pretended deafness. His domestic aviary swirled against the panes and pecked and chirruped as if to say that there was nobody home, but we all knew Peter was kneeling on the floor behind the curtain, unable to pay his rent because he had spent it all on his feathered allies.

In my country, this refusal would have led to police vans and prison. But Miss Desdemona, after waiting for a response, eventually moved on to Julia's cottage and no one said a word. For that was not the English way. Peter's behaviour had been noted, and would not be forgotten. One night the Lord of Goodlove Castle, who owned all our houses, and much of the village, it seemed, and most of the land between Little and Much Musing, would come to call and demand his fee. I had the sense that although they resented the far-reaching powers of the mysterious noble, they somehow felt him to be part of the very fabric of life, with his festivals and his name and his Big House and his nocturnal raids, and they were all connected, or beholden, or related to the invisible aristocrat. Even Julia, unwillingly slipping her envelope into Miss Desdemona's shopping bag, complaining bitterly about the number of birds in Peter's cottage for which 'he did not pay a penny', or the presence in the house of the defrocked Bishop of a little person from the colonies who was undoubtedly some sort of live-in servant, while she rattled around like a lost marble in a cold house she could not afford to heat, with a lawn the person from the colonies would not bestir himself to mow, paying rent to a rich man who gave not a thought to decent and proper conduct, but instead spent it all on a harem of floozies, yet she asked Miss Desdemona to convey her best wishes to her cousin – though how a man of his standing could carry on like some oriental despot she, for one, could not imagine.

To which Miss Desdemona and the Farebrothers and Peter the Birdman, crouched behind his curtains, and I listened and said nothing. For this was the English way; a little tirade was allowed, and even encouraged, but it did not change anything and everyone knew the score. Hate the Lord though they might, even in protest they all still deferred in one way or another to his invisible power. Not, I think because they liked him, or believed in him – but because without him to love or hate, who else was there?

I watched as all the village, decked out in the costumes of yesteryear, climbed aboard the transport provided by the Lord of the Castle, an old wagon, pulled by a tractor, and set off for the festivities. I felt they resented my refusal to accompany them, but the Farebrothers were adamant.

So concerned did they become at the threat represented by the Lord that they began casting about for some hiding place where I might be concealed until the Lord of Good-love Castle had forgotten all about me. The church was just the place, they decided.

I offered the opinion that the Lord of Goodlove Castle, knowing I had been living with the former Bishop, would surely guess where I had been hidden.

On the contrary, the Bishop informed me – the last place anyone thought of visiting was a church.

After dark, the Bishop took me to my place of safety. The church was stoutly barred and carried a great padlock. Local people were in the habit of carrying away anything they could lay their hands on, from the lead on the roof down to the pews and flagstones. It was a rural custom.

Custom or not, I could not help wondering whether he regretted the loss of all his sacred furniture.

He confessed that when he still believed, it had saddened him. But it was a phenomenon which happened all over the world, did it not? Even in my country?

I was pleased to be able to tell him that nothing of the sort occurred amongst my people. We built no churches. Our healers and medicine people wore no distinguishing insignia, and owned no fixed property. They were there to help us at the dance time of the eland bull. Or when a woman first bleeds. To talk and to sing of Kaggen, the praying mantis. To pray to !Khwa, the rain god, and to protect us from Khwai-hem, the All-Devourer.

Ex-Bishop Farebrother said it was quite plain to him that nothing was stolen from my people only because they had nothing left to steal. He would give anything to be in my position. And he hoped I realized how well off I was.

He pushed open the door and we entered the holy gloom which they favour in their churches. When my eyes grew accustomed to the semi-darkness, I saw that the floor of the church was made of the lids of the tombs of scores of bishops. The walls were lined with the coats of arms of brave knights, and with the regimental flags of the local soldiery. Relics of famous victories in foreign parts. I could not help reflecting on their extraordinary sensitivity. Not for them the great brassy trumpeting monuments of other tribes, nor the noisy marching displays of triumph. That would not be their way. Rather, they preferred to incorporate their relics into their sacred places, to lay their battle standards in the lap of their Creator. To recognize that, without the help of their God, they could never have conquered three-quarters of the globe and ruled an empire that stretched from sunrise to sunset.

Each evening the good grounded Bishop paid a visit to

me. We talked of my gods and of his, and of how he had come to be excluded from his Church.

Their religion, as he explained it to me, seems rather crude, though it has some saving aspects. They know nothing, for instance, of the power of the moon as regards hunting or rain-making; nor of the songs of the stars or the dangers of the sun. There is some slight indication that they retain rudimentary memories of true religion because they sometimes refer to the beliefs of their ancestors who paid due respect to our mother, the moon.

Mr Farebrother knew nothing at all of how man came to die. How the hare found his mother lying still in the veld, so still he felt she must be dead. He prayed to the moon to wake her, but the moon said that his mother was not dead but only asleep. However, the hare being foolish, the hare being little-brained, the hare being of the family of man that goes on two legs, he would not listen, would not hear, would not believe the moon and cried and cried for his dead mother, until the moon grew pale and angry and, reaching down to earth with long arms, slapped the hare hard across the mouth, as a mother will do a foolish child. The hare's lip was split, and the hare's mother continued in her sleep, now truly a sleep of death. Oh, if only the hare had believed the moon that his mother truly lived; then the hare, like the moon, would have lived for ever, and all the human family.*

My flightless friend told me that, to them, the moon was just a piece of earth that had split away long ago and now floated in the heavens, cold and dead. He stared at

---

* This story of the hare and the moon is common to many of the San people, but it is amongst the /Xam of the Cape that we find it used most forcefully to explain how death came into the world.

me, open-mouthed, when I told him of Kaggen, who made
the moon, the celestial joker, the nimble god, who shifts
his shape in the blink of an eye, from cobra to jackal. Mr
Farebrother had never seen a praying mantis and shook his
head wonderingly as I described the divine jester, who
appears to man in devout repose with huge eyes and tiny
hands clasped in prayer. He listened in silence when I
related how, one day, the mantis was attacked by meercats,
so sharp of tooth and claw, and how, in his haste to escape,
he pierced the bladder of an eland bull and flooded the
earth with inky darkness, and so escaped. But since a dark
world is no good for hunting, clever Kaggen made light by
throwing his shoe into the night sky, where it hangs shining
to this day, helping the hunter on his way.

It did not look like a shoe, the Bishop objected.

I explained that the shoe carried with it, into the sky,
a cloud of dust from Bushmanland; the dust prevents us
from seeing the moon for the true shoe it is.

He appeared unpersuaded. They have great difficulty
understanding such profound truths.

We talked about God.

Their God is bound up with notions not of the good,
as it is for most other people, but of the useful. Particularly
with those things their genius has created: the steam engine,
the railway, the spinning jenny, the football match, achievements with which they consider they have enriched the life
of man.

Thus it is that one can say that they worship what is
gone. Their God lies somewhere behind them, where he
inhabits an ideal paradise, small, green and clean. Their
God has absented himself. If you wanted a sign that the
English were innately religious, said the former flying
Bishop, you would tell it from the fact that they were for

ever looking over their shoulders asking where he was, why he had gone missing. Would he turn up one day? Again? And come in glory? Was he simply late – like the trains?

But that seemed to me a very pallid god, a polite fiction, a deification of their own nostalgia. I hoped we might discuss it.

Now, they have a great horror of abstract thought. They will do almost anything to avoid it. They hate, above all, what they call 'speculation', that is to say, the effort of thinking hard about ideas. When they do this, it is a very comical sight. Their eyes turn inwards. They scratch their heads. They exhibit all the delightful but helpless perplexity you will find among the baboons, those people who sit on their heels when confronted by our fierce euphorbias in the Karoo, which, pointing their poisonous spines at the sky, stop those poor, thirsty baboons from eating their milky flesh.

Each night I was locked in religiously by Beth, who made sure I had enough to eat and drink, often bringing me delicacies she knew I would like, especially the larvae of ants, being entranced when I told her how we prized this 'Bushman rice'. More and more she asked me about the life and ways of the Red People. Increasingly, she stayed with me after I had eaten, and settled me for the night beneath an old tartan blanket, which she pulled over the stretcher set up for me before the altar, and I noticed the shine to her eye which she had first shown me when I took that bath in her presence on the night I arrived in Little Musing and she had hidden her blushes in the steam and I had hidden my modesty under my hat. Beth now demanded constant stories and instruction in the ways of the Red People, going so far as to say that if her father objected, she would run off to join a Bushman band in the far Kalahari; for she wished to climb out of her skin and enter that of another, where she would be free and alive and far from home.

I suspect my mistake began there. For it seemed to me, in feeding her hunger for tales of the old times, of the mantis and the moon, of hunting customs and the dances of my people, I was pleasing this sad woman who never ventured out of her house and whose duties towards her father were harsh as any servant's. Besides, I hoped that in pleasing her I was repaying her father who had saved me. I meant well, but I did badly.

Her absence from home was noted, and her father began arriving unannounced, demanding she return immediately and cook his supper, or sweep the house, or iron his shirts, saying that I was quite capable of bedding myself down for the night and that too much comfort was likely to spoil me. And what good, then, my unspoiled innocence? But Beth tossed her head and looked determined, and I began to wonder what she was determined on. Furious with her father, she told me she would happily stay right through the night, if I liked. Or, if I preferred, she would help me to leave Little Musing and travel with me through the length and breadth of the kingdom, safeguarding me, as the lioness does her whelps. I thanked her for her offer. It showed that the warmth which her father had hoped would be established between the English and myself was now evident indeed, though perhaps not in the way he had intended.

I made no secret of my admiration for Beth: that magnificent plateau, that great fleshy magnificence of her posterior, that spongiform delight, those two fat heifers harnessed to a lovely plough. What man in his right mind would not feast on such charms? And Beth for her part, instead of hiding this miracle, as she usually did among her own people, positively showed it off, allowed the solid, rubbery bounce of each hemisphere to find its own inde pendent rhythm and harmony, walking away from me with a sly backward glance, knowing I was bewitched by that divine fundament. I understood her essential loneliness and I was not, as I have made clear, immune to her charms. However, philosophical questions arose. Could one, for instance, enter into an intimate relation with a local person and not acquire, or have 'rub off on one', as the English say, some of their less admirable qualities? Then, too, there was the responsibility to my people. What would it profit their cause were I to go native?

But the strength of the attraction was there, and it can be explained, I believe, by very compelling characteristics we held in common: in a world where others found us odd, we saw that we were beautiful; and in a world dominated by height, two smaller persons found each other truly towering.

As it happened, a decision was not required in the matter because, one evening, before Beth arrived with my meal, a crowd of angry villagers assembled outside the church and called on me to come outside so that they could kill me. Among the voices I recognized those of my neighbours Julia and Peter the Birdman. She declared that I had turned the church of Little Musing into a coven of witches and urged the community to burn the place down; and Peter asked me to allow any birds which might be roosting in the church to escape before it was burnt.

I was just thinking that this was not the warming process that good Farebrother had in mind when that gentleman arrived to announce that the most horrible things were being said about me in the village.

Had I not, asked the good Farebrother, his porcupine hair flying into accusing points over his broad white forehead, allowed several children at the school to run their hands over my person?

I had done so – at his urging, I reminded him, as part of the warming process.

Well, it seemed that the warming process had taken something of a knock. He was sorry to tell me that one of those same children, a little boy, scarcely three years of age, had been discovered, broken and bloody, beside the rusting railway track, his body covered by a heap of stones.

I was horrified.

Since I had recently exposed myself to the same children, dressed in little more than the barest essentials, many in the village had drawn most unfortunate conclusions. They had decided I was the killer.

Decided, I said, seemed an odd word for such an irrational decision, leading, from what I could hear, to horrible bloodlust.

Moral perturbation was the phrase he preferred. He was quite sure that when I understood the agonizing moral dilemma of many of the men now baying for my blood, I would feel considerable sympathy. However, such was the mood of the crowd that he could not be sure that time allowed for a proper airing of the subject. He intended to slip away and try to head off the furious villagers. Beth would soon arrive in her motorcar and would smuggle me to safety. In the interim, on no account was I to leave the church. Being the House of God, it was a sanctuary the villagers would not dare invade.

Remembering how little faith they retain for Church or God, I thought this a somewhat optimistic summation of affairs, but the good ex-Bishop insisted, before he fled into the night, that although faith might have died, tradition taught that you did not – if at all possible – disembowel people in church, and tradition would keep the lynch party out long enough for me to escape. With that he squared his shoulders and went out to face the mob.

Now Beth arrived, terrified by the crowd – who had warned that unless she gave me up, she risked joining me in the fiery pyre when they set the church alight – but vowing to save me. She too had a plan, based on long-standing tradition. These were my instructions: I was to pay close attention, or my life was forfeit.

She had parked her car outside the vestry door, and if we needed to make a run for it, I would find the boot unlocked and the area enclosed by a steel mesh, forming a cage. On her command, I was to enter this cage, lie down on the floor and pant heavily; she would attach a collar and lead to my neck and then drive the car through the mob. It might also help if I whimpered loudly. I might be mistaken for a family pet. This would have a calming effect on our pursuers, she prayed, and win the time to accelerate through the mob to safety.

I protested again that the men of Little Musing were greatly mistaken. I had not harmed the child. It seemed unjust.

Beth gave a strange smile. It was not justice that was at stake, but another tradition. The men of Little Musing might have blamed me for the crime – but in truth they suspected themselves. Assaults on children were so woven into the history, the very fabric, of English life. The more painful implications of the custom were eased by putting it about that (a) other natives were worse, or (b) those responsible were quite unrelated to ourselves.

By dwelling constantly on this imaginary predator, they have made him into a continual presence; he lurks in the hedgerows, he haunts the back streets. They have many names for him; sometimes he is 'the man in the van', or 'the horrible uncle', or 'the bad neighbour' or 'the man on the moor'. Frightening images from their pantheon of horrid spirits. He is as fearsome to them as the rain monsters are to us, or the giant snakes which lure women to their death in the bottoms of deep wells, or the vicious baboons who will leap on a virgin the moment her back is turned. The difference, I suppose, is that there is some scientific basis for our horrors, while their demons are little more than extensions of their own guilt.

I began to perceive how unhappy these poor wretches must have been as we sprinted for the car. But, running for my life, I could not give them the sympathy deserved. Beth flung open the boot, snapped on the dog collar, and I lay on the floor of the cage. She whispered that it might be useful if I could bring up the short hair on the back of my neck.

Catching sight of us, the mob began screaming. Lying on the floor of Beth's car, I prepared to be lynched. But nothing happened – except that the screaming turned into singing and cheering. Raising my head cautiously, I saw that they had seized hold of the good Farebrother, and lifted him on to their shoulders, and were carrying him to and fro; some had fallen to their knees and seemed to give thanks.

The ex-Bishop now encouraged us to rejoice. The crisis was passed. The child battered to death and buried beside the railway line had not been, after all, the victim of the usual predator. It seemed that he had been done to death by two of his older classmates, boys themselves barely eight years old. I could see for myself the joyful relief on the faces of every man in the village, who now felt very ashamed indeed of their threats towards me, and wished to make amends by whatever means possible, and he could say that the warming process was back on track.

Beth wept, the Bishop grinned, the men of Little Musing cheered.

And I? I asked, in my innocence, whether there was anything to be done about the murder of children by children.

They considered the question and replied that, on the whole, they thought not.

Try as they might to limit injuries and murders of children by adults, and vice versa, the custom is too widespread, the need too deep, the island too crowded, for there to be anything between the swaggering, proliferating young and the anxious, older generation than a struggle to the death.

But principles of fairness demanded that everyone got a fair crack of the whip. So it was that, increasingly, children were beginning to act in a very similar way towards their parents, and to abuse adults. Especially the old and the ill, who were attacked at every opportunity. And children were giving every sign of being better at injuring the elderly than their parents had been at harming them. This must be considered an advance of sorts.

Now it seemed that a third front was being opened up, and children, finding the older generation a less interesting target, were attacking each other. Painful as this sometimes might be, it showed that democratic principles were still very much at work in England. For however frightening the experience of near-lynching might have proved to me, the ex-Bishop hoped very devoutly that I had learned something from it.

I was happy to set his mind at rest. Certainly I had done so. In my few months in England I had learned two essential lessons of survival: when faced by a murderous mob in a suburb of bastards, pretend to be a donation; when faced by villagers baying for blood, there is no more soothing behaviour than to pretend to be a household pet.

Chapter Six

Beth goes native; dances with elands and the tale
of an omelette; learns the difference between adultery
and incompatability; Beth vanishes, and Booi runs
into a horse of a different colour

For reasons not clear to me at that time, Beth began
accompanying me into the garden of an evening.

My decision to sleep outdoors came about for the
following reasons. After my near-fatal encounter with
the villagers of Little Musing, when they suspected me of
some devilish part in the tragedy of the child stoned to
death, I took the view that there was safety out of doors,
and informed the Farebrothers that henceforth I would be
camping in the garden.

If caution dictated this decision, nostalgia also played its
part. I found I simply could not sleep in the great bed
assigned me, warm as blood, soft as *kapok** and as deep
as death. I tried to honour their hospitality but, as I had
found in the Royal Guest-house where I had awaited Her

---

* Karoo word for snow, since its flakes, seldom seen and an
occasion for wonder, remind people of feathery, floating
eiderdown.

Majesty's Pleasure, their beds are not sleeping places but warm lakes, into which they dive at night and float, but in which I felt myself drowning.

Months folded together like feathers in an ostrich's tail – impossible to tell one from the other. And my unhappiness and impatience grew even greater.

Many nights I lay in the bed, broad as several donkey's carts, in the soft English darkness, so exotic, so foreign, and I smelt again the hot brown perfume of rain as it splits the baking desert dust; I heard the rustling music of the busy dung beetle, putting his shoulder to the wheel of his pungent cargo and rolling it roundly home. I would feel in my heart the approach of the springbuck in the hunting season, with little lady steps, perfect on its tiny toes, closer and closer, until it was within bowshot, and its heart began beating in my chest.

And I could not bear it. I told my friends, the grounded Bishop and his dark-haired, delectable daughter, that I would sleep no longer under their roof. I begged them to understand my feelings. I would hang my grey suit in their cupboard; my boots would sit in their keeping; they would safeguard my cardboard suitcase full of treasures until such time as I set off for London. I would take my loin flap, my bow and arrow, my good broad hat and pitch camp in the garden, under the apple tree. A couple of strips of corrugated iron would do very well, a hollow for my hips scooped from the soft earth, a nightly fire over which I would cook whatever I caught in the fields.

The Bishop tried to dissuade me, but I told him, speaking very frankly, that it did not much soothe me to be told that the men of Little Musing were now quite over their anger at the death of the child; that none were readier than the people of those parts to forgive and forget; that they were not the sort of folk who bore grudges; and that the warming process was now back on track. I preferred to fix the sun above my head by day and the sky on my back by night and to study the lives of these Remote-area Dwellers from a secure distance.

I had still that nagging, unprovable, yet irresistible feeling that I was being secretly watched; if this were indeed so, I wished to face my observer on the terrain of my choosing, and not walled up in the breathless confines of an English cottage.

The effects of this move outdoors were twofold, and surprising. First, Beth, announcing that she too was giving up the indoor life, pitched a small blue tent at the other end of the garden and began to mimic my life, right down to her clothing, which now consisted of a small skirt, sandals and the deliberate removal of everything else, so that her very good breasts, formerly so strangled, now showed clearly by day and by night, to the astonishment of the neighbours and passing natives. Beth announced that she was adopting the dress of the Red People and asked if there was some special ornament or substance she might add to the very fine figure she already presented. I said that, truly, I could think of nothing – except perhaps a layer of sheep's fat, for this, traditionally, contributed lustre to the women of the Red People. Being in good sheep country, this was easily arranged.

How very beautiful she looked, by moonlight and by sunlight, with her skirt swinging across her thighs and tracing the flowing, swinging outlines of that prodigiously lovely posterior; her upper body was now a column of light, richly gleaming and delicious with the faintly greasy, meaty flavour of newly shorn wool.

There really has been nothing like it since the wall

paintings of our ancestors, where sturdy figures straining nose and knee cap, showing exquisite posteriors, race after fleeing gazelles, and loose their arrows like bees.

Such was the transformation in Beth – from a swathed female in her father's shoes to this shining creature, living in a blue tent pitched near the box hedge in an English country garden. But there was something else. In place of the shy, tortured woman who never showed herself except when she was sure no one could see her, there arose a gleaming beauty, listening raptly to the stories I told her of my people, and showing her breasts to the world in the way God intended. In short, it could be said that Beth possessed something I had not seen in her before: she was happy.

Others were not. Young males in the village alehouse, the Brass Monkey, grew increasingly noisy as tales of Beth's new life spread. Night after night I heard the bang of the drums, as young bloods swayed and swooned and stamped to a beat so primal, so savage, we may trace its origins to the beginning of the world – and the publican, fearing some form of raid or attack, sent a runner to the Bishop's house, warning him that the natives were growing restless and begging him to keep his daughter out of the garden. But she would have none of it. She was free at last, she told her father.

Beth was eager to experience all the customs of real life as it was lived by the Red People – all, that is, but one: she preferred food from the refrigerator to anything I caught for her.

I sympathized. After all, their diet is not one we would find very agreeable. And they have irrational distastes. Although, like us, they prefer meat above anything else. Yet they turn up their noses at caterpillars. The English caterpil-

lar, I can confirm, lightly fried, is the equal of anything I
have tasted in Africa. Strange to tell, they know nothing of
the delicacy of iguana meat and do not even cook and
eat the small lizards to be found on the island. Honey, they
take as we do, though they seldom eat it directly from the
comb. And they will pass it amongst themselves in a way
which our people would perhaps find promiscuous. They
make no beer from honey, though legend has it that their
forefathers once made a liquor based on honey, as we do.
If so, they have lost the art.

The news that Boy David was 'living rough', as they
put it, and foraging for grubs, roots and tubers, became the
talk of the village. Guess what Dave's having for dinner, I
heard them calling. Come, quick! And in no time at all a
gaping audience crowded the garden.

I enjoyed their dismay; I confess it. When a swarm of
flying ants passed through the garden I caught several handfuls of these succulent little titbits and fed on them before
an astonished crowd of children, farmers and old women,
some of whom were audibly upset at the sight.

When word spread that the Bushman was eating termites, so many villagers crowded into the garden the Bishop
made them enter in relays. The children were particularly
entranced, pretending to gag into the bushes and shouting
encouragement. To them, it was a kind of repulsive magic.
I felt quite ashamed of myself afterwards. Your average
native is a credulous soul; he *wishes* to believe. For him it
is Bushman magic. And although there is good sport in
this, I cannot believe it anything but cruel to play upon
their childlike natures.

To begin with it was a game, pure and simple, as well
as a relief, this brief return to the diet of my country. But
I was not expecting anyone else to enter the spirit of my

game. What, then, was I to make of the ostrich egg that mysteriously appeared outside my shelter one day, donated by some nocturnal visitor who knew something of hunting, for he left no spoor on the wet grass of dawn, having dragged a broom over his tracks to erase them?

I looked at that huge, pearly shell, so like the moon. So perfect it could only come from the gods, who, in their goodness, pity the people of the world who must go on two legs. So they made another two-legged person. The ostrich. Who else runs so fast? Who else roars so loudly that even the hunting lion stops to listen? Who kicks the sniffing hyena in the head? Who is the fiercest defender of its baby against everything from snakes to elephants? Who first learnt about fire and would have kept the secret to himself, hidden in his warm armpit, had the scheming god Heisib not known how the ostrich loves to dance? They danced together, Heisib and the ostrich, and the clever god waited until the ostrich's head began spinning from the dance and his arms lifted to the sky and then, from deep in his armpit, Heisib plucked the ostrich gold, the fire that warms the Men of Men.

Now, I should have asked myself: who would give me such a present? And where in England ostriches lived and laid? And what my visitor's motives might have been. I should have heeded good Farebrother's warning, when I called him to see my prize, and he urged me to return to my bed indoors; it might be safer. He had done what he could to protect me from the less agreeable aspects of English life, but – and he jerked his dark, sharp locks at the world beyond his garden – it was a jungle out there, and while most people I met were basically decent, kindly folk who were beginning to warm to me, he wouldn't fancy my chances if I ran into a horse of a different colour.

But I did not ask. Or reflect. I simply rejoiced. It does not do to question a gift fallen from Heaven. And to waste food is to make hunger your brother. And so, beneath the curious eyes of the neighbours, I prepared a meal.

First, I drilled a hole in the roof of the egg, using the sharpened point of a rose-stem. Next, I scooped in the rather damp earth a hollow, and in the hollow I built a fire of small twigs. Lifting the egg, I carefully poured the belly of it into the sandy hollow where my fire had folded itself into a bed of tasty ash and soon the wonderful aroma that the ostrich omelette alone possesses began floating in the air, sufficiently strongly for even their weak, untutored nostrils to take hold of the fruit of it. Lest there be any misunderstanding of the delight to come, I engaged in a little dumbshow, rubbing my belly and smacking my lips.

I drew from my ashy oven a few minutes later a soft and steaming marvel, a fleshy loaf baked to perfection, salted with a little ash, and offered it to the watchers. But they grimaced and gagged. I heard it said that my omelette was poison; and some covered the eyes of their children when I ate a little to show how good it was.

I offered a slice to Edward Farebrother, but he frowned and declined. Only Beth was prepared to try my fine omelette. That was a grave mistake. Ever afterwards this dinner of innocent golden meat was seen by her father as some horrid magical spell that had changed his daughter from a decent woman of ordinary tastes and sensible disposition into a freak.

Between Beth and her father relations began to sour. She taught me this charm or spell which I was to say out loud in order to ward off the hostility of the villagers: you cannot make an omelette without breaking eggs.

I said it out loud, but it failed to convince.

Beth now rounded on our noisy audience, extending the debate beyond the egg in question by declaring that she would also be breaking the mould, new ground, and, for the record, she would be breaking with tradition.

To which our audience replied in a great chorus: Oh, no you won't!

And Beth responded: Oh, yes I will!

I did not know it, but I was witnessing the primal ritual warfare in which the English traditionally engage before any transformation may begin.

It is not, as I was to learn, a question of whether anything actually changes. In fact, it hardly ever does. What is important is the noise raised for and against the idea of action.

Beth's transformation began innocently.

She would visit my campfire, sit beside me and listen to tales of Kaggen the mantis and of how he, turning his eyes, big as saucers, on the sky, created the moon who is our father and also our mother.

How could this be? my student demanded. Father and mother in one? Unless the moon were also our God and so contained female and male in one person.

They have literal minds and become confused very easily when expected to think on several planes. Explanations must at all times be gentle, clear, yet firm, and present often difficult facts in an elementary, or what they call a 'sensible', fashion. This can be taxing and often frustrating, but I can assure anyone who should follow me to these shores that your average native, with careful and patient direction, can be coaxed towards enlightenment, always provided that swift progress is not expected.

By my fireside, of an evening, I would explain, as simply as I knew how, the very complex belief of the Red People that the moon was not our God but that by the moon's light people could observe the work of God in a world which would otherwise be too dark to discern His high and holy ways. Our father the moon and our mother the sun. The lights of the great sky, lay together each night and gave birth the next day to a new sun and moon.

Who gave birth? she demanded.

I replied, the moon, and she was instantly cast down because that did not sound very sensible to her, as I had said the moon was our father.

You cannot give to people who have lacked essential religion for centuries the elements of the true faith in a few encounters beside a campfire. In my estimation, the reintroduction of these people to the essentials of true polytheism is possible. It can be done. But it will take many years. Missionaries, Dedication. In that English country garden, I preferred to concentrate on my own expedition, which showed alarming signs of having become bogged down.

Beth asked about dancing, and I explained to her the beauties of the Eland Dance, which she immediately proposed that I should teach her. Now, this presented certain practical difficulties, since the dance in question is usually held at the hut of a girl's maternal grandmother, at the moment when she is ready to be initiated into the customs of the band.

To the resourceful Beth the missing grandmother would be no problem. She cheerily assured me that she knew just the person to stand in for her.

He came. He sat in Beth's blue pup tent, and he agreed to wear a shawl over his shoulders to signify his age and sex, but he refused point-blank to smoke a pipeful of strong, black tobacco, even though I pointed out that, in real life, Beth's grandmother would have been doing so, as she awaited the arrival of the eland bull. At this eminently sensible encouragement, I am afraid that Mr Farebrother quite broke down.

A plaintive litany of woe issued from beneath the shawl. Little Musing was scandalized by Beth's behaviour. If the villagers were upset, the neighbours were livid. Peter the Birdman was frightfully concerned about his crows, which roosted in ever smaller numbers in the episcopal elms. The crows had declined since Peter waged a one-man war in their defence against the gamekeepers who killed goshawks. Gamekeepers did so because goshawks attacked their pheasants. Now, thanks to Peter's war against gamekeepers, goshawks multiplied. Unfortunately, goshawks had been attacking his crows. His crows had been attacking the nests of game birds. Mayhem was everywhere and matters were not helped by two semi-naked people running around the garden feasting on insects. If human beings belonged to a higher order of life than birds – Peter the Birdman protested – then it was their duty to set an example.

And Julia had complained to Miss Desdemona, our rent collector, that the former Bishop appeared to be carrying out some form of agricultural activity in his garden and she felt sure this must be against the terms of his lease and would be prohibited under local bye-laws; what was more, the smoke from my fire got in her washing; and when she had rented a house from the Lord of Goodlove Castle, she hardly expected to find herself living beside a gypsy encampent.

I see, looking back, that I paid too little attention to the emotions aroused by my removal to the garden.

I was happy, however, to have such an adept pupil. And
Beth was too obsessed with learning the steps for the Eland
Dance, which required her to move in a figure-of-eight
formation, circling the fire and her hut, where her beshaw-
led father sat morosely on the ground, asking plaintively if
it was all over yet.

Now I entered the dance, as the eland bull himself,
lifting my forefingers above each temple, pawing the ground
and panting in pursuit of my lovely, fat eland, while she
ran before me, lifting her skirt from time to time to expose
her magnificent buttocks. Have you ever seen two fat rain
clouds, bursting with the liquid of life, bowling along the
horizon, pushed by a stiff breeze which palpitates and jug-
gles and kneads these precious containers so that they seem
to throb and quiver with the lovely weight they contain?
Well, that is the sight I saw before me as Beth, lifting her
skirt as if she had been doing this all her life, disappeared
around the back of the blue pup tent with the eland bull
in pawing, bellowing, stabbing pursuit.

All was happiness – until the good ex-Bishop, suddenly
jumping up and ripping off his shawl as we were passing
his hut for the seventh time, demanded that I follow him
into the house for he wished to have a word with me, in
the strictest confidence. Leaving the lovely eland dismayed
in the garden, I adjusted my loin-cloth and followed him
into his study, where he sat behind his desk, though he left
me standing while asking me what my intentions were
concerning his daughter.

I did not understand his question and told him so.

Very well, he replied in a grating voice, he would spell
it out for me. I was chasing his daughter around the
garden clad only in a leather loin-cloth; she wore a skirt
not much larger; and, to boot, my *qhwai-xkhwe* was in a

state which left him in little doubt as to my physical ambitions.

I had to fight to control my face. How very instructive it is to see that they assume, always, that their worst characteristics are present in others. Because women in England were terrified of rape, murder, various cruelties at the hands of their menfolk, the ex-Bishop was certain that I felt for his daughter a form of hatred which, from what I understood him to imply, far from making me detest her, was, in English terms, a prelude to love and therefore could, and would, be followed by some liaison. As if this was how they conducted their love affairs – cruelty, assault and abuse being both the forerunners of, and accompaniment to, the married state.

I controlled my desire to laugh. It would have been funny had it not been so desperately sad. He seemed to have little doubt as to what would happen to the eland once the bull caught up with her.

He need have no such fears, I assured him. The role of the eland bull was always played by some elderly relative, well beyond marriageable age. As for my intentions towards Beth, they were as honourable as I was sure his were towards me.

In that case – boomed the frockless prelate – I was making things damned difficult. How was he to save me from myself if I went on being myself? The essence of his plan was to persuade people that I was actually not unlike them. That meant learning to live in England as the English would expect. It did not mean running around his garden in the altogether, making great calf-eyes at his daughter. Instead of becoming more like them, I had deceived his only daughter in to becoming more like me. How on earth did I expect to get ahead when I carried on in such a fashion? He had worked long and hard to lure the locals towards the impression that I was, basically, a deserving case. And he had bent over backwards to convince the powers that be of my genuine refugee status, assuring them I was in sore need of every scrap of asylum I could muster, being virtually hunted to extinction within my own land and destined, if ever I had the misfortune to be sent home, to be shot by the Beastly Boer and my hide pegged to the farmyard gate.

And this was how I repaid him! By darting about, mimicking a bloody stag in the rutting season. It was too bad.

And for these nightly cavortings to be happening just as things were going right was a tragedy. People were coming round. The temperature of the warming process was up by several degrees. Certainly we had had our little set-backs, but these were things of the past. The villagers of Little Musing, even if they did not yet quite see me as one of them, were increasingly of the view that, given time, one day I might almost *be* one of them.

But now, he was sorry to tell me, there were mutterings. The sight of a foreigner making free with their flying ants, at a time of scarce resources and high unemployment, had upset them. And could they really be blamed?

Then they also complained about what he rather mystifyingly called my 'relationship' with Beth, for, difficult though it was for me to grasp, the young men of the village felt about this almost as badly as they did about my theft of their flying fauna.

I said that Beth's fear of the mockery she excited in the village whenever she showed herself hardly suggested a feeling of kindness or real interest among the males of Little Musing.

Smiling a less than convincing smile, Edward Farebrother remarked ruefully that we did not seem to be getting through to each other, did we? It was not a question of kindness, as I put it, but of scarce resources. In an area where young men struggled to find wives, I was seen as reducing the available pool of females of marriageable age, thereby depriving young men of the chance of procreation.

Remembering what we had seen and suffered on the Green Meadow Estate, at the hands of the offspring of just such young males, I said that even if it were true that I had removed Beth from the marriage pool, was I not doing everyone a service by preventing yet more unwanted progeny and sparing the wretched young women, whom these young males got with child and then deserted, from further pain and suffering? And fairly regular beatings?

It was exactly this sort of attitude that marked me out, fumed the good ex-Bishop, I was seen as a threat, not only to local flora and fauna, but to the traditional English way of life.

The retired sky-pilot pushed his black quills of hair off his pale forehead and grew gloomier still. Already there were fears that if more of my sort settled in Little Musing, it would be only a matter of time before flying ants appeared on the school menu, and people were expected to worship the moon, and women ran around the streets showing their behinds.

People would not take this lying down. Oh, no! I had been reported to the authorities as a bogus asylum-seeker. A grave charge. Teams of investigators were combing the country, determined to root out such fraud and save the Exchequer millions of pounds, and here I was, flitting around the garden in the altogether, consuming precious local resources. I was asking for it, wasn't I?

What I was asking for, I explained in simple terms, was the answer to a mystery which intrigued much of the civilized world. The Children of the Sun, those they thought of as the men of half creation, buff and ochre, cream and yellow, white and mauve, had long wondered and speculated about the River of Promises that had flowed out of England for centuries. Where did it rise, this mighty river? We did indeed believe that the source lay in the Palace of the Monarch. I had been sent to confirm this, and I was determined to keep faith with my people and travel to the source of this mighty river which had once watered half the globe.

Unless I journeyed to see the Queen I would be said to have failed my friends and sponsors, who had backed my expedition. I would make a last attempt to reach the source of the River of Promises. Even if I perished in the attempt.

Perished. He took the word out of my mouth, you might say, and, in a fashion we would perhaps find vulgar, began rolling it between his rather full lips as if he tasted in it some rare savour; beginning his meal with the great P that had about it, say, the nutty tingle of roasted ant-bear; lingering lovingly over the main course of the rolled R, followed by the silken hiss of snake flesh; finishing on a tiny D for dessert, that had the salty bite of lizard's tail.

Per-ish-ed! Once again the ex-episcopal lips pursed, with the explosive little sound of the bowstring, and propelled the word into the world. Perish the thought! said the good grounded Bishop. Though I could not know then what he wished to perish. But I noticed that he shook his head like a sleeper troubled by dreams of snakes. And then, in that rather endearing way of the English caught in the grip of some emotion of which they feel a certain shame, or embarrassment, he immediately changed the subject to one in which they are quite at home and expect the foreigner to be discomfited.

What did I and my kind believe to be the best form of sexual congress? the gravity-struck missionary demanded. Single or multiple spouses?

Indeed, the question had the desired effect. My surprise must have shown on my face, and the fallen one pressed his advantage. Surely there was nothing strange in a desire for knowledge of our customs? And surely he was entitled to ask? Beth was his daughter, after all, and he was permitted to know something of me before I made him a grandparent.

The sexual obsessions of the English seem to us distressingly narrow. Any of our people coming after me may wish to know that English sexual activity seems to fall roughly into two parts: those convinced that people wish to rape them; and those who wish to rape someone themselves.

Wishing to return to Beth and the Eland Dance, and being unwilling to encourage this nonsense, and feeling little certainty that the subtleties of our relations would be understood, I explained, very simply, that among our people one partner sufficed, but others married many wives. Among the !Kung, for instance, the rule was single wives when the food was scarce, many when the rains were good. Either way, partnerships were lifelong, unless adultery was proven.

This surprised him. In England, said the ex-Bishop, adultery played an important role in the God-given scheme of things. Men were designed for promiscuity. One did not condemn married partners for consorting with others – as he was sorry to hear we did in my part of the world.

Therefore one did not regard my lusting after one's daughter as anything other than quite sacred, really.

This surprised me. Why then was he protesting about the Eland Dance?

In England, the good priest replied, his voice rising like the ascending swallow's, lust, in and out of marriage, was regarded as very natural: a Minister of the Crown, for example, who fornicated with a female camp-follower was only obeying the direction of his genes. However, adultery was one thing; incompatibility was quite another. A chappie from a different background who took advantage of a simple country girl, dressing her up in skins and playing hump-the-heifer in his own backyard! That put all heaven in a rage. And he was playing with bloody fire!

And then he fell again to making a meal of the word PERISHED, repeating it over and over. Realizing he had lost sight of me, I left him to his lipping and pouting and returned to the garden, somewhat cast down by this inexplicable outburst.

More surprises were in store for me. Instead of my fair, fat eland, ready to recommence the dance, I found the garden empty and the fire dying.

Watching me over the fence were my neighbours, Peter the Birdman and Julia.

Cooking and eating that ostrich egg, said Peter, was a bad thing. Meat was murder, but cooking and eating an egg was infanticide. One person's egg was another creature's agony. An omelette was a massacre of the innocents — and, man of peace though he was, a person who went around eating innocent ova deserved all he had coming to him.

If I was looking for Beth, Julia smiled, I had come to the wrong place.

Then Miss Desdemona, the rent collector, came by, swinging her shopping bag, and Peter went and hid inside his house, and Julia announced that she would not be paying rent to live beside an ex-Bishop who kept a menagerie in his garden.

Miss Desdemona looked at me and in her quiet voice she said that if I was looking for Beth, I would find her in Goodlove Castle, to which her father had delivered her. Her cousin, the Lord of Goodlove Castle, had accepted her, on loan, as it were, and because the ex-Bishop believed she would be safe there from people like me. I had arrived in the nick of time. Pointing north, where lay the great estates of Lord Goodlove, she urged me to save her. If it was not already too late.

Removing my shoes, I set off at a trot we can keep up for twenty miles, without effort. I ran through the church-yard where the dead lay sleeping; crossed the stream where the ducks gathered and shouted; padded over the hump-back bridge; passed the station; and set off through the fields, crossing over vales and hills, lonely as a cloud that floats on high. On and on, until I arrived at a long, tall wall and a great black gate, so high it seemed to imprison even our mother and father the moon, throwing black bars across that holy face.

From somewhere behind the wall I heard a sound which stopped me in my tracks. I heard it not with my ears; that sound bites straight through the stomach walls and seizes the heart. I stood unable to believe it. I was in England, yet I heard the full-maned, sharp-fanged music of the hunt-ing lion.

I stood too long. Somewhere in the darkness now I heard it: the snorting, galloping pursuit of a horse of a different colour. A large hunter with little sense of smell and bad eyesight, thinking he moved silently while he signalled, with every crashing step, his purpose.

As I turned to run something sharp as a porcupine quill struck my right shoulder. Even as I plucked it out, I knew what I would find. My pace was slowing, my legs turning traitor, as those of the springbuck will do when the arrow strikes and points the poison on its way. I plucked from my shoulder a sharp, ugly, little dart, light as an arrow, and as deadly. From far off the lion roared somewhere in the darkness into which I now fell face first, the taste of earth in my mouth.

Chapter Seven

Welcome to Goodlove Castle:
Africa in England: the conservation of fauna:
the life of the True Pulse: Lord Goodlove
amongst his women

Struggling out of that darkness into which I had been plunged by the ugly barb fired into my shoulder, mouth dry, eyes sticky with sleep, I realized I had been manacled to the steel floor of a moving vehicle reeking of dog, rubber boots, shot-gun cartridges and over-ripe game bird, a species I reckoned to be something like our *korhaan*.*

Once again on my English travels I had come to my senses to find myself a prisoner. Hands and feet strapped as tightly as the ant-bear who, trussed with sinew by the hunters, is slung from a spear, and marched home to the cooking pot. In my drugged state I wondered if I had been taken by cannibals.

The hunter who had brought me low – his rifle propped against the dashboard – bent over the steering wheel. I could not see him clearly, for a mesh of steel protected his driving compartment from my prison. But I could smell

---

* Afrikaans in the original: tr. guineafowl. In fact, probably pheasant.

him well enough, for his dung signature rose pungently above the competing scents of birds and boots. He blended whisky, honey, cow-dung, tobacco and ashes.

I studied his neck. And learnt a great deal. A stiff neck; a proud nape; a neck that knew no bounds: and felt itself to be head and shoulders above all rivals. And was pleased to say so. It was no mere mute column of flesh and bone this neck, but an oratorical advocate of its own grace and strength. I had known such necks. I had heard their speeches before: high and mighty words that led one ever downward to the prison cell and to the grave.

Strange are the meetings that evoke memories of one's native land! And make a terrible joy. The steel mesh, the gun and the burly driver, far from depressing me, gave me a surge of happy recognition. How many times had I not made a similar journey? Trussed hand and foot, on the floor of a police van? Homesickness of a kind replaced my fear and, finding my voice, I bade my kidnapper a loud Good Day!

Swearing a mighty oath to the founder of his religion, he brought the van to a skidding halt. Hurrying from his seat, he threw open the rear doors of my prison, and stared at me in astonished delight.

A huge man, dressed in oily hunter's uniform,* all rough green, from boots to hat. Much of his head seemed made of hair, out of which his face peered like a rabbit caught in a thorn-bush; a great brassy thatch, like the upside-down-tree† which wears its roots on its head; below his jaw, it trailed like the branches of the willow which stoops to wash its face in a waterhole.

---

* I suspect this 'oily' uniform is, in fact, no more than the typical country fashion of Barbour and galoshes.
† Probably the baobab tree.

Indeed, this paragon was bedecked, as Kaggen is my witness, with as much hair below his head as above, it hung in a curtain from his chin, so dense small fowl might happily have nested there. Here then was a warrior as bold in his plumage and his pride as in the bloodcurdling ferocity of his manners. He spoke as if raised up on some lofty pedestal, from which eminence he was accustomed to addressing not only the hard of hearing, but also the weak of eye, for he spoke boomingly, moving his lips around his words very slowly, followed by a belligerent gleam of the eyes, as if his words were wasted on his audience far below. His teeth flashed gold. He was, I swear, as fine an English buck as ever I saw. Even if I was obliged to observe this choice specimen from an enforced recumbancy upon the cold steel floor of his vehicle.

Let me say, too, that I managed, discomfited though I was, to solve several small mysteries about the natives. Firstly, it is claimed that it is only the English abroad who are fat. Everyone will be familiar with the old maxim – if you would war with the English do it after dinner. For as the !Kung rightly observed, they eat not to live but to sleep. They are observably amongst the most adipose of the pale strangers who invaded our land. However it was long believed by our sages that in their own country they were bred for running and hunting, as are proper people every-where. I can confirm that this is not the case. They tend to the rotund, even in their natural habitat. My captor was shaped rather like the blood pudding we make of the giraffe's second stomach; much liquid inside a thin skin. His girth was as round as the moon's, as full as the flooded waterhole's, as prodigious as that of the hippopotamus. We may infer that this innate tendency to spread, corporeally as well as territorially, is no less pronounced At Home, than

Abroad. And that, in their order of values, weight is a component of status.

Then, his colour. I stress that only his uniform or cloak, vest and boots, were green. We were familiar from childhood with tales that there lived in England troops of green men, hairy and wild, half-gods, half-apes, who fed on honied liquor in forests of oak and alder, and worked magic or murder, as primal whim moved them. It seems to me entirely probable that our misinformation about such verdant manikins, gnomes, wodwos or forest sprites, is based on tales related by travellers after encountering individuals such as the prodigy who shot and imprisoned me. I can well understand that myth may be the only refuge of a shocked sensibility, for truly one imagines, on first meeting certain varieties of native, that one had discovered some new and alarming species, only distantly related – if at all – to civilized beings.

Watching this enormous distended barrel examining me, I was suddenly made aware of the reason way this island race is fond of referring to their land as 'the old country'. The island is full of old people! My hunter was no exception. At an age when most men are beside the campfire or have long since departed to the land of locusts beyond the Orange River, elderly souls continue to pretend that they are as flush full of youth as young lions: cheer themselves for avoiding at home the corruption, venality and debauchery rife in less fortunate lands across the water; declare they will fight like tigers if Johnny Foreigner dare show his face, and do almost anything to maintain the illusion of youth and strength. And having seen the fate meted out to the old of the tribe I think we can understand why this should be so.

These fruitful reflections were interrupted by my captor, rifle in hand, looming above me like an overfull raincloud and addressing me as if I were an entire tribe, not a trussed and helpless prisoner on the floor of his van. He demanded my name and, when I answered, his delight increased all the more. With trembling finger he lifted my upper lip and studied my teeth, as we do with a donkey to determine its age; prodded my tongue, as if scarcely believing that I had the power of speech; and fell to examining my bow, quiver and arrows. Fortunately, he did not think to look inside my hat.

Introducing himself as Goodlove, Lord of all I surveyed, he declared he would have been happy to shake my paw, had said paw been available. But perhaps I might like to confirm that I was, in fact, by golly, a true specimen of the San people? One of the far-flung, far-gone, decimated bands of foragers who inhabited the hot, dry wastes of Southern Africa?

I replied that I preferred plainer speech. The term 'San' meant no more than a rogue and vagabond. I was a Bushman.

And from which bushy region, precisely, did I hail?

To such a strange question, I gave the obvious answer: from Home.*

Out of the hairy hole of his mouth a laugh clapped like happy thunder. From henceforth, he vowed, my home would be in Goodlove Castle.

---

* This reply is less 'obvious' than it may appear. For Booi is alluding, or perhaps dimly recalling, another lost Bushman, the convict known as //Kabbo, a member of the /Xam Bushmen of the Cape. The prisoner//Kabbo, when asked by a friendly interrogator in the 1870s 'What is your place, its name?' gave this answer: 'I come from that place, called Home' (see Stephen Watson's wonderful renditions from the original/Xam: *The Return of the Moon*, Cape Town, 1991).

When Farebrother had announced that he had acquired a genuine Bushman, he'd laughed. To be frank, he'd yelled his head off. Farebrother might be a living bridge, a descending angel amongst the dregs and the destitute and all that. But blind. A busted flush – not so? A floored flier; the sort of bloke who could not recognize a real San hunter-gatherer if one bit him in the backside. He might be sound in the God department, but in the matter of the Life of the True Pulse, the holy originals of existence, he was a joke. So how could one be sure of my authenticity?

At last I began to understand. A test had been devised?

A most efficient test, confirmed the bearded one. Only a genuine specimen of the San people would have cooked that ostrich egg as I had done. By their omelettes ye shall know them, my captor intoned. My cooking skills had given me plain away. After that it was only a matter of acquisition. He had offered Farebrother large rewards, but the batty old apostle had turned them down. So he had watched and waited.

I remembered the hidden watcher observing my movements. The eyes in the darkness. And now here he was. A wild and booming man who shot passers-by and locked them in the back of his police van.

Farebrother, said the hairy gunman, had rejected all offers. He had gone bloody religious on him. Insisting that he had promised his Bushman a visit to the Queen, and it was vital that we all dealt in a fair manner with the developing world, and other stomach-churning sermons.

He had very nearly despaired of laying hands on me, said my kidnapper, when, Lord be praised! Farebrother changed his tune. Claimed that his daughter Beth was planning to run off with his San lodger. And while he was determined to keep faith with the developing world, he was not having his daughter wed a Bushman from the Karoo who fancied his chances of marrying into a passport and living the life of Riley off the back of the family fortunes. And so on. All of which ex-Bishop Bonkers had sworn was about to happen ever since his daughter had stripped off and begun running around his garden in a mini-skirt, flaunting her not inconsiderable posterior at the moon.

It was then, said my captor, that he presented himself as the answer to a Bishop's prayer. Did I savvy?

Certainly, I had begun, as he put it, to savvy. Beth had been traded for me?

Exactly.

I had been lured into a trap.

Got it in one.

And where was Beth now?

Back home, he very devoutly hoped and prayed. In the bosom of the busted Bish. Fair exchange no robbery. And not a moment too soon. Appalling woman.

And all this – he waved a hand towards the horizon – was mine. His estate was at my disposal. To hunter-gather in to my heart's content.

I was about to reject his dubious offer when I seemed, once more, to lose consciousness. For a moment I felt as one does in the Trance Dance, when the spirits of the animals, who were once people, rise up and dance in your heart. For I beheld an unbelievable sight, yellow-and-black, lovely, long necks arching up as if they would bite their way through the grey clouds, so low over their graceful heads, a wondrous, impossible sight – a family of giraffe at play in the muddy green field of the Lord.

Now it was my turn to laugh in astonished joy.

And, propping me up in a corner from where I could

see better the marvels of his castle, my hairy captor leapt back into the driver's seat and we continued on our way.

We had barely set off when our vehicle was again halted, this time by a herd of elephant crossing the road. Next, as naturally as if they were galloping across the hot sand of the Karoo (rather muddy, it must be admitted, but undoubtedly the genuine bird), came a procession of ostriches, with their slow, tall step and exasperated look, turning their heads from side to side as if they had lost something of great importance.

Better still was to come. For there, grazing quietly upon a grassy incline – oh, the skip of my heart, the dance of my hooves, the swing of my dewlap – I spied a family of eland, children of Heaven, sisters of God, adorable people with their broad shoulders, fine horns, and meat for a month. No wonder I had heard the roar of the hunting lion before the dark descended: in this place was food for all! Here was Africa – in England!

More and more, they came – our people! My heart sang as there floated past, most graceful of all, a herd of flying springbuck. And I felt again, as always when hunting, the dark stripe that divides its pretty face, running, as if it were my own, from my eyes to my mouth. The buck's hair was red, which is its winter colour, the reason being to warm their blood. In our land it grows white again in spring when the sun returns. But these wore their red coats still. I felt sorry for these little persons, since all their lives in England must have seemed one long winter.

Next a flock of blue cranes, most beautiful of birds, who wear their disguises so well that you can no longer see – unless you know the truth – that once long ago they were girls, in the Early Time when animals were still people; yet the truth is there to be spied in their long thin necks,

delicate voices, the modest trailing of their blue-grey tail
feathers along the ground, like women sweeping the earth.
Elder sisters of the god Kaggen, protector of children,
friends of frogs.

A miracle! That great-walled, black-gated park teemed
with our relatives from Africa. Perhaps the grass was too
green, the sky too low, the rain too frequent and the mud
too plentiful; but, even so, here were baboons who like to
imitate men, and then attack them for laughing at their
crooked tails or their straight foreheads. Hyena, which we
do not eat. And hartebeest, the heart of which pregnant
women may not eat. Hartebeest which is the prey, some
say, that the moon hunts and from whose hide makes a
new cloak for himself; but each morning the moon's
troublesome wife plucks and fidgets with the new coat,
fraying it down to nothing in no time at all – so the moon
must be out again each night hunting a new cloak.

The Lord of Goodlove Castle declared himself delighted
by my delight. He clapped me on my shoulder, saying
he welcomed me as one conservationist to another. He
had dedicated his energies and his fortune to preserving,
within the safe enclosure of Goodlove Castle, all creatures
who lived the life of the True Pulse. He collected not
only endangered specimens from Africa, he had also been
instrumental – in his own small way – in rescuing many
indigenous forms of island life as well.

Not animals alone, but where there rarity warranted it
he conserved human specimens also. He drove me now to
the brow of a small hill from where we looked down upon
a village – a poor place, stone huts, blackened by smoke,
occupied by shuffling figures wearing orange helmets over
curiously begrimed, sooty faces.

He had built for these remnants an original village, the

sort of habitat only they lived in, and therein he gave
sanctuary to a community who were once to be found –
if I could believe it! – in vigorous breeding colonies
throughout England. Fearsome warriors. Capable, in their
prime, of bringing the kingdom to a standstill, but now,
alas, almost extinct. They had once lived in happy warrens,
delving deep underground like moles to extract a treasure
no one today wanted any longer. Very sad. These men had
been a terrifically successful example of adaptation to harsh
habitats. But their holes had been closed by an uncaring
generation, their skills despised. And with the destruction
of their environment, this fine example of English wild life
– the miners – had dwindled until they existed only in
isolated pockets. Why, cried the Lord, there were today
English children who had never seen a miner in his natural
habitat! Hence his decision to set up this protected haven
in the grounds of Goodlove Castle.

I was moved by his passion. I was reminded, by these
remaining miners, very much of our white rhino, the
slaughter of which people felt able to oppose only after
the bulk of the tribe had been destroyed. And there was the
black-maned lion of the Karoo, extinct for want of wisdom.

Exactly! the Lord agreed. And the thing was to get in
first, before it was too late. Many other groups were
threatened too. They would go the same way as the quagga,
the dodo and the miner if we were not bloody careful.

He was very concerned, for example, at the poor survival rates of the traditional English clergyman. He planned
an ecclesiastical reserve where these gentle, inoffensive creatures might safely graze, in all their vivid plumage, free
from harassment. Numbers had shrunk so drastically, they
were as endangered as the red squirrel or the Iberian wolf
or the black-maned lion of the Karoo. He had found it

impossible, thus far, to locate suitable breeding pairs. But he would scour the kingdom, for English life would be immeasurably impoverished without the local vicar – a horrible thought: as bad as England without muffins or the monarchy!

For exactly the same reason – the Lord smiled fondly down at me, trussed like the ant-bear – he was determined to save what he could of the remaining San. In our small way, had not we lived the life of the True Pulse as authentically, if not quite as successfully, as the Zulu?

Such foreign specimens also deserved protection. Here he beamed at me again. If I settled down, he would set off to Bushmanland, there to find me a mate, a little Bush-woman with whom I would create the first Bush infants born in England!

His journey to Bushmanland, I told him, would produce nothing of the kind. He might walk for a hundred days in Bushmanland and glimpse nothing but thorn-trees, or the little white-and-purple-striped flowers we call 'baboon shoes'. He might see a hundred thorn-trees flower and know from it, as all civilized people do, that the honey will be fat. And not find a single Red Man to lead him to the honey. He could ask the jackal, that clever person whose hair turns silver when the moon is on his back. And receive no reply. Or the baboons, the people who sit on their heels, and learn nothing. He might whisper his question into the pointed ears of the quick, red cat.* But he will only blink his green eyes and say nothing. He could ask the blue crane that sings as it walks, 'A white stone splinter, a splinter of stone so white!' The blue crane who walks the walk of peace will tell him little. It might confess that when the animals

---

* The lynx – a common predator in the Karoo.

were people, in the First Time, it had the form of a lovely girl. But it will have nothing to say of the Red People. Let him ask the little honey guide who hovers before the overflowing hives of the yellow people who thrust their honey fists into the rock cliffs; or interrogate the ant-bear who sleeps underground. None will point him to those he seeks; so few and far are we, and vanished the lands where we dwelt.

He received this information with silence and a disbelieving look, started the engine, and we continued on our way. We came at last to an ancient castle, surrounded by a moat. Crossing over the drawbridge, we passed beneath a triumphant arch of elephant tusks, and entered through a gateway guarded by lions carved from black marble. He helped me out of the police van, and urged me to make his home my home. African Bushmen were probably the living link between animals and humans. Which aspect was uppermost in me was anyone's guess. But I was free to roam the grounds, as the animals did. Or, if I preferred living under a roof, then indoor facilities had been prepared. The choice was mine.

I replied, rather pointedly, that I was bound and chained. Imprisoned. What was the good of offering choice where I had none?

He looked pained. Imprisoned! But I had *not* been captured; I had been *collected*. On no account was I to think of him as my captor.

He had shot me, roped me and transported me like a goat to the butcher, I cried: that made him my captor.

He had selected me humanely, came the reply. Using a tranquillizing dart guaranteed to have no lasting ill effects.

If he was not my captor, I demanded, then what on earth was he?

My curator, said the Lord.

And, as if to prove his kindness, he unbound me and fixed around my neck a leather collar with a large cardboard tag, of much the sort the farmers in Zwingli use to designate sheep bound for the abattoir. On it he wrote in a fine aristocratic hand: '*Bushman David*. Collected in the vicinity of Little Musing. Property of Goodlove Castle.'

I understood something then. Africa was not so much a place as an *adventure*, which they made up as they went along. And truth was never allowed to interfere with the pleasures of certainty. This wise policy ensured their progress in Africa for generations, their ideas so firmly fixed that no subsequent experience was allowed to disturb them. How else does one explain how they succeeded so well, and saw so little?

I declared then, without more ado, that his welcome amounted to detention and he had better tie me up again, or I would escape at the first opportunity.

He responded amicably that at Goodlove Castle wild life took precedence over humans. Though visitors were permitted, they were warned to observe the rules of the Castle. Yet people would not learn. Inquisitive children were regularly savaged by hyenas. The screams of those taken by lions were clearly audible in the nearer villages. Every year some simpleton clambered in amongst the gorillas and was hugged to death. Lord Goodlove often found himself angrily condemned for his commitment to the Life of the True Pulse. But he stuck to his beliefs; the greatest threat to life was man!

However, it was only fair to point out his writ ran only inside his walls. In the surrounding countryside a certain dislike, even hatred, was felt for the creatures of the Castle. Any item of his collection – and my collar and tag marked me as such – found beyond the walls might be shot on sight. He hoped I took his drift?

Then he begged me to excuse him. His women were greatly excited by my arrival, and a grand reception awaited me later, when I had settled in.

The quarters he had prepared were commodious. My room was the length of six donkey carts, with a bed broad as a ship, surmounted by four great masts to which were attached richly brocaded sails of red velvet, as large, I swear, as the great curtains that cover the screen in the bioscope in Lutherburg.

When the green, hairy Lord left me, I flung myself into my great ship of a bed and wept bitterly. If golden lads and girls all must, like chimney sweepers, come to dust, so too then Bushmen! I was still as far from the object of my journey as I was from the endless plains of my country. My role from now on, it seemed, was to amuse the madding crowd, just another exhibit in that green and menacing Africa, a curiosity a little less interesting than the ostrich, a little more amusing than a monkey.

The sole consolation I drew from this grim state of affairs was another morsel of enlightenment about the tribe among whom I found myself. I recalled ex-Bishop Farebrother's treachery with fearful admiration. He had sold me to the good and the great of the land for half the latter's fortune. This had made him feel good. I had once believed that the English are a rare people, in that they believe that having money adds moral status, yet that status increases when you give your money away. But they also believe it increases when you do not give your money away. And the good ex-Bishop had now sold me into a menagerie for the price of his daughter's happiness — and must have felt morally better than ever!

However, a warning, offered by the former flying Bishop, had proved true: it really was a jungle out there. Just as I had been warned. Now I had run into a horse of a very different colour.

Later that evening, when I had rested, Lord Goodlove sallied from his quarters, accompanied by a host of guards, pages, hangers-on and other supplicants, and, passing by my room, sent one of his servants to request my presence. I made myself as presentable as my few poor garments allowed, brushed my hat and followed the retinue to the lake where cranes played and hippo frolicked and where the Lord held court, in the open air, seated on a bench of full, fat leather, much padded and puckered and broad as an eland's back. He was the centre of a large crowd of concubines, or 'wifelings', as he described them.

They wore loose garments based, he said, on his own design taken from the warrior queens of old England, and designed to free the limbs for battle or love or childbirth.

Two dozen sets of lustrous, humid eyes focused on my person, at which the Lord, at first, laughed and said how eagerly his wifelings looked at me because they expected to see me accompanied by a woman of my own colour. But he was not jealous and invited me to sit beside him. But now the cause of their excitement became very evident; they stared quite shamelessly at the flap of leather which preserved the loins.

Their Lord now smiled less, and called them to order.

Not for the first time, I concealed myself as best I could behind my great tawny hat, while his flock of wifelings, chirruping and pecking, endeavoured to jostle for the best view.

Their Lord and Master, grown suddenly angry,

demanded to know, in a huge voice, what should cause them to stare like idiot children. Was there anything present in David Mungo Booi, besides his slanting eyes, yellow skin, peppercorn hair and tiny stature, that they had not seen more nobly present in their Lord?

I am sorry to say the answer was stifled laughter, which I can only describe as indecent, bordering on the downright lewd. He commanded silence – but the merriment continued in the ranks. And I saw that they were as much prisoners as I was. There was something in them that did not love their Lord. Something that pledged itself to silent disobedience. But they lined up for inspection like a guard of honour for a foreign head of state. And that was exactly the way the Lord described the ceremony. He inspected the ranks, but the mocking smiles persisted.

He took me down the line of women, pointing out an ankle here, there a buttock he considered particularly admirable. He was, explained the Lord, a hunter, a hedonist, an artist, a polygamist, a gambler and a conservationist. His wifelings were chosen for their genetic endowments. Each was expected to be ready at all times for the summons to one of the Lord's weekly seedings. He asked me to notice how his wifelings had been trained to fall on one knee as he approached and at no time to look him directly in the eye: this was the Zulu manner. He was a Zulu 'By Appointment', as it were, a privilege conferred on him by the King of the Zulus and an honour which had been accorded to no other living Englishman. He showed me his assegai, his knobkerrie and his cowhide shield with which he had been presented at his induction into the tribe. The Zulu were among the last who lived the life of the True Pulse, who washed their spears in the blood of enemies and died happy. The English, once upon a time, had enjoyed a blood–brotherhood with the Zulu, based upon the finest compliment nations might pay; they had gone to war and killed each other. Nothing quite so cemented a friendship. Did I not agree?

I might have replied that the Red People made war on no one – except those whose cattle ate our land – but I remembered where I was, and held my tongue.

The life of the True Pulse, to which he had devoted himself, beat to a stern drum. Each day of the week saw some solemn ceremony.

There were for example, his art Mondays. In his private apartments every available surface, the ceilings, the walls and even the floors, were daubed with his 'cave art'. How very grateful he would be for any help I might give him in this regard, knowing as he did that Bushmen held the premier position in the painting of rocks and walls of caves. In these images resided the secret religion of his pagan forefathers, the fruit of a lifetime's dedication to the life of the True Pulse. In truth, most of the pictures depicted his Lordship naked, sometimes painted blue, frolicking with his wifelings in vales, verdant dells and dingles of an earlier, merrier England, or fornicating among oaks and holly. His *qhwai-xkhwe* might be shown in full promise, adorned with a sprig of mistletoe (for that is their sacred plant); or he was dressed in the hunting or soldierly costumes they hold to be closest to divinity. In others he was naked on horseback wearing only the peaked hunting cap, blowing a small trumpet. Allegories, he said, for the sacred blood sports, hunting, shooting and fishing.

On Tuesdays, Lord Goodlove became a White Zulu. In leopard skins and cowhide shield, assegai in hand, he

was up before breakfast, practising short, stabbing movements on the front lawn. Later in the day he would invite
me to teach him to hunt like the Red People. Without the
support of his own tribal hunting regalia, tools and animals,
his progress was slow, and painful the death of his victims
(once a giraffe). But I turned his child-like efforts to good
account and, amazing him, from time to time, with a
reminder that we kill out of necessity, not for our diversion,
I would demonstrate how to convert slaughter into a sus-
taining meal. But, as ever, he had much to teach me in
return.

When he moved around his estate, he was followed, a
couple of paces to his rear, by a young man carrying a plastic
bag which held a damp dishcloth. It was the duty of
the young man, Lord Goodlove explained, to cleanse his
posterior parts, whenever the need arose.

In days gone by, the great Zulu Kings, said the Lord,
were always accompanied by an officer whose privilege it was
to perform this intimate service. It was one of the lovely
coincidences that their blood-brothers, the English, in their
own special way, had long practised something very similar.

Since I had no experience of the ways of kings, I
wondered whether he found it difficult to attract young
recruits. Where was the nobility or the profit in so debasing
oneself?

Debasement? Rubbish! came the good-natured reply.
People competed for the privilege. It was one of the few
remaining things that made the country truly great. A trait so
deeply ingrained, he doubted it could ever be rooted out. It
was the basis of the monarchy, as well as of a properly
functioning aristocracy based on wealth, land and breeding,
and of the least corrupt civil service in the world. Thank
God! Others had tried to emulate the practice and failed. It

was a tradition. It flourished naturally. His country, he was proud to say, still produced people willing to roll up their sleeves and do the necessary. People who fully understood the importance of carrying the towel. Difficult as it might be for me to understand, to get ahead in England, one generally started off by bringing up the rear. For this reason ambitious parents put down the names of their offspring at birth in the hope of winning a place in special academies where youngsters acquired the training essential to correct perform-ance, of which there were complex variations, probably impenetrable to the non-native: how to judge the precise position of the towel relative to the job, of the carrier relative to the king; the business of acquiring the all-important demeanour – cool, reserved, discreet; proper application of the towel, never to be overestimated, always downward and *towards* the carrier, never towards the great one, so that in the event of an accident it was always one's mentor who enjoyed the sweet smell of success and his towel carrier who accepted the load of responsibility. This was the essence of good rearing. He was proud to say that many of those numbered amongst the movers and shakers of the nation had learnt their trade by wielding the ceremonial towel on his Zulu Tuesdays.

On Fox Wednesdays, he became the Master of Hounds.

Early one morning I was set in a tower of the castle to watch this ancient ritual. His wifelings began preparing glasses of strong drink to fortify the hunters. I saw the horses, neatly groomed, being led from the stables. I saw the hunters meet in the misty hour and mount their horses. I was entranced, at first, to notice that they wore red coats, not unlike the coats that the English wore when they came to the aid of our people and kicked the arses of the Boers from the Snow Mountains to Murderer's Karoo.

It was beautiful, the tongue-pink beauty of the coats, the black, pod-like peaked helmets of the huntsmen, the sun bright on their little bugles, strange instruments that give off a sad cracked tootle, not unlike the harsh croak of the blue crane, though nothing like as lovely.

The hounds, once unleashed, boiled like newly made tea, their nostrils seeking the scent which hung in the air in tiny droplets. The hunters carried no arms, and I wondered how they planned to dispatch the prey. Suddenly, skipping through a hedge like a red shadow, the quarry was sighted, and hounds and hunt were off in hot pursuit. The fox is regarded as being very clever, and they need to make sure he has little chance of escaping them. He will use any hole to go to earth, they say. And so they stop all those he might think of using.

To some extent they see this creature as a mystical animal, blessed with the cunning we attribute to the divine joker, Kaggen, the mantis. From my captor's talk of the Zulus, I realized that it was part of their religious sense to believe that nothing more dignifies your adversary than having sport with him. Unless, of course, it is killing him.

I saw from my tower the hunters slipping like pink smoke across the damp green fields. I felt the fox's heart beat inside my breast. And I remembered my home and my mission. I heard the little cracked bugle ring out, and the excited baying of the hounds, and I had no need to ask what had caused the excitement far across the fields.

And I heard the song of my red brother. He sang an old truth. That among these people the saving of life is death. And the preservation of dying species, and the keeping of wifelings, and the celebration of brother warriors, and the admiration of Bushmen – all is death. And the salvation of miners, and the redemption of clerics,

and the costumes and the customs and the life of the True
Pulse are all of them — death.

The song of my red brother woke me from a fatal
dream. I had travelled in England to find freedom, a new
life, a living faith. I had found those who wished to help
me, hold me, advise me, guide me, teach me, save me —
but all their helping, holding, advising, guiding, teaching
and saving amounted to was a tearing of living flesh, the
small cry, the long darkness.

All this the fleeing Red Man sang. His death was our
death, this other Red Man, running before the hunters'
dogs. Our fate was to be chased from *kopie* to *kranz* by
soldier and farmer and traveller and collector. Driven from
our water-holes. Robbed of our honey. Smoked out of our
caves. Parted from our children. Cursed for our tricks.
Feared for our arrows. Shot down in our hundreds.

They say of the fox that he is very cruel. And so it was
said of us. That he will take what he cannot eat, six lambs
at a time. And so they said it of us. That he kills for the
fun of it. And so, they said, did we. That he is cunning,
dangerous, dirty. So, they said, were we. That the hunter
who destroys him is friend to all.

These memories and pains sat heavy in my heart as I
watched from the tower and heard the fading screams of
the dying fox as the hounds tore him to pieces.

By the time the Lord and his party returned, jubilant
from the kill, I had remembered my manners sufficiently.
It was only right, surely, that an explorer in a foreign land
should not stand in judgement but try wherever possible to
understand their native customs? But it was right, too, that
a traveller in this antique land should be aware of the
dangers, lest he be killed by custom, or kindness.

Chapter Eight

Among the wifelings of Goodlove Castle:
participates in a series of 'hands-on' experiments:
learns something of their sexual practices,
and rather more of fox-hunting

I was that evening alone in my room, shaking my head with astonishment at the strange turn of events when, without so much as a knock at the door – carried, as it seemed, within a thunderstorm of giggles, whistles, blushes and flashing eyes – there burst into my room a gang of immensely cheerful wifelings, which introduced itself 'collectively' as the 'Goodlove Science Group' and individually as Beatrice, Jade, Victoria and Tracy.

Beatrice was a buxom matron whose ankles I had heard the Lord speak of with adoration; Jade, very petite, but somewhat faded; Victoria, dark, full-lipped and, I thought, sharp as a jackal; Tracy, a heavy-bosomed, sleepy blonde, who had performed, in some relief agency, a form of manual labour by which she 'helped' men in some way I did not quite understand; one day the Lord had chanced upon her and taken her on because she was very good with her hands. I looked at her small, smooth, pale fingers and found it hard to believe Tracy had ever been a manual worker.

The Goodlove Science Group, explained Beatrice, their spokeswoman, wished to offer me a deal and to ask a favour. One hinged upon the other. I would have noted the demeaning confinement of the Lord's wifelings. They, in turn, had noted my servile status, the tag around my neck, the suffering in my eyes and perceived I was not enjoying the iron hospitality of their Lord. Well – here was the deal: do them a good turn, and they would help me to escape. The favour she had to ask of me was related to the offer of freedom. But it was such a small favour she would not even mention it, since she felt sure that I would find their offer far too tempting to baulk at the little service they asked in return.

Naturally their offer was very interesting, but I told them that I desired to know the favour before I considered the deal.

Very well, said Victoria, the Science Group wished to carry out an experiment.

For I seemed to them, declared Beatrice, to contradict one of the essential laws of physics.

That what went up, smiled Jade – except in my case it didn't – must sooner or later come down.

Now the four women fixed their eyes upon my *qhwai-xkhwe* with such passionate interest that I began to understand why people of the New World have a reputation for scientific advancement. They believe all must be put to the test.

Proceedings must be strictly confidential, Victoria continued. The Lord had forbidden any close inspection of my endowment.

Jealousy, Beatrice opined. Plain and simple.

Absolutely typical, said Victoria.

Until I had arrived, declared Jade, the Lord had felt

himself to be a seeder without rival, an inseminator extra-ordinary, father of half the damn country. Suddenly here was a creature, only half his height, who appeared eternally primed for seeding purposes.

His Lordship's instrument — declared Tracy — was, in fact, flaccid, slow, unwilling and required patient stimulation before it ventured forth, as the schoolboy, creeping, like the snail, unwilling to school. Then, no sooner had it appeared than it performed, and vanished, shy as the tortoise that pulls its head into its shell. But now they had found a horse of a different colour! And Tracy reached out a hand.

But this was altogether too sudden for me. I was still considering their offer. To win a little more time, I now asked how they could be sure that the Lord would not arrive home at any moment and disturb their experiment. Or turn murderous, as jealous men can be.

Jade laughed and declared, mysteriously, that the biter was bit.

Just as puzzling was Victoria's gleeful remark that the fox was not in the chicken coop that night; he was detained elsewhere.

And serve him right! cried Jade.

So there was plenty of time to conduct the experiment undisturbed and in fine detail — as true science demanded, said Tracy, rubbing her soft, pale hands.

It was the matronly Beatrice, of the ankles, who took pity on my confusion at their mysterious remarks. For years, she explained, Lord Goodlove had deserted his ladyloves at night. By long-established custom he ranged through the countryside like a hungry wolf, seeking fresh pickings. All were regarded as his property. There was scarcely a barn, a hedge, a hayrick where he had not tumbled some village maiden; not a byre, a bed or a barn where he had not tupped some local matron; not a cellar or a stable where he had not spent his noble seed. He took all and any: single women, old wives, and ailing grandmothers.

Or, at least, so he boasted, Victoria explained.

They saw scant signs of it closer to home, sighed Jade.

It was as if, said Tracy, their Lord could unfurl only in foreign parts a flag he seldom flew at home.

The women of Goodlove Castle said they hated these nightly gallivantings. And these raids were also detested throughout the region, from Little Musing to Much Musing, from Much Musing to the Black Mountains.

Sometimes a maddened lover, father, brother waited with a horsewhip at the gates of Goodlove Castle, threatening to thrash the errant Lord within an inch of his life. But the bearded old reprobate merely laughed in their faces and vanished into the fastness of his castle, crying that indeed he deserved horsewhipping – but first they must catch him!

A feeling of helplessness spread far and wide. By what spell had he turned farmers' wives and post-mistresses and village policewomen into bewitched slaves into whose willing wombs he nightly deposited a cargo of little lords a-leaping?

None could answer this question. Or prevent their own humiliation.

Not the wifelings sequestered in their quarters.

Not the angry husbands and fathers, and brothers, and lovers with the horsewhips, itching to thrash him within an inch of his life.

Not even, it seemed, the Lord himself, who, though proud of his nocturnal prowlings, was just as puzzled as to the motives behind his predatory raids. On the one hand, in a show of candid soul-searching, he confessed that his morality was perhaps not everyone's. But then he was not everyone. He was the Lord of Goodlove Castle, and the glimpse of a well-turned ankle, a delightful bosom, excited him. He grew excited often: in barns and taxis, in trains and in foreign parts. And, being honest, and vigorous, and in touch with the life of the True Pulse; being the only White Zulu in England; soldier, philosopher, hunter, gambler, curator – he let no shadow fall between desire and action. He took as he chose – and a good thing too!

And so it might have gone on for ever, sighed matronly Beatrice, but I had arrived – the pygmy from Heaven.

Their Lord, praise be the Lord, was hunting that night, as usual. They had come to take advantage of his absence, confided Jade.

And to offer me the hospitality of the Castle, said Tracy.

And to satisfy their scientific curiosity, declared Victoria.

Before I could stop myself, I had given my agreement.

Cheering and applause greeted my acceptance.

Would I please recline so as better to facilitate their examination? Beatrice asked. And, without waiting for a reply, she lifted me in her strong arms and, raising my loin-cloth to facilitate their view, laid me tenderly in the middle of my acre of a bed.

The women took up positions around me, and the experiment began with a barrage of questions. Tracy, stirred perhaps by some dim memory of her former trade, took hold of my *qhwai-xkhwe* in practised hands, and presented it for inspection by her colleagues. Victoria was intrigued by the little holes, one on either side of the head. What did they signify? Beatrice asked if it stayed unflagging, even while I slept? Little Jade simply stared.

It is a wonderful – God wot! – to address an audience aflame with scientific curiosity.

I explained that my permanent semi-erection was a

perfectly normal phenomenon among the San, whether the People of the Eland, or the river Bushmen, or the mountain Bushmen; this sturdy dependability was a celebrated fact in Bushmanland. And was often shown in our paintings. To demonstrate the purposes of the shafts through the crown, I took from behind my ear a needle of porcupine quill and threaded it through the flesh. What a commotion ensued! What a chorus of screams, a throwing up of hands! And a burst of applause when the needle successfully negotiated the narrow gateways and emerged on the far side of my *qhwai-xkhwe*, and yet that valiant stalwart did not slacken in the least.

Beatrice asked the purpose of this penile fenestration. Jade intimated that she would welcome the application of some similar procedure to the Lord of the Castle. And Tracy just stared.

Among certain Red People, it was the custom, I told my fascinated listeners, removing the quill and replacing it behind my ear, when a boy came of age, to have the spike inserted and to wear it whenever the member was not in use. The porcupine quill was the sharpest dart known in nature and a gift of the daughter-in-law of our god Kaggen, the praying mantis. She was given these admirable darts to protect herself against the hunger of her father Kwhai-hem, for, without this essential armour, the All-Devourer would have gobbled her whole. The test of pain was a measure of the endurance of the hunter; I was sure her people had some similar custom.

Beatrice corrected me. Pain was used less as a test of endurance, and more as an aid to sexual stimulation. Many males were incapable of arousal except by inflicting pain on women. I might have noticed that in their culture, bound into the notion of romance and marriage, was the expectation of assault.

Remembering, with a pang, my first exposure to Beth Farebrother, I said I had noticed it rather early on.

Tracy said that among some classes of indigenous male, inflicting pain on women took the form of beatings, strangulation or even murder. Or variations on these themes. And it was seen as quite natural. Often it was the only way of achieving enjoyment. On the other hand, more expensively educated males preferred to inflict pain on themselves.

Among such males, said Jade, you often found that the preferred practice was to do without women at all. Either by confining relationships to members of your own sex, a custom widely encouraged in the best schools, with the male taking over the woman's role.

Or, as an alternative, Beatrice continued, by taking over the woman's role oneself. This was generally done by stripping naked and donning one or other intimate item of female underwear, tying a rope around one's throat, then, after covering the head with a plastic bag and attaching the rope or ligature to some handy household fixture, such as the curtain rail or the banisters, leaping into space. This method of arousal sometimes achieved the degree of lift which my *qhwai-xkhwe* maintained so effortlessly.

But sure, I objected, this risked strangulation?

That was just the point, replied Beatrice. A miscalculation could be fatal. The risk attracted many ambitious men, or 'high flyers', as they were called, for obvious reasons. Those who failed perished. But those who succeeded in these solitary practices often went on to make considerable names for themselves in politics. It was a code of conduct: better-bred men did not strangle their wives, they preferred to strangle themselves.

I said I understood the code of conduct, but since death was the result in either case, I could not see the distinction.

Perhaps not, said Victoria, but that was because I was not English.

But now Beatrice announced that it was time for their experiment. The hypothesis advanced by the Science Group was as follows: if my *qhwai-xkhwe* was employed for a number of times successively, it was bound to slacken. This theory had been vigorously debated. Now the time had come to put the theory to the test.

Before the experiment began there took place what I suppose I must describe as their equivalent of the gift-giving ceremony. However, it was not as with us, where the lover will present his desired one with the gift of a tortoiseshell, or a springbuck skin, or shoot little love arrows in her direction. No, they presented me with a little rubber hood, or balloon, smaller than, but shaped rather like, the bladders of goats that our children use for footballs.

When locals were about to copulate they rarely observed these formalities. Tracy explained.

But as I was from Africa, said Victoria, certain precautions needed to be taken. Terrible afflictions had spread from my country and laid low many of their people who had no resistance to the plagues.

This is something which must weigh heavily on our hearts. How many European nations have been decimated by our diseases? Without any resistance, these simple souls perished like flying ants. Was it not from the Countries of the Sun that the Black Death had come? And venereal disease? Now another disease struck them down. For which we must again accept responsibility.

So I wore my little hood with gratitude. It was a shade of fiery red, giving the lie to those who claim that these people have no great liking for bright colour. It was Tracy, so good with her hands, who fitted the device, slipping it over my *qhwai-xkhwe* with the practised ease of the true scientist. And I could not help thinking, when I looked, that I rivalled in hue the tubular flower of the flame-lily.

Each wifeling in turn now removed her clothing and the experiment began in earnest. I had just time to notice an interesting physiological difference between their women and ours. They have no natural apron of skin, covering the tunnel of children,* the entrance to which is more hirsute than we are accustomed to.

But I had no further time for reflection. The experiment was in full swing, with each scientist attempting to assess whether, when exposed to regular and rhythmic stress, my *qhwai-xkhwe* might eventually flag and fall, and, finding to their mounting excitement that what went up did not always come down, they recorded their discoveries in cries of joy.

As for myself, the passive partner in these experiments, I did the only thing possible. I lay back and thought of Bushmanland.

As I lay resting the following morning, after a long night of concentrated experiment, I was surprised by a visit from the Lord. His upper lip looked somewhat stiffer than usual. Staring down at me as I lay in my ship of a bed, he expressed the hope that I had not been too bored in his absence.

I replied that his womenfolk had been kind enough to include me in discussions of a scientific nature.

He seemed pleased. His wifelings had been chosen for their inquiring minds. Not the sort of women who lay

---

* Accounts of the Cape San people suggest that women displayed a fold or 'apron' of skin concealing the vagina.

back and left it all to the chaps. Not at all. The sorts of people who rolled up their sleeves and got down to it. By George, yes.

He seemed very friendly. And of my close scientific co-operation with the Scientific Group he appeared happily ignorant. Far from exhibiting any animus towards me, on the contrary, the Lord of Goodlove announced that he proposed to honour me by giving me a privileged position for the great hunt which was to take place on Fox Wednesday.

But, remembering my pain the last time I had witnessed this particular event, I begged to be excused.

The Lord was eloquent in his plea that I take part. Surely I would not disappoint him? My hunting brother? From me he had learnt the hunting rites of the San, killed his first giraffe and supped on its brain. Now he was offering to repay my kindness by introducing me, at first hand, to one of the most ancient of English ceremonies.

He urged me to think of those who suffer among my people – of the /Xam people of the Cape, gobbled down like ant larvae, by the invaders black and white. Vanished they are from the land to which they belonged, he reminded me, fled like water in a thirsty time!

How could I refuse? Put like that. For, after all, if we do not support their traditions, will we not have only ourselves to blame if one day such specimens of traditional English rites vanish as surely as the hunters of Bushmanland? Where today are our medicine ceremonies of childhood? Who beats the drum when a girl has her first issue of blood? Where is the solemn naming of the fountain by the father in the presence of the son to whom it is being given? Who can remember the respect-names of the animals? Who knows the secrets of rain-making? Where is the Trance

Dance? Who observes our food taboos – that woman will eat no part of the red cat, that children must not taste the tip of the springbuck's tail? That no one shall taste the jackal in case they become cowardly like him? Or the baboon because he is too much like us?

Very well – I told him – I would attend, but I would not hunt. I would watch, but I would not kill. This he agreed to very happily.

He stood me in a fine position just over the brow of a little hill, where I could not see the Castle any longer but where, he assured me, the quarry must pass, when he had been flushed into the open. I would see him run before my very nose.

We were brother hunters, the Lord proclaimed. I had helped him to bag his first giraffe. He would repay me now with my first fox's brush!

But what would I do with the tail, I wondered, in that green field, on that glorious morning? Hunters, when they are true, need their quarry more than it needs them. They love what they kill. But these people hunted what they hated, much as they did in love and marriage.

I mused on these things in the early morning light, waiting to see the black helmets and pink coats come over the hill, looking for all the world like the red tubular tips of the aloes that stride like men across the Karoo. I heard the distant baying of hounds and the far-off cracked notes of the hunting horn. The call of the hounds grew louder, and I saw the pack begin to climb the long, green slope where we had killed our first giraffe. Behind them came the huntsmen. The sun shone on the little bugle that Lord Goodlove raised to his lips. What I could not see was the fox, and I shaded my eyes for a better glimpse of the wretched quarry.

The horses' hooves drummed on the wet turf. English soil is soft and sounds well across a considerable distance. By laying an ear to it, you can read the state of the hunt while it is still afar off. The dogs were now in clear view, the pack almost hysterical. They had the scent, were heading in my direction – their jaws wide. The hunt was on to something.

Still no sign of the fox. I reminded myself that Lord Goodlove was not keen-eyed. Many was the time on our hunting expeditions when he had mistaken a hartebeest for a springbuck. But he never minded, saying it didn't matter a damn, so long as he made a kill.

Still the hounds came on. I now thought it wise to put some distance between myself and the hunt. My pace, I am pleased to say, was as good as ever. As a young man I could run down a springbuck. I am no longer fleet, but I am still fast enough to outstrip the hounds they like to use, given some small advantage. I increased my pace as I moved past the giraffes' enclosure and at the same time shifted my direction, aiming for the small wood. As I did so I felt the pack behind me change direction too. I heard the cracked bugle sound again. There was no doubt in my mind now. The dogs, the horses, the hunters, these things were aimed at me. Some mistake had been made. After all, the English redcoats in our land had been fooled by the appearance of the red-tipped aloes striding across the land and mistaken them for black warriors. My skin prickled the way it does when the sharp-toothed, red hair-clipper spider feasts on a man's curls when he lies asleep at night. If the English had mistaken aloes for Xhosas, I told myself, why shouldn't this hunting party now mistake a Bushman for a fox?

The foremost dogs were closer now. The little dark wood still sat way up the incline, and I was conscious that

I was slowing. The dogs were faster than I on the hill. And I knew my little lead was vanishing. I remembered the fever of the dogs when at last they close on their quarry. I remembered the cries of the Red Man as he was torn to pieces by the intoxicated hounds. I thought how sad it would be if I should perish this way, on green, foreign soil, without ever having delivered my message to their Queen, my notes gone, my travels among the English buried with me, my very memory lost in the darkness of this island.

I reached the safety of the little wood ahead of the field. Here, perhaps, was some chance to go to ground. Many a time have I tunnelled into the ant-bear's hole. The badger's lair would be no different. Of course, the creature itself might object, but what with the clamour of the hounds above ground, he might not care to ask too closely why another should want to share his home.

Alas, for the luck of the Bushman! The badger sets I found without trouble. But the entrances were firmly barred against me. Too late I recalled that this was the custom of the Master of the Goodlove Hunt: to block the entrances before the sport began. Another ancient hunters' tradition.

This, then, was a place of death. The badgers sealed in their sets would die slowly. The fox, denied refuge, would go more quickly. I turned at bay and I took from my quiver an arrow. They were too many, I knew that. They had always been too many. But some, at least, would die with me.

It was then that the wood erupted into a screaming, exploding, whistling, jeering, ratcheting, hooting, fire-cracker world. The hounds yelped and snarled and turned tail. The horses, coming up fast behind, shied and several threw their riders. I saw Lord Goodlove fall slowly, as if he was used to this, and his cracked little bugle described an arc of the sort you still see when the Evening Star fades from the sky at the first light and falls into the veld, ready to be born again the next night.

The huntsmen were being attacked by an army who came out of the trees and blew whistles and banged drums and rolled beneath the horses' feet the sort of marbles that children play with. I felt myself seized by the hair and passed from hand to hand, from man to man, above the heads of the warriors, down the line, until I was deposited safely in the rear. Who my rescuers were I had no idea, except to know that they had saved me from the jaws of the hounds.

As I was carried off by the raiding party, I heard some-one say in tones perfectly throbbing with satisfaction that the hunters of Goodlove Castle would rue this day for a long time; that the Lord himself would be as sick as a parrot; that there was after all, perhaps, goodness and justice and peace in the world; that the Goodlove hunt was spitting blood and a damn good thing too because the travellers of Happy Common had just stolen their fox.

They took me to their camp. A long line of ancient vehicles in a muddy field. There I was directed to one I took to be their king or chief or clan captain, for he lived in a vehicle much grander than all the others. The sort of magnificent conveyance usually seen only among the very rich Karoo farmers when they set off for their holidays on the Cape coast. It had a water tank on the roof, a bed, a stove, a chair; it was an entire house on wheels. I knew as soon as I set eyes on the visitor that here was a luxurious traveller, a rich explorer, and not one at his wits' end like me. I was suddenly very conscious of my poor appearance. Living, as I had done for weeks now, in the green veld of Goodlove Castle among the giraffe and the lion and the tiger, I was acutely aware of how I must look to this handsome stranger, in my short skin skirt, my cloak and my spear.

He wore a fine blue suit and carried an umbrella against the rain. But his other characteristics were immediately recognizable. He was short, like me. His hair and eyes and complexion were mine, perhaps a little darker; a Nama, I reckoned with a clash of Griekwa blood. He stepped forward with hand outstretched and spoke to me in my own language: '*David Mungo Booi, ek se?*' Which I can translate, more or less, as meaning 'I say?' But, more accurately, this stranger from my country addressed me as follows: 'David Mungo Booi, I presume?'

Chapter Nine

David Mungo Booi, I presume? An historic meeting;
he is confined in an English asylum and is favourably impressed;
returns happily to Little Musing

Yes.

With that simple reply, I confirmed my identity. A scrawny, ungenerous response, as it must for ever sound to 'posterity' and 'history' and 'generations to come', all of which would be enthusiastic spectators of our 'momentous' meeting, in some future time when news of it reached the outside world. So I was assured by the stranger in the fine caravan who greeted me so unexpectedly after my escape from Goodlove Castle, and who seemed disconcertingly, but distantly, familiar.

What should I have answered, faced with a question so colossally foolish? I was 'presumed' to be David Mungo Booi; at first sight, such tentativeness suggests courtesy and the diffidence of good manners on the part of my 'discoverer'. Look again, however, and the spurious nature of the question is plain. 'Presumption' implies room for doubt; yet where in ten times ten thousand miles might he have found another Bushman in the remote and treacherous reaches of darkest England?

All this I reflected upon while being pinned to the ample chest of one Hendrik Mamalodi Kosi (for that was the name of my visitor), who filled the air with delighted cries. As soon as we reached civilization – he vowed – the good news would be flashed to the editor of the *Zwingli Advertiser*; and people back home, from Eros to Compromise, from Lutherburg to Pumpkinville, would rejoice at the knowledge that their countryman had been found alive in these terrible green wastes.

Mr Kosi's instructions from the editor of the *Zwingli Advertiser* had been very direct: 'Draw ten thousand bucks, right? And go find the lost explorer.' If the money ran out, Hendrik Mamalodi Kosi was left in no doubt as to how to proceed. 'Draw another thou. And another. But *find* David Mungo Booi!'

And he had done so. God be praised! And once more I found my face making close acquaintance with Mr Kosi's rich shirt front. And I remembered then why he seemed distantly familiar. The suit, the diamond ring, the air of large confidence, all these had been absent when I had seen him last. He had had an official air, certainly, but then it would have been surprising if he had not done so, for he was the clerk in the magistrates' court over Eros way, and his job was to bring charges against Ashbush People suspected of stealing firewood from abandoned farms.

I'm afraid we disagreed from the start. He claimed to have found me. I did not regard myself as being lost. What is more, I did not wish to be bound. In my time in England I may have been detained pending Her Majesty's Pleasure; I certainly had been found, gagged, almost deported, dropped on my head, saved by a flying Bishop, nearly lynched by Remote-area Dwellers, tranquillized, collected by the Lord of Goodlove Castle, experimented upon by the women of the Castle and hunted to within an inch of my life . . . but I had always known where I was, why I found myself in a certain place and what I was doing there.

Until now. We were moving slowly, but steadily, ever deeper into the countryside, bringing up the rear of a convoy of ancient vehicles; we were sole occupants of a spanking motorized caravan sailing along very grandly in a line of elderly vehicles, many rusting buses and vans, lovingly coaxed to a show of speed, hiccuping and belching smoke. The aim of the rescuers, it seemed, was to put a goodly distance between ourselves and Goodlove Castle, lest the Lord mount a counter-attack to reclaim his fox.

Hendrik Mamalodi Kosi was one of us; that is to say, he bravely mingled in his rich person many family features. But there all similarities ceased. His fine blue suit sported creases so sharp you could have sliced bread with them; the diamond ring I had spied on his thumb flashed rainbows of light; and a thick gold chain snaked around his hairy wrist. I had not seen such prosperity since my one and only glimpse of a Government Minister who, having lost his way, turned up unexpectedly one day in Lutherburg and was persuaded to show himself, briefly, to a crowd of sceptics. That pale Minister had worn a brown suit; his well-oiled hair was much admired; and the sun made rainbows of the diamond in his tie-pin as he stood for a few uneasy minutes on the balcony of the Hunter's Arms before being hustled back inside because the crowd began pelting him with stones.

And this was strange. For the clerk of the magistrates' court is powerful – but he is not rich.

Yet Mr Kosi's suit was richer, his diamond larger, his well-fed prosperity far exceeded in girth the person of our fugitive visiting Minister. Only in one aspect did the two resemble each other: they were both sure of themselves. The furtive Minister that he was in the wrong, and my 'rescuer' that he was right.

As our convoy rolled through the green countryside, lashed to a frenzy of luxurious growth by the promise of summer, this intrepid explorer told me why he had come to find me.

A deputation of nomads, calling themselves the Society for Promoting the Discovery of the Interior Parts of England, had turned up one day in the offices of the *Zwingli Advertiser* and told the editor a most extraordinary story. One of their number, a certain David Mungo Booi, had set out on an expedition to darkest England, there to seek the Queen and to ask her to redeem the promise made to the Red People by her great-great-grandmother – namely, to send her soldiers to the rescue of her beloved San. He had been instructed, also, to locate the grave of 'Little-Boy' Ruyter. And to report on the suitability of the country for Bushman settlement.

Many months had passed without word, and they feared his expedition had tragically miscarried. Rumour was rife among members of the Society. Some believed that I had been killed by savages for violating food taboos. Another, more cheerful, myth held that the Sovereign so favoured me that she had given me a thousand sheep and I dwelt by her grace and favour in a palace, at no cost, along with other faithful courtiers, and I had forgotten the sufferings of my own people. Still others maintained that I had become a champion Royal Jockey, until killed in a fall from my mount while taking part in some ceremonial race.

Hendrik Mamalodi Kosi had therefore journeyed to England, sponsored by the *Zwingli Advertiser*. On landing in England, he had attempted to recruit staff for the trek inland. But his expedition had been plagued by terrible difficulties from the start, when he had attempted, as he told me, very emotionally, to put some backbone into the miserable wretches whom he had taken into his service. But labour relations had been poor.

I told these men, cried my rescuer, that they were fortunate indeed to find paid employment in a noble cause. I assured them that I would be fair but I would tolerate no shirkers, or malingerers, or dumb insolence. I attempted to awaken a spark of pride in the brutes. They were to take on the important roles of bearers and porters. The terms of their employment were generous and followed the guidelines established by past expeditions from their country to mine, and I expected them, at least, to respect their own traditions of exploration.

Everything would be done in conventional fashion. Each would receive four months' salary, in advance. In the event of accident or illness, they would be nursed, where they dropped, by a qualified member of the expedition. Each of the porters would be given a pack, never above thirty kilograms, and assigned a place in the line. A man's pack would remain his personal responsibility, and exchanges between porters would not be permitted. Porters who showed promise I might permit to wait at table, where they proved quick enough in anticipating my wants.

Next, I explained the procedures of the march. I proposed to dispense altogether with their names, as these were difficult to remember and to pronounce. I would number my men instead. The lead porters, with my supplies strapped to their backs, were numbered One, Two and Three; there would follow my bearers, numbers Four to Seven, carrying my sedan chair, behind whose silken curtain I would repose, reading one of the useful texts of the early explorers.

My sedan chair was very lovely, built of solid teak with red silk curtains against the heat of the sun, and useful for privacy.

The carrying poles of my chair were mahogany, rubbed to a dark sheen by the calloused palms of bearers long ago who might, I imagined, have carried it from the Cape to Cairo, from Lake Victoria to Stanleyville.

But his staff, cried the magnificent Mr Kosi, were quite blind to the honour he did them. They had failed at the first obstacle. They had come to a small lake, which he had ordered them to cross. Their leader, a fine specimen standing well over six foot in his bare feet (bearers were not allowed shoes), broke down and wept like a child when ordered to advance into the centre of the lake. It was the fear of water – the island-dwellers' phobia.

Terror overcame him and he froze. I saw the box on his head begin to slide and knew that strong action was called for. Accordingly, I fitted an arrow to my bow and told him distinctly that if he did not move, I would shoot him where he stood. I am pleased to say that the effect was salutary, and in a few moments he splashed on to the further bank, a well-baptized porter, his burden still intact. One hesitates to use force towards them, but sometimes it is only force that is efficacious.

Mr Kosi's expedition soon foundered in recriminations and unhappiness. His porters absconded; his bearers stole his provisions. One morning he found himself alone and in England.

Too late, declared Mr Kosi, I realized that the local tribes will always have more in common with each other, even if it is only hatred, than they can ever feel for the people of Bushmanland or the Children of the Sun.

Finding the wretches either unwilling to work or ignorant of their own country, he had decided to travel alone rather than trust his life or his purse to rascally natives, riddled with inertia, greed and duplicity.

He had begun to believe I had perished when, one day, he met the band of vagrants with whom we were now travelling. They told him the way to the Castle and of rumours that a little creature, half man, half monkey, with pendulous posterior, crisp curls and slanted eyes, had been added recently to its wild-life collection. When these vagabonds confided that they were planning to sabotage the Goodlove hunt, he saw the perfect diversion by which to cover his entry into the estate in order to check on the truth of their stories. Imagine his delight when the fox, snatched from the jaws of the Goodlove hounds by the hunt saboteurs, turned out to be none other than David Mungo Booi!

His discovery came not a moment too soon. He had suffered terribly. His hair had gone quite grey in a few months. Fever, suspicion, hatred had walked with him every step of the way. This land had been called, truly, the Red Man's Grave. Your average native was a hopeless fellow. If you gave him an inch, he took a yard. If you treated him with elementary kindness, he took it for weakness. Firmness, cried Hendrik Mamalodi Kosi, was the only language these people truly understood.

I said, as one who had no answers at all, I would like to hear the language these people understood.

His reply came like the cobra's kiss, so quick, so toxic. *Exterminate the brutes!* He saw no other way. As one civilized man to another, the sooner we got out of this poxy little kingdom and back to a big country where a man could see the stars, where there was a future, and the beer was cold, the better for both of us. And this was his great good news. The Boer was defeated! Very soon, our people would expel him and set up a council of all the people, freely chosen for the first time ever. A new government would take over. *Viva* the new Freedom! *Viva* the new government! *Viva* the *Zwingli Advertiser!*

I waited for him to dry his tears before I gently told him that this was just what I feared. How many times in the past had the travelling people, the hunters, the wanderers the Ashbush People, heard rumours of a new government, and of its plans for their future? First came the Dutch New Government; then the French New Government; then the English New Government; then the Boer New Government. Now, if I understood him, there was to be yet another New Government. Each administration gave way to the next, the way identical beads of ostrich-eggshell are threaded on sinew. One thing, however, always remained the same; the more of governments, the fewer of us. I saw no reason why our latest rulers should be any more tender towards the people of the far plains, the high places, the great road. They were too tall, and we too small. We were so far beyond their gaze that we had fallen off the edge of the world.

His response was to brake sharply, bringing his splendid vehicle to a rude halt. Then, leaping from the driver's seat, he stood before me, his clenched fist waving in front of my nose like a jackal's tail. I thought he was going to attack me, but it seemed he wished again to make a speech. He spoke wonderfully of something called the New Freedom. Our people would live in free houses. Our children would go to free schools. Water should be free. And electricity. Quite, *quite* free! There would be telephones in each house, and we would call each other over long distances, quite free of charge. He, Hendrik Mamalodi Kosi, promised this. Would I call him a liar?

I thanked him. Far from calling him a liar, I felt that, as a man who made promises, he would appreciate that I had given my word to my sponsors. And I intended to continue my journey until I reached my destination and fulfilled my promise.

He raised his fist, now, very slowly, and unclenched from that bony club a stabbing finger. It pointed to the road. And then he delivered an ultimatum in a loud voice: I was to leave his vehicle immediately. Clearly my long exposure to the English had sent me mad. If I wished to remain in this benighted land, then all he could say was that I deserved whatever I had coming to me. Little as he liked the Boers, he was obliged to admit that he understood now why they called the San people wild, treacherous vagrants who could not be taught or tamed, a pest, a vermin, a disgrace to human kind.

Following the direction of that stabbing finger, I clambered down the steps of his marvellous caravan: on the roadside, I watched as he furiously reversed in a violent screaming of tyres, over which I just made out his last malediction, flung at me as he raced away. You might take the Bushman out of the bush, yelled my erstwhile rescuer, but you could not take the bush out of the Bushman!

Not for the first time, I found myself on the road. But I had an idea I should not have to walk for long. The convoy of antique gasping vehicles we had so abruptly abandoned could not have gone very far.

So it proved. Within an hour I came across the old wrecks huddled like a flock of storm-drenched sheep in a muddy cornfield.

The travellers reminded me in many ways of ourselves.

They called themselves the tribe of peace: I met Nobby and Nosh and Stoney, as well as Sue, Emma and Miranda, who was in an advanced state of pregnancy; and, darting around them like locusts, muddy, tousled children who stared at me frankly and unabashedly, with a kind of limpid curiosity, as if they had never in their lives seen anything like me. I had noted this before – it is the custom to stare with an intensity which is uncomfortable, but which in them is unstudied and completely natural.

Nobby, their leader, was gorgeously colourful. His hair had been shaved severely along the sides of his head into a great wedge, rubbed with grease until it stiffened and it stood up from his skull like an axe-blade. Moreover, this hatchet of hair had been dyed the colour of a locust's wing in the sunset, gold, violet and blue. His thin face, like a long lantern, showed a form of scarification common among the peace tribe, who like to mutilate their nostrils and ears by piercing them with rings, pins, old nails or any metal scrap they find. Their appearance can seem rather frightening when you are first exposed to it, yet I found these people to be the gentlest of souls; hardly ever raising a fist in anger, or a finger for themselves, they look as brazen as butcher-birds – but they are really as gentle as doves.

With *one* exception: they were sworn enemies of Lord Goodlove and all those who hunted the fox. To disrupt this barbarous custom wherever they found it, and to curb the slaughter of innocent animals, was the religion of the tribe.

I admired, as well, the ingenuity with which they gave their flimsy shelters the appearance of substance.

If their household furniture was rather vague, its end use was perfectly clear. Doormats of straw, curtains of string, boxwood cupboards, ingenious extending beds, tin-can chimneys, enamel-basin baths, paraffin lamps, and even real pictures on make-believe walls. A spurious, yet somehow steadfast, domesticity was achieved. The cumulative effect of which was to construct from the flimsiest pieces of scrap a home as well founded as a castle. A castle built of dragon-fly's wings, quick to fold away.

They took me to the fire where they cooked their daily gruel, a stew of lentils and beans they call 'hippy slop'. They used meat – but rarely, finding it very expensive. They preferred to buy their meat at the local shops instead of hunting or taking rabbits or squirrel by snare or trap. I was surprised to learn that these were plentiful enough in the nearby fields. Yet they did not teach their young to hunt. Even bagging birds was forbidden. Nosh pointed out that their disapproval of hunting made poaching quite impossible.

Nobby, his gold earrings flashing in the sun, explained that working for money was also against their religious belief, right?

Right, said Nosh.

But how did they manage to feed themselves? I asked.

No sweat, said Nobby. They went to a special office and were given money for being without work. Or for being with children. Or if they were ill. But they were also given money if they were well.

It seemed to me a far more enlightened idea than our pensions, which are paid only to the old who have worked a lifetime. In England they pay pensions to those still young enough to enjoy them.

Now the pregnant woman, Miranda, whom I saw was similarly stabbed about the nose and ears with the tribal motif which favoured nails and fish-hooks, stepped forward and declared that it had been decided that I should share her caravan during my stay.

All their lives they had struggled towards a natural life,

one combining the visions of the Aboriginals of Australia, the austerity of the Eskimo, the nobility of the Sioux, the songs of the whales, and the healing magic of the Cape Bushmen. And now, right here in their midst, with his cute slanty eyes and his lovely wrinkles and his orangey skin and his adorable rump and his heaps of healing magic, was their very *own* hunter-gatherer, from whom she and Nobby, and the whole tribe, would learn so much. She was at that very moment so overcome with gratitude that she simply had to go and spike a joint in the bender under the trees and listen to the stars singing. Because stars *did* sing if you had Bushman ears, didn't they? And she could feel her Bushman ears growing with every passing minute spent in my company.

And Nobby said, yeah, he thought he'd head up a little Horse, maybe, and pick a little guitar, and if I felt like having a little bit of Horse or Sue, to feel free, because he would be pretty honoured and so, he was sure, would she. Or him, for that matter. No problem. Under a bender, there was no gender.

A lesser-known hazard of travelling among the English is their impulsive desire to fornicate with strangers. It is sometimes difficult to decline without giving offence. But San people are advised to travel with their members well covered at all times.

Fortunately, I was not obliged to refuse. Our delightful conversation was abruptly ended when a young man with two chicken bones threaded through his nose and a face painted in dark-red and white and blue (which, incidentally, are the sacred colours of the rain eland), who had been posted as a guard, came running into the centre of the camp crying in a very agitated way that there were, as he put it, pigs on site!

Imagine my surprise when I saw, cutting a swathe

through a field of corn, not a herd of pigs, but a police car. I watched, amazed, to see the campers fling themselves into its path, climb on its roof and bang on its bonnet.

The police retreated and took up a position on the edge of the cornfield.

Addressing us through a loud-hailer the officers announced they had reason to believe that the tribe was giving shelter to a bogus refugee or asylum-seeker, who planned to enter the Queen's Palace; this man was Boskoid★ in appearance, below average height, semi-naked and in possession of a dangerous weapon, namely, a quiverful of poison arrows. Anyone fitting that description should come forward so that he could be eliminated from their inquiries.

It was Nobby who put into words the very thought passing through my mind. How had the police found me among the peace tribe? The answer came in Nobby's words – for ever afterward to ring in my ear:

Mr Kosi – he squealed!

Clearly, since parting company from me, my country-man had not been idle.

I had no wish to bring the force of the law down on the heads of my friends. I proposed giving myself up. But the tribe would not hear of it. I was *their* Bushman! Miranda declared. And if the pigs wanted me, they would have to come and get me.

Once again the convoy of police vehicles advanced towards us.

I watched as the youth so artfully threaded with bones ran forward, rolling a tree trunk into the path of the lead vehicle; and then, leaping on the trunk, he began beating

---

★   A Victorian ethnologist's term for people of the San and Khoe-Khoe groupings.

his chest with his fists in the way that the baboons do when threatened by leopards. The women of the camp banged saucepans together, and the children, in what was evidently a rehearsed manoeuvre, relieved themselves on the wheels of the police vehicle.

In a few minutes the cornfield was a battleground. Even the children joined in, biting the officers wherever possible. And the women poured jugs of urine over their heads, pushing a number of them into the noisome latrines of which the nomads were so proud.

Wielding long truncheons, masked and armoured police joined battle with the peace tribe, whose weapons were loaded chamber-pots and whose troops were squads of children. I was reflecting on the interesting principle of their warfare, in which unarmed police and unarmed citizens beat each other severely but seldom fatally, when I was approached by a police officer who asked me to accompany him to the station. I agreed to do so, whereupon – as if to seal the contract – he struck me on the head with his truncheon and, despite some small protection afforded by my hat, not for the first time, night fell suddenly.

I opened my eyes in a room which, for one joyful moment, made me think, in its comfort and security arrangements – bars on window, steel door – that I was back once more in the Royal Guest-house where I had been accommodated – oh, so long ago! – at Her Majesty's Pleasure. My great hat, together with my bow and arrows, had been placed neatly at the foot of my bed, in which, for reasons not clear to me, I seemed to have difficulty moving.

There entered a woman, dressed in white, who called me 'dear Booi' and urged me to lie back, relax and make myself at home. She introduced herself as Head of Care and hoped I would be very happy in my new home.

'Home', I fell to reflecting, is a terrible word in the mouths of others and worst of all in the mouths of the English, who are the only people in the world whose very country is called Home and for whom the homeliness of other peoples' homes is hatefully foreign where it is not absolutely incomprehensible.

Was this place to which I had been brought a Palace of Detention? I asked. Where one awaited Her Majesty's Pleasure?

The Head of Care looked horrified. I was not in jail. It was not the English way to imprison people in need of special help. She consulted her notes. The police had brought me in while I was unconscious. Could I confirm that I was one David Mungo Booi, a bogus asylum-seeker suffering from the delusion that I would be received by the Queen?

I tried to raise myself, only to find my body strapped to the mattress with the same dexterity as a hunter will bind the legs of the baby giraffe before butchering it on the spot. I asked for my precious hat and it was brought to me, rather battered, I fear, as a result of the blows from the police truncheon, and from its cranial hook I retrieved the Paper Promise from the Old Auntie with Diamonds in Her Hair and read it aloud, taking comfort from the majestic rhythm of the phrases, and the certainty of English honour.

And tell me, dear, urged the Head of Care, when I finished reading, what were we planning to ask Her Majesty?

Her look should have alerted me. I had seen something like it in the eyes of many a farmer when I had asked for an advance on my shearing money, or the loan of a suit of clothes, or the gift of a sheep for a fence-mender who had broken his fingers and could no longer work. A mixture of astonishment and disbelief, tinged with anger. But I was sleepy or blind or stupid, and I answered that I planned to ask Her Majesty to send troops to my country to kick the arses of the Boer to Kingdom Come, in accordance with her promise.

She seemed satisfied. Addressing me by the pet-name 'Sonny Jim', she said, that anyone who believed that would believe anything. She was satisfied that, for my own protection, I had been delivered to a place of safety. In my new home I would find patients with similar delusions had been brought together and were encouraged to share them. Obsessive behaviour could be moderated by exposure to opposing aberrations. While I was prone to royalist fantasies, many of her patients suffered from something very different – a disease of logic.

In less advanced countries people were driven mad by unhappiness, or drugs, or cruelty; in England it was excessive common sense that unhinged them. This made mental illness as difficult to detect as it was to treat. There were more of the reasonably insane in England than anywhere else on earth. Sorting out the demented from the sane required great skill; to all but the specialist's eye, they seemed so very alike.

Her method was to bring certain patients face to face with me. The shock might be salutary. I seemed to have no trace of sense whatever. I was insanely romantic and pathologically credulous. I suffered from a view of England which no one else in the world, least of all the English, believed in. I yearned, I aspired. I dreamed of Royal Receptions, of *justice* and red-coated soldiers. Doubtless I also believed in decency, honour and cricket. I was absolutely barking, but who cared? Brought face to face with the patients under her care, something of my madness might rub off, in the way that the best antidote to a poison is a little of the same.

I wanted to interrupt and say that, frankly speaking, this might apply to their poisons, but ours were antidoteless, until I remembered those long-ago lessons Beth had given me in how to be nice, and said nothing.

And I remembered enough to know that the Head of Care was being nice to me, and I should be very much on my guard. As I had learnt from the Farebrother family, the impulse to do good is, among the English, a very dangerous inclination. Once set upon the path, they are merciless. There is nothing more fatal, except the need to be kind.

Consequently, I feared the worst when the Head of Care told me, kindly, that she hoped I would not object to being used as a form of therapy.

I replied that, since I was bound hand and foot, objecting would not help me.

She thanked me for my understanding, and they wheeled into my room a young man, blindfolded, in a wheelchair.

The Head of Care reached down her strong arms; her biceps rose full and white like the rills of fat on a *kudu*'s kidney, and she took hold of the blindfolded man on his stool and turned him, east and south and west and north, to reassure herself that he was sightless in all directions.

This young man had been a very brilliant government servant until mental illness struck him. Even now he must always be blindfolded, or he saw things.

I asked what he saw.

Her answer surprised me. Links! He saw links. A sad

story. He had once had a fine job – he had been in charge of all the donations, grants-in-aid, the country made to foreign, less-developed, poorer peoples in distant lands. Such gifts were handed over freely. Nothing whatever was expected in return. Unfortunately, sophisticated charity was not easy for developing peoples to understand. The generosity of the donation was polluted by the very thing it was meant to alleviate – the backwardness of the recipient nation. People felt obliged to feel grateful; worse still, they showed it!

Very well. Account needed to be taken of this uncalled-for gratitude: it should be monitored. Accordingly, a civil servant had been appointed to take charge of Foreign Gratitude. He begun hallucinating soon after he took up his post. He conjured up a clear link between, say, the donation of a dam and the grateful purchase of a battleship. Worse followed. Soon he was convinced he could correlate the degree of gratitude felt, using a special scale. After this his condition deteriorated so sharply that he actually began rewarding recipient nations able to display most gratitude. Soon he was seeing connections all over the place, and he had been admitted to this place of safety, where he was kept in the dark and blindfolded whenever taken into the light.

I was puzzled, facing the man blindfolded in the wheelchair. Surely, all he had done was to face facts? Gifts brought tangible expressions of gratitude. Generosity was rewarded. Would it have been better to lie, either to himself or to his country, by denying the existence of a link between donations, grants-in-aid, no-string gifts and a thankful recipient?

The Head of Care laid her strong hands on my shoulders. Sadly, I was not one of them. Or I would have known that failure to tell the whole truth is not the same thing as lying. Oh, dear, certainly not. Truth was, in fact, a precious commodity – and should be used sparingly. To be economical with the truth was the public servant's duty: how else was the public to be protected? Or foreign friends dealt with whose standards of probity fell far short of one's own?

One glance had told her I was the ideal' medicine in this unfortunate case. Aversion therapy, that's what I was. I was a member of the receiving peoples. I was foreign, simple and pitiably poor. The treatment she proposed would consist of convincing the deluded official that there were no links between gifts freely given and gratitude expressed. Thereby restoring not only his sanity, but the reputation of Her Majesty's Ministers, who were, alas, no longer seen in some quarters as the most honest, upright and uncorrupted in all the world.

The treatment required privacy. The Man in Charge of Gratitude would perform only if he believed he was dealing frankly and in the strictest confidence. I was please to remember that the important thing was to destroy, in his mind, any notion of a link. Then, without further ado, she removed the young man's blindfold, slipped from the room and left us alone.

The young man, smiling, recognized me immediately as a member of a receiving nation, and asked in the most interested fashion about my people. He was sure that most of us were dead, dying or scattered to the winds. Had we not thought of resisting our enemies?

We had fought those who invaded our country, I assured him, but arrows were little use against rifles.

Exactly, came the answer; heavy machine-guns would have been a better idea. Surely life was hard in our desert places without modern weapons?

Today, I said, it was not weapons we wanted, but water.

First-class, said he. Had we considered building a dam?

I replied that we would do well enough with new windmills to pump underground water.

I barely saw his hands move. Faster than anything I had ever seen since a striking cobra. A blur of motion and he had slipped a wad of bank notes beneath my bedclothes.

Then, very calmly, as if nothing had happened, he produced a piece of paper on which appeared these pictures: a bomb, a tank and a battleship. And, in a very winning and modest way, he asked for my help. Would I look at the paper and indicate my feelings by ticking the appropriate symbol? A bomb meant 'mildly grateful', a tank 'very grateful' and a battleship 'grateful beyond words'.

I replied, truly, that I felt no gratitude whatever.

Not even one little bomb's worth, he demanded. For all that money?

What money? I asked.

How quickly his madness flared. Suddenly he was shy and diffident and modest no longer. He began to rave, calling me a fraud, a yellow swindler; and I believe he might have injured me had men in white coats not burst into the room, gagged him, replaced the blindfold and dragged him away. The swiftness of his hand was not lost on seasoned observers, however, and they took the bank notes too.

The Head of Care entered now and pronounced herself very pleased. The young man would expect to be back at his desk soon. I had helped a patient with very serious problems of illusory linkage, and she would like to help me too.

Tell me what you want, dear Booi, urged the woman in white, and I will take care of it.

There was only one thing I wanted, but I feared it was not in her gift: my freedom.

The Head of Care laughed her generous laugh, saying how little I understood of their ways. If she could release a man who could not tell the difference between gratitude and battleships, who thought that people should pay for free dams with jet fighters, then she was not going to baulk at a little fellow who imagined he had an audience with the Queen, now was she? And so, she promised, I would be free by the end of the day.

Her answer astounded me. Out of England, I cried, there is always something new!

She agreed. No more the barbaric custom of locking up the mentally ill. Discharge them as soon as possible, that was their way. Send them back into the community. Kinder, really. And more economical.

Delighted as I was at my own good luck, I was also confused. Did this not mean that there were many lunatics roaming the streets of England? What did other people think of this?

Again there came her tolerant laugh. No problem at all. So easily did her patients slip back into the community that it was soon impossible to tell them apart.

The way they release lunatics into the community is really rather touching, both in its informality and brevity and in the mutual relief felt by both sides. It is difficult to decide whose pleasure is the greater: the departing patients' or that of those who wave goodbye.

Patients being discharged are given a bottle of pills and a train ticket to the city of their choice. I had asked to go to that place, where, my heart told me, my long adventure was soon to be concluded.

Inmates about to 'graduate' from a Place of Safety undergo a simple, dignified, private ceremony designed to attract as little attention as possible. The Head of Care addresses graduates, urging them, as they go back into the world, not to let the side down.

And to remember the sensitivities of those amongst whom they were being released.

At this point, several graduates, overcome with joy at the prospect of release, fell on the warders with wild embraces. I thought this might lead to the suspension of the ceremony, but they were discharged as soon as they had been subdued and their pills wrestled from them; the Head of Care explained that these graduates were taking unsuitable medications. They may take ours, or theirs, but never both. Never mix your medications, Mr Booi – it becomes a horrifying cocktail of unhappiness.

It also led to a regrettable slander. After a spate of stabbings, assaults and even murders in the receiving communities, it had been put about by ignorant or malicious observers that the culprits must be crazy – when, in truth, they had simply forgotten to take their pills or mixed their medications.

I cannot stress too strongly, Mr Booi – the Head of Care smiled, as she unlocked the doors to freedom – that there are no discernible differences between people like you and the community about to receive you.

Then, as she handed me my bottle of pills, she added: no discernible mental differences, at any rate.

Without more ado, she pushed me gently into the street and locked the door behind me. I was accompanied to the station by a large man in a white coat. He explained that as I was both a graduate and a foreigner, I warranted the special escort due to the doubly disadvantaged. His orders were to ensure that nothing stopped me from leaving their care. I thought such attention very kind. My escort insisted on waiting until the train was slipping from the station before handing me my tickets, running alongside the train and bellowing a last reminder: I was to take my pills – unless, of course, I was already taking my pills; in which case, I was not to take my pills.

Anyone wishing to study the English might do worse than to spend time in an asylum; I had learned useful lessons about the psychological contours, colours and phantoms of their mental landscapes. I saw, for example, that I had misread their capacity to help a stranger travelling in their country, even when they wished to do so. I had failed to recognize how little they know about their own culture or geography. The average native is probably more confused about his country than the most ignorant traveller, since the traveller, by his very ignorance, is free of the lamentable superstitions, fed by fear, that afflict these people and blind them even to their own virtues. Certain taboos and phobias are so deeply ingrained that to expect them to think coherently, or to behave usefully, is to lay an impossible burden on what is after all a very little country, more badly traumatized by loss of empire and loss of earnings than they are willing, or even able, to admit. How would they have characterized the intentions of an alien San ambassador who proposed to trek boldly where no San had gone before, through bewildering, dangerous terrain about which they themselves knew little, to call on a Monarch about whom they knew even less? As arrogance, foolhardiness or madness? Probably as all three.

One might say that they regarded my mission as bound to fail, not because of any particular animosity towards me (above a generalized distaste for foreigners and travellers and distance) but because the configuration of their brains makes them prone to despair. Their instinctive belief that nothing *can* be done shades so closely into the belief that nothing *should* be done that one cannot drive even a porcupine quill between the two.

What they prefer is to take any sharp weapon that comes to hand and repeatedly, and obsessively, to stab to death their best beliefs, to assassinate their virtues, to puncture their own confidence and self-esteem, and to bleed to death their most cherished institutions. This has led some to contend they positively enjoy failure. This is a mistaken view. There are signs that they may enjoy succeeding as much as we do. What they fear, however, is forward movement, whether of peoples, of ideas, of time; in short, what they fear is the future. And themselves.

The explorer is wise not to be deceived by this constant, pitiless self-denigration; the unwary visitor sees them wolfing down their favourite dish, which they call 'humble pie', and mistakes their dinner of despair for the true state of affairs. Rather, as the unwary traveller in the veld sometimes cannot spy the difference between the mottled sun-splashed rocks and the monstrous puff-adder, until he steps clumsily and the common rock rises up with horrible fangs, so they may rejoice in their belief that they are a pretty ordinary nation, but they reserve their ancient right to kill foreigners for saying so. And when they bemoan their decline, it is always from their own standards that they decline, and these are set higher than any others on earth.

I had chosen as my destination the only place in England I might call home and in a spirit of compassion for the ex-

Bishop who had so nearly lured me to destruction in the jaws of Lord Goodlove's hounds. He would be eaten up with anxiety, I felt sure. The fallen Bishop had been my guardian in England. He had given his word to the Sovereign that he would not let me out of his sight. And he had not kept his word. He would, no doubt, bitterly regret his weakness; but now that I knew a little of their ways, I saw that he had been maddened by the fear of sexuality that lies at the very essence of their being, for I had learnt that the English believe love to be dominated by one factor above all – battery. Of the female partner among those who marry, or of themselves among males who do not, and of children by almost everybody.

And he had taken me for one of them. How bitterly the former flying Bishop must have regretted his behaviour. Despite Lord of Goodlove's alarming tale of a father trading his daughter as one might a sack of tobacco. I felt sure that his joy at seeing me would overcome any lingering animus. In his simple mind, my instruction of his daughter in the ways of the Red People had come to seem threatening. I blamed myself for failing to pay enough regard to the primitive terrors of the native mind.

With these thoughts humming in my mind, I arrived in Little Musing.

Chapter Ten

London at last!
Penetrates the Mother of All Parliaments;
sees a Minister destroyed;
hears Mr Conbrio put a question;
lavishes hospitality on Her Majesty's Ministers
with unexpected results

Not since old Adam Blitzerlik, who did a bit of gardening for the Mayor of Puffadder, was found astride the Lady Mayor, wearing only her husband's golden chain of office, have I witnessed such an explosion.

I walked up the path and knocked at the door of Edward Farebrother's cottage.

Julia was leaning over the fence. Well, well, she said, the prodigal returns.

Peter the Birdman, out in his garden, said nothing but pretended to be watching a sparrowhawk killing a fat racing pigeon.

The wingless wonder, the failed flier, my old friend and mentor Edward Farebrother opened the door and stared at me the way a man does at the snake he finds in his shoe; his face blushed like the flame tree, then, seeing his neighbours watching, he pulled me sharply inside the house and slammed the door.

And why, David Mungo Booi – he demanded – are you here?

I had arrived prepared to overlook the behaviour of a man who had sold his friend, traded his daughter and broken his word to his Sovereign to placate his tribal taboos. I returned a truthful answer to his question – Goodlove Castle had very nearly claimed my life. I had escaped only by the grace of Kaggen.

That is when he exploded. Pointing a shaking finger at my heart, the former holy aviator declared in ringing tones that I summed up in my hateful little person all that was wrong with the Third World. He had managed, with enormous difficulty, to place me in the house of an aristocrat to teach and tame and fashion me in the ways of the upper classes; knock off a few of my edges; give me a taste for horseflesh, a whiff of shot and shell; a sense of the sacred ceremony of the tea-towel; of roast beef, of common sense; of the knowledge that things will be all right on the day, and we'll muddle through; and of what was, and was not, on; of true-blue Anglo-Saxon love of the loam, the cow and the copse; of that ancient attachment to English acres; English ale; English attitudes which so distinguish the landed gentry of England from those pale shadows across the Channel, the effete, landless, loveless Eurotocracy of other, less fortunate, lands.

And how had I repaid him? I had gone over the wall like an absconding schoolboy.

No wonder that people like me could not feed or clothe ourselves. Give us entry into one of the great houses of England, and we went AWOL. Give us a finger and we took an arm and a leg. Give us millions and we frittered them away. Give us asylum and we began seducing their women; give us a brighter tomorrow and we elected a darker yesterday; give us dams and we bought guns; give us the honey of Northern ingenuity, the cream of Western intelligence, and we preferred dumb insolence and disease; give us clean water and we kept coal in it; give us condoms and we wore them on our heads, lightbulbs and we used them as penile ornaments, tractors and we lost them, trade credits and we spent them, nuns and we raped them, tanks and we used them to invade our neighbours; give us grain, millions of land-mines, electoral observers, bags of compassion, aid agencies, relief agencies, humanitarian agencies, fighter bombers, field ambulances, dollars, Mercedes Benz, international mediators, marines, and we chewed them up and spat them out and things were soon a lot worse than they had been before we started. Look at Rwanda... Somalia... Angola... Liberia...

And here I was again. Asking for more. Well, he had news for me. Not now. Not ever again. He had treated me as a lost son, trained me, groomed me for better things. And how had I responded? By suborning his daughter, leading her in lascivious dances, preceded by omelettes and lechery in his own back garden. These were his thanks for plucking me from the fists of the authorities as they were about to return me to that distant, god-forsaken, murderous, uncouth, fly-ridden, disease-struck neck of the woods I called home.

He left me then, returning moments later with my brown suitcase and threw it down, without care, on the floor, and it broke open, spilling its precious contents, and I scrabbled to collect my bow of *gharree* wood, my arrows, the ceremonial digging sticks and fire sticks and necklaces of ostrich-eggshell and, most important, the fine copper bangles. The small leather bag, given to me by my cousins the !Kung from the Kalahari, split open. I gazed on the fabled star-stones that Europeans are said to love more than life or love, and which I had quite forgotten. Very indifferent pebbles, much like gravel you see scattering across the road when the farmer races down the dusty roads in his quick white truck.

Then a silence descended. Where was I proposing to go? the former Bishop suddenly inquired. Not merely had his tone changed but his voice was close to my ear, and I was startled to discover he was down on his knees beside me, searching the darkest corners where the stones had rolled.

To London, I replied. And the Palace.

How could I manage in the capital without help? Surely I needed help?

By those who do not know them, they are said to be a passive, stolid people. Do not believe it. Within the space of moments, for reasons unclear, the once-winged priest had moved from outraged denunciation of my person and all its works into a mood of almost wheedling kindness. Truly they are a mercurial, volcanic, turbulent tribe!

I had learnt a good deal about survival during my time as a guest at Goodlove Castle, I answered.

And did I propose, then, to visit the Queen in all my tribal finery?

My heart pained me so that I could manage no reply. But silently nodded my head. Once upon a time, I dreamed of a far more magnificent progress to the Palace, borne aloft, in the traditional manner of the great explorers, in a sedan chair, carried on the shoulders of four white bearers; as the expedition progressed towards the Palace of the Great She-Elephant, I would recline in the yellow shade, behind my heavy satin curtains, reading some appropriate text from my portable library: *Travels to Discover the Source of the Nile*, by Bruce, or Henry Moreton Stanley's unique primer, *In Darkest Africa*. Bringing up the rear would struggle my porters, toting their bales crammed with every conceivable necessity: quinine, tea, coffee, sugar, salt, pepper, canned vegetables, dried meat, fruit, bottled water, and champagne, in which to toast the health of the Monarch.

Alas, now this was not to be. My small funds had dwindled to nothing. So, yes, I would present myself at the Palace in the clothes I stood up in.

And when I had achieved my goal and presented my credentials to Her Majesty, what would I do then?

What I had always intended – I would return home.

Would I give him a categorical assurance?

Before I could reply, the room erupted for a second time.

Beth, who must have crept upon us silently, and heard most of our conversation, burst upon us and flung her arms around my neck. Her lustrous behind, seen from my vantage point, my nose buried in her neck as she hugged me, showed like two great boulders, smoothed by a mighty river into perfect melons, and carried together by that same torrent to repose side by side like identical twins.

How could I even contemplate exchanging the safety of their garden for the horrors of home? Beth cried. I must promise to do whatever possible to stay with them for ever.

It is a happy people who live under a delusion, quite impervious to reason. They, who by any measure may be said to lead lives of poverty, sadness, fear and restriction on an overcrowded island, sometimes never seeing the sun from one week to the next, at the mercy of increasingly savage young who would tear their parents limb from limb for a sixpence, and frequently do so, marooned at the mercy of clever and more powerful neighbours, enduring in the twilight of their past glories and fearful of the future, still contrived somehow to believe themselves the happiest people on earth and their system the best that the sons of man ever invented!

Beth was scarcely recognizable; what a dismal descent from the proud, upstanding, free-swinging beauty of the Eland Dance to this wan, tousled-haired person, breasts strangled, haunches swathed in some crumpled, hairy skirt reaching all the way down to her feet which, saddest of all, protruded to show she was again wearing her father's old shoes.

As I examined his daughter, the flighty holy man examined my star-stones, giving little cries as he did so, 'Well, I never,' and 'If I'm not very much mistaken,' and other signifiers of happy astonishment, and I began to realize that the !Kung had been wise to include these fripperies among my baggage. The ex-Bishop's manner had altered utterly, from stone to water. He ran through his fingers the white gravel as if it were food, honey or tobacco, or something almost as valuable.

If I was ever to attain my ambition, warned the ex-Bishop, I would not do so by sticking out like a sore thumb.

Boy David, quoth he, when stalking your quarry, is it not essential to blend into the background? And the best disguise when hunting the lion is his mane, worn as a cloak. And the ostrich is beguiled when the hunter carries, above his head, a beak on a stick, and ties a circle of feathers to his rump, so the ostrich thinks it spies a brother, plodding, sedately over the veld towards him. Like calls to like.

A becreeping cap, said I.

Precisely, returned Heaven's fallen sky-soarer. If you are to succeed on your final safari, you must so blend, as you pass through England, that your own mother would take you for a native. If you succeed in your safari, and no one, believe me, hopes more heartily than I that you should do

so, then you will return from whence you came. I shall see
to it that you are fitted out in the best damn becreeping
cap money can buy. Can you think of a better plan?

I saw the flaw immediately. I had no money.

He ran the star-stones through the funnel of one hand
into the palm of the other and reassured me that with these
charms, money would flow like water.

Let me put on my good grey suit, which he had kept
very safely for me during my time away; I might carry my
tribal dress and my gifts in my suitcase. Now, if I would
excuse him, he too would go and slip into something more
appropriate to the trek that lay ahead.

We were going somewhere – together?

He seemed astonished by my question; How else would
we travel? He would never abandon me, now that my goal
was so close. Soon – very, *very* soon – I would be setting
sail for home, my task accomplished, my journey done. To
which he could only say, God speed!

Beside the grocer and the little butcher in the dying village
of Little Musing stands the old stationmaster's house. Given
over now to the doctor who calls twice a week to serve
the dwindling needs of an ageing population. There is
always a crowd outside the doctor's surgery; people who
are not ill anxious for a word with those who are. A
communal occasion to talk happily about illness, past and
present and to come. The English have, I think a lovers'
quarrel with disaster.

When I arrived at the station, suitcase in hand, Farebrother was pacing the platform, dressed in a voluminous frock
the shade of pinky purple you see in the Babbian flower
(which baboons love for its nutty corns). This lurid costume

was, apparently, the uniform of a practising prelate in the Church of England. He had not worn it since his official grounding by the authorities.

I could not help wondering why he dressed so vividly for what I had understood was a secret mission.

That was the point, came his reply. By wearing such regalia he appeared to be what he was not – a full bishop; and since bishops were seen as odd, but essentially harmless, his cloth would enable him to move about London almost unnoticed. Custom would ensure that we were admitted to all the best places, but no one would pay him the least attention. This was his own becreeping cap.

We rumbled away from Little Musing on the rusting rails bound for London, watched by curious cows which now and then fell down and died. Their cattle, which they prize hugely, suffer from a falling sickness, the cause of which is unknown, but which they attribute to the evil machinations, or even spells, or poisons, of forces 'across the water'.

Strange how the mention of trains evokes a spasm of pain. The mere sound makes them flinch. In their tongue, not for nothing do the two words rhyme with each other: 'train' and 'pain'. They repeat these rhymes to themselves in a kind of furious despair.

Why should this be? In response, Edward Farebrother related one of their oldest tribal myths. They were the inventors and originators of the railways. As they gave so much else to the world. Their genius provided tribes less fortunate than themselves with gifts which no other nation could match. The steam engine belonged to them as surely as the spinning jenny and the football, sweet achievements of the tribe. But then, like sleepy travellers, overburdened with genius, they put down some of their baggage along the way, and never found it again. Like so much else, it was stolen by jealous competitors, copied and travestied, passed off as their own by mixed assemblies across the water, the racial ruction,* whose trains were bigger, faster, better, and about which they boasted continually, forgetting his too modest people to whom they owed their success.

Was that fair? he implored.

I told him of the honey-finder. This tiny bird spends his life watching for the secret places where the bees, those yellow people with noisy noses, make and hide their honey. Flying to the hunter, the bird points the way to the golden treasure. The hunter will hammer pegs into the cliff face, climb to the hive, and smoke out the yellow people and scoop handfuls of the sweet gold water into his mouth. But he will never forget to thank the honey-finder with a good piece of the honeycomb. It looked to me as if his people had acted as honey-finders to the tribes across the water. Then, instead of gratitude, the barbarians took the English honey-finder and broke his wing.

I had understood, cried my friend, and his tears ran under his white plastic collar. And not one wing only, but both! For not only had they stolen – now they repaid kindness with a vengeance.

And also his beak! the good priest continued. And spat in his eyes for good measure. That would be closer to the

---

* The allusion is to Kipling:

I have drunk with mixed assemblies, seen the racial ruction rise,
And the men of half Creation damning half Creation's eyes
I have watched them in their tantrums, all that pentecostal crew,
French, Italian, Arab, Spaniard, Dutch and Greek and Russ and Jew,
Celt and Savage, buff and ochre, cream and yellow, mauve and white,
But it never really mattered till the English grew polite;

('Et Dona Ferentes', 1896)

ₛcale of the ingratitude with which foreign savages had repaid his people. The mutilation of a nation of honey-finders, the persecution of gentle, useful, enchanted creatures . . . And when I understood more of their history, I would comprehend that through the ages England's kindness had been her downfall.

The journey took us much of the day, as English trains are as sensitive as the people who make them. Leaves on the track are enough to bring the system to a lengthy halt.

From time to time broadcast announcements informed passengers, with an enviable frankness, and with frequent expressions of regret, that the train was delayed due to unnamed events over which the authorities had no control; and they were thanked time and again for their patience.

That the passengers did not believe a word of these announcements was perfectly clear. They barely listened to them, preferring to grumble gently amongst themselves. Yet the worse things got, the more cheerful they became. They even took a certain rough pride in these tests of endurance.

I was amazed by the civil way in which the travellers tolerated these delays.

Edward Farebrother was puzzled. Surely, when setting out on a journey we left the arrival time to chance and the gods?

Certainly not, I replied. When setting out on a march of several days between waterholes, a journey that took a band of fifteen people across mountains and deserts, the travellers would know, to within an exact position of the sun, when they would expect to arrive.

Well, said he, in his country individual freedoms far outweighed group expectations. And the most cherished of freedoms was the right to set one's own pace. And if this resulted in lateness, loss or failure, why, these setbacks were likewise cherished. Even celebrated with a fierce triumph. Thus failure, amongst them, was relished for its individual bouquet, like a fine wine. It was part of their genius that everyone was permitted to fail at his or her own pace. Of their continental neighbours, Germany had paid dearly for too great an insistence on order. And Italy had suffered terribly for making the trains run on time. It was different, thank God, in England. Perhaps when my people had reached a greater stage of technical advancement we would begin to appreciate that hard-and-fast demands were luxuries we could no longer afford.

It was an awesome journey, that expedition into the heart of London. As you travel you might be like the even tinier creatures who live on a water-spider, floating haphazardly down a stream. You feel you are in the world as it was in its primeval beginnings. Every so often we would stop at stations and a group of young warriors, male and female, would board in a kind of explosion, a whirl of white limbs, a mass of hands clapping, of feet stamping, of bodies swaying, of eyes rolling.

I was delighted to have a chance to note the peculiar characteristics of the natives as we rolled slowly southward. The females are notable for the small development of the mammary organs. Few have small waists. Both sexes pierce their ears. Some of the young warriors cut their hair, as do those of the peace tribe, so that it commands their heads like an axe-blade, which they colour with a variety of strong hues. Often they employ scarification, and amongst the most popular of the clan-marks is a stippled line along the temporal lobes from the external edges of the eyebrows to the middle of the cheeks or the lower jaws.

With each stop, a fresh invasion. The chants went up

anew, and I felt as if prehistoric man was cursing us, praying to us, welcoming us — who could tell? Their cries were incomprehensible. My friend interpreted for me, saying that some commented on the failures of the French, or the deformities of foreigners generally.

I should not be in the least bit afeared, as this was a perfectly normal practice — bands of sport lovers travelling abroad to support their country.

Love of country among these young men was unashamed, as they repeatedly chanted the beloved name of their sceptred isle, which they pronounced with a curious double beat, accentuating both syllables, ENG-LAND! ENG-LAND! Many carried flags. Not only was the proud standard waved at every opportunity, but many of them had made clothes of the national emblem and wore it as a shirt, or as a scarf or even as trousers. Some flew the flag on the tips of their stout black boots, or had tattooed tiny flaglets on each knuckle. One fine young buck, clearly a super-patriot, had emblazoned the beloved red, white and blue on his shaven skull, and the precious emblem flew wonderfully against the granite gleam of bone. Another had taken matters a step further and, perhaps because he was a great singer, he bellowed out 'God Save the Queen' in a rough baritone, showing, as he did so, that each of his teeth had been stained red, white and blue. This display of what we might call dental patriotism impressed me deeply.

None the less, I had to confide in my mentor that the sight left me secretly appalled, as a sane man would be before an enthusiastic outbreak in the madhouse.

On catching sight of me, they became very excited. Some leaped from their seats, lifting their arms and scratching in their armpits as if troubled by furious itching; some threw monkey nuts in an artillery barrage of shells, ending with a large banana which struck me on the forehead to the accompaniment of loud cheers. They howled, they leapt and spun and made horrid faces. Ugly? Yes, it was ugly enough, but I felt in me a faint response to the terrible frankness of that noise. It was something that we, so far from the night of the First Ages, find so hard to comprehend, that someone from another part of the world should be traditionally saluted with fruit and nuts.

Good Farebrother, seeing my perplexity, assured me that it was all quite normal, really, a regular occurrence, I should not mistake ceremonial displays of aggression for anything more than healthy high spirits. It was not a war they were preparing for, but a sporting ritual. Certainly I need have no fear for myself, since bloodshed was something they generally preferred to pursue abroad, and, wishing to reassure me of this, he now waved and smiled at the young people.

Perhaps this was not helpful, for the crowd began to take a closer interest in my episcopal companion. One young brave, his hair closely shaved, who had until then been preoccupied with the task of carving his name, DARREN, into the seats with a sharpened screwdriver, now tapped the ex-Bishop on the chest and, indicating his lovely purple frock, demanded to know if he were the Pope. The question accompanied by a large wink at his mates, indicating, I felt sure, that here was a sign of that fabled English humour.

The good Farebrother responded equally gaily with a gentle smile that he was Not Guilty! That, to the contrary, he was Church of England, Eng-Land!, giving to the name of his country just the same double emphasis as the young warriors had done, showing that he was emphatically of their kind.

Unfortunately, the joke did not now, as I had expected, lead to general laughter and good humour all round. Not at all. Hearing the word 'Pope', the others began chorusing their desire to perform sexual intercourse with the Pope, whom I took to be some person who inspired deep physical desire in Englishmen. That the young fellows were aroused seemed clear. Calling repeatedly for carnal relations with this Pope person, they grunted, whistled, stamped their feet and brandished their colours; I saw flags in the air, flags in their hair, flags on their fingers and flags on their toes. In this way they arrived at such a state of sexual excitation that some began tearing up the seats and throwing them across the carriage; others began pelting us with coins, and all the time they gave out this curious greeting or salute, perhaps an unconscious expression of their physical erections; that is to say, they lifted stiff arms before their chests and pointed their fingers into the air, as if to suggest the direction from which they expected this longed-for Pope to appear.

I was fascinated. Why, I asked my friend, were these people so filled with desire for the Pope? Did they love him?

On the contrary, came the astonishing reply. They hated him.

Then why did they wish to lie with him?

I had misunderstood the subtleties of the language, said the Bishop, rising from his seat as the missiles rained down on us, and urging me towards the door. The good old Anglo-Saxon expression used did, indeed, refer to coitus, but it was also synonymous with the desire to destroy.

Alas, we were forced to abandon this fascinating etymological discussion, for several coins had struck the Bishop about the head and he was bleeding into his white collar.

Seizing my hand, he pulled me into the safety of the corridor, and we beat a retreat to the far end of the train, and locked ourselves in a lavatory.

It was later – oh, so much later – that I remembered, too late, my suitcase and its gifts for the Sovereign. I comforted myself a little with the hope that they might at least be bestowed, by these seeming admirers, on His Majesty the Pope.

And very much later, when I told the good Bishop of my loss, he consoled me by saying that the star-stones at least were safe in his keeping.

We spent the rest of the journey to the capital in the lavatory. I did my best to staunch his bleeding, while he told me how very shocked he had been by such behaviour on what he called his home turf. Sad was a word he used. As well as setback. And scandal. It was also really most unusual. Normally these young people reserved that sort of behaviour for trips abroad.

But they had seemed to be enjoying themselves, I suggested.

This saddened him further. I must be careful not to give way to unwarranted cynicism. We had been exposed to the hooligan element, a tiny hard core of thugs, who were not representative of the great mass of ordinary, decent sports lovers. These sorts of people not only brought the national pastime into disrepute but dragged the country down to a level one was more accustomed to expecting from less civilized people. Still, we must look on the bright side. I had been taught several useful lessons about the patriotism of the young. Having seen what fate awaited the Pope, I could imagine the treatment I would receive if these young patriots took against me. My training in Little Musing had given me the outlines of the camouflage needed if ever I was to travel safely in England. Now the time had come to put a London gloss on the good work.

London looked to me stiffly joined at hip and breastbone, one dwelling to another, a city set hard from end to end. The Queen, explained my guide and mentor, lived at the centre, and from her great Palace (or Royal Kraal, as he believed I would call it) the capital spread in concentric rings, rather as if one had dropped a stone into a waterhole and the ripples had set solid like concrete.

Our first stop was at a tailor shop. Not, you understand a man bent over an old Singer sewing-machine, like Mr Goolam over at Compromise, but someone who advertised in his window that he provided clothes to Her Majesty, by Royal Appointment. I began to glimpse just how cunning was to be the bait mixed by my frockless friend. The tailor ran around me, laying hands on my person, much like the children of Little Musing had done, exclaiming happily on my miniature but lovely measurements, saying that sir had a most original pelvic formation. In my natural state, I probably ran around in a penis sheath? A very short sheath. But we couldn't have sir walking down Oxford Street in a penis sheath, now, could we?

When Bishop Farebrother whispered that I was on my way to see the Queen, he declared he had known it the moment he set eyes on me, saying to himself that here was a wealthy foreigner with a love of Higher Things. Only such individuals still possessed the style, the fortune, the breeding to appreciate classic English tailoring. In fact, without clients like sir, he would most likely have to close his business; and he had little doubt that Her Majesty felt the same way.

They removed my MAN ABOUT TOWN suit and my rubber boots. I was decked out in my hunting outfit, a heavy woollen suit, dark blue with thin little stripes. The jacket had a long, ungainly vent which, they explained, was to allow the buttocks free play, as the better class of male is often prominent there; a white shirt as crisp as a Karoo daisy with a collar stiff as a dominee's choker and a tie pink as morning. For my feet soft, brown suede shoes, rather ungainly, flowing like cowpats. They wanted me to give up my big brown hat and adopt one shaped like a piss-pot, which, Mr Farebrother explained, though rarely worn any longer, was affected by aliens trying to ape the locals and so marked me out as an aspirant of real status. But I would not part with my hat, repository of my notebooks, protector of my modesty. And in the end Bishop and tailor agreed to let me keep it, saying it was a permissible foreign eccentricity in what was otherwise a near-perfect ensemble.

Only a last item had to be added, said Edward Farebrother, and that we could collect at our next lesson.

To begin with I found it difficult to work inside my disguise; the becreeping cloak was heavy, smothering and ugly. Especially difficult to manoeuvre in were the broad, flat, shapeless shoes, and I fell over my own feet, but this they said was a good sign. Tailor and cleric added that foreigners frequently found it difficult to adapt to English costume. When faced by discomfort, in myself and others, I should at all times simply barge ahead. If opposed, it helped to raise one's voice, most especially if asked a question one had not understood. If in doubt, one disagreed. Or disapproved. I confessed to feeling rather ridiculous in the cumbersome outfit, but this too they said was perfectly natural in the early stages of transition. Even indigenous folk took time to get over the feeling. Were people to laugh at me, I should ignore it, for they were the sort who did not know any better. By heeding these simple guidelines I would so closely resemble a native of some importance that it would be impossible to distinguish me from the genuine article.

When my costume was complete, the good Bishop declared he had made me the best damn disguise in the world, an English becreeping cap, by George!

Now the final item would be added, said the flightless Bishop, nodding his big head up and down so that his nose sawed the air like a weaver-bird's sharp beak; an irresistible titbit to bait our trap.

He took me in my fine new outfit to another part of the city, a noble place thronged with men dressed in just the heavy, creased costume I was wearing, and I blended into the large, pink, important, noisy herd so well, these individuals went about their business of barging ahead and raising their voices and did not even lift their heads and sniff the air when I appeared downwind of them, so I knew that my disguise was working well.

We arrived before the most magnificent edifice, with marble columns and a steeple and statues of pensive goddesses, which I knew must be a church or temple. I saw a change in my once-airborne friend's demeanour which seemed to confirm that here was a place, holy and enchanted.

Remember, Boy David, advised the frockless holy man, that there is a distinction between religion and faith. Religion is the province of the Church of England, but the guardian of faith is the Bank of England. Faith is the shared belief, deep in the soul of the nation, that our currency is sacred, remains, in a word – and what better word could there be for it? – STERLING! Never to be sold short, off or out. Never to be polluted by mongrel admixtures, or supplanted by foreign impostors, or shunted aside by Euro-surrogates, or ambushed and buggered, absolutely buggered, by those who do not share our faith. Who believe money is merely a common-or-garden coinage, a means of whor-ishly easy exchange between foreigners, instead of the life and soul of a people!

And with a promise that he would show me what real money was, he took from his pocket my little leather bag of star-stones. When I asked what he was doing with it, he replied that he was working a miracle. He vanished into the temple, to emerge some moments later carrying a fat leather satchel bulging with money, and not just any old money, but, as he proudly showed me, English money, coin of the realm, said he, though all were bank notes, each painted with a picture of the Sovereign, and very welcoming she looked, a strangely confiding look in the Royal Eye, as if she said to me: David Mungo Booi, at last! I cannot wait to make your acquaintance.

I was so glad and humble and moved all at once to see that there was something of my world that England wanted more than life itself, even if it was these little pebbles that lie in the desert.

I realized that my patron had entered not some temple, to effect this miracle with my star-stones, but a bank.

When I confessed my mistake he said, very kindly, that it was typical of foreigners, really, to get these things wrong. I would not get far in England if I could not tell the difference between a church and a bank. Banks were in the main devoted to upholding morality; that was why the fall of a bank, which happened rarely, thank God, was an occasion for national mourning. Churches, on the other hand, closed every day. But then they were mostly given to raising money and worrying about affairs financial. The better sort of English bank hardly ever mentioned money, while the Church of England talked of hardly anything else.

Field-craft lessons followed. These consisted of learning how to disgorge cash effortlessly from the leather satchel without ever COUNTING IT, MENTIONING IT and, above all, MISSING IT!

He taught me, also, a set of phrases which he recommended I make my own: *Being abroad makes me ill; Oh, really?; It's just a German racket; No, no, no, no! It's just not on*; and *Personally, I blame the French*. By varying these phrases, he assured me, and becoming expert in the decorum of the satchel, I would soon blend naturally into the background and pass easily amongst all classes of English society.

When my teacher was satisfied that I looked the part, he took me to their ruling council of elders, or chiefs, who assemble in their Great Place beside the river.

Let us test-fly your becreeping cap – cried the ex-Bishop – in the Palace of Westminster, before we send you to the Palace itself. And he assured me that nowhere in the country was there greater experience of chicanery and deception. If I fooled these connoisseurs of camouflage, I would fool everyone.

Their national assembly is, I suppose, a cross between a church and a railway station, demonstrating how, in their culture, the sacred and the pragmatic are intermingled.

We were met by a Member who, my friend whispered to me, had the ear of Her Majesty's Government, being himself one of her Loyal Ministers. A smooth, affable, beardless, balding fellow with eyes in which, from their gleam, it always seemed midnight by moonlight, and the dark-brown laugh of the foraging hyena.

His name, said my guide, was Mr Conbrio. And he was widely admired for his knowledge of essential parliamentary procedures. A Member of the highest integrity. If my case interested him, he might be prepared to put a question on my behalf.

Oh, really? I replied, in the manner I had been taught. Well, the question I wished to put was the following: did the Monarch not have a duty to honour the undertakings given by her predecessors to the San people of the Cape of Good Hope, and would she admit David Mungo Booi, their accredited representative, in special audience to discuss the matter?

Addressing me as 'squire', a tribute, I assumed, to my disguise, Mr Conbrio explained that before he could even consider putting a question on my behalf, time-honoured procedural customs in the Mother of All Parliaments must be observed. Certain formalities, if I took his drift . . .?

I did not take his drift. Which formalities did he mean?

Mr Farebrother came to my aid, throwing a meaningful glance at my leather satchel. With studied nonchalance, grateful for my coaching, I handed him several large bank notes amounting to one thousand pounds, casually expressing the hope that this took care of the formalities.

Leaping backwards, as if he had been presented with a cup of scorpion poison, Mr Conbrio's handsome face turned that ruddy ochre in which our artists once used to portray a *kudu* speared to death. In icy tones he announced that such behaviour was just not on. It might be all very well in shoddy little assemblies in far-away lands where bribes and dash and kickbacks and pork-fat, as he believed such things were called, greased the wheels of corrupt governments. But we were present in the Mother of All Parliaments and he would do nothing to sully the fairest, finest, freest democracy in the world. He had no doubt I had meant well. But to take this gift from me? Never! It might look to the cynic, or the foreigner, as if Her Majesty's Ministers could be bought. He would sooner die!

But there was no question, the ex-Bishop interposed silkily, of anything so gross, so offensive. All we requested was the benefit of his advice. Did he know someone who might help us?

That was a very different matter, Mr Conbrio replied. By a stroke of good luck, he was himself a professional consultant specializing in Royal Connections: Marques, Charters, By Appointments, Honours, Yachts, Palaces and Equestrian Events.

More than a stroke of luck, Farebrother assured him in the same manoeuvre by which a trapdoor spider generously extrudes the gossamer noose with which he plans to throttle his prey. It was a prayer answered! As a professional consultant, then – what advice would he give us?

As a professional consultant, Mr Conbrio smiled modestly, he was obliged by the rules of his professional association – Select Lobbyists, Experts And Zealous Enablers plc – to levy a charge before parting with advice.

From a professional consultant, said Farebrother, he would expect nothing less. And with a movement so mercurial I never saw anything so neatly done (except perhaps the even greater speed with which the notes disappeared into Mr Conbrio's pocket), he slipped him his fee.

I knew I had seen a display of skill which must have taken many decades to perfect. It was not something that came easily or naturally. And, as the ex-Bishop had demonstrated, it was certainly not something that came cheap.

After brief reflection, Mr Conbrio parted with this

advice: the best way to advancing my cause would be to table a question in the House. By a stroke of luck he had intended to put just such a question that very day, and I was very welcome to watch from the Visitors' Gallery the majestic proceedings of the Mother of All Parliaments. I might perhaps learn something to pass on to my people. Who could say?

I answered sincerely that I thought I had already done so.

They have two political parties: the first of these is the Party of the House, which divides into different sides or teams, each identified by a colour, much as young herd-boys, when they hunt doves, identify their loyalty with a red hibiscus behind the ear or a daub of blue chalk on the forehead.

The leader of each team is called something simple, such as 'John',* to remind Members that though the game requires opposing policies, these are as interchangeable as the leaders.

Opposing teams face each other across a fighting floor, seated in green leather benches which rise in ascending tiers towards the roof. The air is criss-crossed with a fine tracery of spittle as arguments are sent this way and that in a form of ceremonial warfare in which a few may emerge rather damp, but no one is seriously hurt. The further back Members sit, the higher their position on the tiers and benches, the louder they shout, and the greater their moral standing. This they call 'claiming the high ground'. To ask which team is 'right', the Right Reverend Mr Farebrother explained, was to miss the point. The object was to score points by holding your opponent up to derision. Members

---

* Booi's visit to the House of Commons must have taken place *before* the death of the Labour leader, John Smith, in July 1994.

often said the first thing that came into their heads. Tore into each other tooth and nail.

But surely, I observed, this must lead to terrible clashes among their supporters in the country?

It might have done, my guide explained, if the noise from the Chamber reached the outside world. But it seldom did so, and people were able to get on with their lives. It was a magnificent achievement, was it not, to conduct fearless public debates on the great issues of the day while ensuring that the private lives of citizens were barely affected? He felt sure I had seen nothing like it.

Well, now, things grew a little clearer. And I had seen something very like it. I had watched opposing troops of baboons on the hillsides, under a huge, indifferent African sky, mocking, gesticulating, howling at each other, while each troop attempted to gain the higher ground, from where warriors rained down missiles on their enemy or presented their colours, by directing their brightly hued posteriors at the other side. These debates achieved a subtle and satisfying result. The sky remained utterly unaffected by the activities of the apes. Yet all sides of a question were aired without fear or favour; and at the end of the day nothing whatever had changed.

If the opposing teams of the Party of the House were really on the same side, where then, I wondered, was the true opposition?

He pointed to a small group of individuals who sat in a special gallery well above the reach of the brawling teams below. These were the members of the Party of the Press, which never missed a chance to question, to harry, to attack and, where necessary, to destroy Members of Parliament who fell below the high standards laid down by the owners of the public prints, often retiring individuals, usually invisible, yet the true guarantors of English democracy.

The Party of the House may propose, explained my episcopal guide and mentor, but it is often the Party of the Press that disposes. The Party of the House must, from time to time, however briefly, pay attention to its electors. The Party of the Press is answerable to no one, except its owners.

And with that we took our place in the Visitors' Gallery, and he urged me to watch and learn and to carry myself always as an important visiting native with Anglophile impulses; in short, to remember that I was almost English. We were in luck. That very day we were to see a Minister being destroyed.

The Minister whom it was my privilege to see being destroyed that day was a sad, rather portly, nervous man, habitually looking over his shoulder with the jerky, panic-stricken movements of a rabbit transfixed before the flaring hood and glittering eye of the golden Cape cobra; he bore the portfolio of Minister for National Contentment.

Now I saw unfolding below me, in all its splendour, that flower of their democracy, the parliamentary debate. Mr Farebrother advised me to watch particularly how the loyalties of Members of the House Party were stirred to heroic defence when one of their colleagues was set upon by the Press.

The charge against the Minister was complicated. From what I gathered, the Press reported that he had been seen, disguised in a woolly muffler, bobble-cap and boots, emblazoned with his country's colours, entering the house of a young woman. The Party of the Press believed a Minister charged with the contentment of the nation should not be playing away or indulging the national game, in particular, shooting and scoring. There was jocund debate as to whether there had been much dribbling. This drew laughter, even from the Minister himself, and one realized how civilized are these debates, despite their apparent bloodiness.

Then the Minister rose to defend himself. He had indeed visited the young woman – and he deplored the salacious reports which emphasized the gender of the therapist involved – to obtain a professional massage of the feet, attending particularly to the toes, which were especially sensitive. He strongly refuted suggestions that anything improper had occurred. A Minister charged with National Contentment had a duty to safeguard his own well-being. A happy Minister had happy feet. And a foot was only as happy as its toes. As to the wearing of the national colours, he had been planning a trip abroad immediately after his massage. Whenever setting out for foreign parts he always donned muffler and cap, a traditional costume of the Englishman when crossing the water, and he wore his colours with pride. He wished to assure the House that he loved his country so much he felt ill whenever he travelled abroad, and wearing the colours improved his health – and his happiness.

This struck a chord with the House and he was loudly cheered on all sides, and I was interested to note that the press joined in the acclamation, showing, yet again, how these people will sink their differences when the national interest is at stake.

But then, as Bishop Farebrother made plain, in Parliament one's enemies are seldom found amongst the opposition. I was baffled by this comment, when, to my great surprise, there now rose a Member to the rear of the Minister who asked an apparently innocent question: he wished to know where the Minister's duty lay. Whether or not the Minister had been playing away was a matter of conjecture; however everyone seemed agreed on the fact that wherever the Minister might, or might not, have scored (laughter), it looked very much like an own goal (cheers). And if the Minister had the interests of the nation truly at heart, he would not have ventured so far offside (cries of Shame!). Was it not the duty of the House to show him the red card and to say to him that the only honourable thing to do was to leave the field?

Of the ruthless effect of this attack there was no doubt. A dagger to the heart. The victim turned at bay, but I think we all felt the wound was fatal. His colleagues scented blood and knew that one of the big cats of the political jungle was badly mauled and bled mightily.

Now the Minister looked to me much as a sheep does that has been set on by hyenas. One catches his victim by the throat; several more take deadly hold of legs and tail. And it becomes a race to see whether those with their teeth deep in its flesh will gnaw their way through to the heart before their comrades, at the other end, tear the wretched victim limb from limb.

In the early days of my expedition, I might have baulked at such apparent barbarity, such cynical cruelty, but I was, increasingly, an old English hand, and had learnt that you do not judge these people by mores and conventions suitable to the Bushman traditions of amity and solidarity. Rather, one saw things from an English perspective, which, if carefully examined, revealed a form of fellow-feeling, in Members on both sides of the House, who, rather than allow a colleague to be slaughtered by the Party of the Press, preferred to destroy him themselves.

It was with great emotion that we watched as the former Minister stumbled blindly from his seat and vanished into the outer darkness. A moment charged with emotions; several Members unashamedly blew their noses and stiffened their upper lips. I imagined that now they would offer up some short form of thanks for the divine grace which safeguarded the Chamber, or observe a minute's silence.

But, as so often, I was proved wrong. For there, on his feet, was none other than young Mr Conbrio, our professional consultant, and he put the following question to the Prime Minister.

Is the Prime Minister aware that, in some of our cities, the numbers of indigenous inhabitants have dwindled to a minority? And that every day, by devious routes, illegal immigrants are being smuggled into the country in numbers no civilized people will tolerate? Will he comment on information passed to me by reliable sources indicating a fresh invasion by so-called Bushmen or San nomads from Southern Africa? The same vagabonds who had sorely troubled Her Majesty's forces during their late occupation of the Cape of Good Hope? When they were described as a pernicious and vexatious vermin. And that were these nomads to settle in England, they will send stock-theft figures soaring, as well as being a drain on vital resources? Will he not agree that the time has come to say *no* to illegal immigration, *no* to the slackening of border controls; *no* to creeping metrification that threatens to replace the imperial measurements of free men with the thumb-in-the-scale mumbo-jumbo of a discredited Bonapartism. *No* to those who urge that after centuries sharing the homes of others, on islands, peninsulas and archipelagos around the globe, sharing with them our virtues of loyalty, honesty and common sense, we should now share with them our island home. Enough is enough. Will he assure the House, better still will he tell the country, that the time has come to put a wall of English oak between ourselves and bogus asylum-seekers, and assorted aliens of every stripe – from Bushmanland to Bongo-Bongo-Land.

Such was the excitement aroused by this question that pandemonium reigned in the Chamber; Members jumped to their feet and waved pieces of paper in the air and cried out, 'Knock 'em for six!'; some cried, 'Shame!' though that looked the least of their feelings; and they broke into that curious chant I had heard among the sports lovers on the train to London, that double-beat of the war cry 'Eng-land! Eng-land!' accompanied by the steady stamping of the right foot. And I realized that the Members on the green benches were but the parliamentary faces of the gangs on the train. Several were staring hard at the gallery where we sat, and I murmured to my mentor that I thought Mr Conbrio's question showed a lesser understanding of parliamentary process than I had hoped.

The ex-Bishop, rising quickly to his feet, indicating that it might be polite to withdraw from the gallery at this juncture, muttered that, far from misunderstanding our needs, Mr Conbrio had showed a knowledge of parliamentary process, and a feeling for what the House wanted to hear, which would take him a very long way.

Getting out of the gallery was not easy. Several members of the public took hold of the Bishop, showing no respect for his cloth; others tried to grab me, though Heaven's ex-aviator thrust me behind his skirts.

It was then that my field training came into its own. Turning to the menacing crowd, I announced in pleasant tones that, personally, I blamed the French. Whereupon those who had tried to stop us leaving fell into such a prolonged state of nodding approval that we were able to slip safely away.

Once outside, I was astonished to see, hobnobbing with members of the Party of the Press, who had so recently contributed to his downfall, the very ex-Minister who had slunk from the Chamber crushed and defeated. Yet he exhibited a gaiety which seemed extraordinary.

How was it that he had recovered his spirits so quickly? Minutes before he had been ruined. Yet now he was shaking hands with the very people who had destroyed him with a series of accusations, merciless and unprincipled, unleashed with the sole aim of driving an effective Minister from office. How could he extend the hand of friendship to such individuals?

What I was seeing, Mr Farebrother explained, was not the hand of friendship; it was the handshake of the newly employed journalist on a good contract. For such was the strength of English democracy that a politician destroyed by the press on Monday would very often be asked to write for them on Friday.

But what would happen, I demanded, if this individual then accused his accusers?

My guide replied that I still had some way to go before I really got the hang of things. If the ex-Minister attacked the press in the press, why, that was his democratic right. More likely, he would defend in print the right of any newspaper to destroy him. That was why no other country could hold a candle to the freedom of the English press – if I did not mind him saying so.

I did not mind him saying so. After what I had witnessed, I would have said so myself.

I had seen that a man is not cast aside when he falls from grace, but is taken up by his enemies, who bind his wounds and set him on his feet. How very different from our poor country, where a man broken on the wheel will be thrown to the butcher-birds or made a supper for jackals.

My reception in the Mother of All Parliaments had not

been all we might have hoped for, declared the wingless holy one, but we were not cast down. Not a bit of it. A spot of local difficulty, certainly. But once more into the breach ... My camouflage was sound, my demeanour acceptable, my phrasing spot-on, my leather satchel stuffed – all vital attributes marking out the man who was going places. What we needed now was a fast track to the top, and he knew just the one for me.

Oh, really? I replied.

While commending my mastery of the language, he deplored the scepticism he detected in my voice. Small men with facial tailings, or language difficulties almost as bad as mine, culturally deprived, financially challenged, from preposterous countries with unpronounceable names, had found England the land of opportunity. Some had begun in the Old Country in a modest way, selling raincoats; others rubber goods, or batches of cheap newspapers which they had parlayed into a press empire, and pension funds so magnificent people could not see where they began or ended. A sheaf of aliens had risen to become peers of the realm in two shakes of a duck's tail. In our case, time was so tight the proverbial duck would be allowed no more than a single shake. And he said this with that curious glance I had earlier noted and had not much liked.

He took me then to a grand hotel, a palace in itself, situated beside a park they call Green, guarded by a jolly fellow dressed in crimson coat and tall chimney-pot hat who greeted each guest at the door, swearing what an honour it was to have me staying with them once again, as if I had been doing this all my life. He showed me to a room as large, I swear, as the old synagogue in Calvinia, and a bed as big as a potato field. Any misgivings about my friend's curious haste to leave me at such short notice were swept away when I saw that this very establishment, at its southern extreme, provided a wonderful view of Buckingham Palace. He seemed to have thought of everything. My fears were stilled, my resolve steeled, my ears ready to hear his plan. Which was as follows.

I must be marketable, said the failed aviator. I must appeal widely. So he would announce me to the great and the good as an Egyptian gypsy. A millionaire from the slums of some dusty desert place. And now dreaming of settling in England. Yes. For, once upon a time, I had been plucked from my hovel by an elderly maiden Englishwoman who had taught me the language and the National Anthem. Ever since, I had harboured feelings of affection for the Old Country. My huge fortune, acquired selling English tea and roast beef – in a word, groceries, so dear to the English heart – was a burden to me. Now this grateful Egyptian gypsy wished to repay his dear dead benefactress, and the greatest country on earth, by making a series of donations to important national institutions.

From that point on, it would be plain sailing, the ex-Bishop promised. And he would quietly bow out. He had absolutely no doubt that I would receive the rewards of generosity. In fact, he would not be surprised if – very soon – I found myself kneeling before the throne, while Her Majesty enjoined me to Arise, Sir David! Even as likely, he continued, warming to his theme, was my elevation to the nobility. If you looked at the numbers of those business people ennobled for giving generously to certain funds, you saw that such wise donors were destined for greatness far more often than any other branch of society.

I was caught up in his enthusiasm now and begged him to stay at least until the call came from the Palace, but he lifted a lofty hand and reminded me that he had erred in making me follow his timetable. He now held to his resolution to encourage Third World persons to run their own lives. He was providing aid without strings. Did I fish? No? Well, if I had done so, I would have known that when you give a man a salmon you feed him for a day, but give him a fishing rod and you feed him for life.

Then he fell on my neck, begging me to remember him to Her Majesty if ever I found myself kneeling before her or, more likely still, when I donned ermine and took my seat as Baron Booi of the Karoo or wherever it was I came from . . . Running his hands through his dark, sharp tufts of hair, which reminded me again of the spikes of the aloe, and turning his anxious eyes full on me for one last time, he bade me goodbye, for ever. And he set off to spread my name amongst the greatest in the land: a grateful grocer come to town with a well-stuffed wallet, eager to express his appreciation to Queen and Country.

I am ashamed to confess I barely missed him because within hours I was besieged by visitors, party chairmen, fund-raisers and political leaders of every complexion, who took me to their bosoms; all of whom, after brief opening compliments about Egypt, its pyramids, its warmth, its culture, followed by succinct expressions of admiration about Romany life, its mobility, its caravans, its lively dances and so on, went on to say how very touched they were to meet a foreigner so wedded to England and English institutions: cricket and clergy and monarchy and groceries and so on. How very much they hoped I would make my home amongst them. How very grateful they would be for any donation I made to party funds. If I took their drift?

I took their drift. I had met Mr Conbrio, had I not?

Yet I was still foreign enough to be amazed at the extraordinary adroitness of these political chieftains and their wonderfully understated acceptance of my donations, very often non-vocal; the wink, the barely perceptible nod of acknowledgement, the ghost of a smile or twitch of the nose. And, before you could blink, my leather satchel was suddenly lighter. Some of my visitors so enjoyed meeting me that they spent the night in the hotel, accommodation which I was careful to pay for, and I drew from the chieftains much praise for my legendary gypsy hospitality. So many foreign benefactors confined their offers of free hospitality to important persons in hotels abroad: it took rare insight to offer free hotel rooms to important persons where they needed them most. At home, in England!

I was delighted with the speed at which my pouch emptied. What had seemed so plentiful vanished like snow-flakes that fall in the desert. And once all my money had gone, my visitors stopped arriving to enjoy my hospitality. It was, I supposed, testimony to their calibre. Again that delicate understanding of the English gentleman showed itself. One simply did not barge in on a fellow who has given his all and is awaiting the call.

But someone did barge in. A very vulgar fellow, the guardian of the hotel, who without even doffing his hat, demanded money, saying that I had settled for the rooms of my friends, but I had paid nothing on my own account. And he was not having Egyptian gypsies running up huge bills in his hotel.

With quiet dignity, I informed him I would not be a gypsy for much longer.

Once a gypsy, always a gypsy, the hateful fellow replied.

Maintaining my dignity, I said that my application for citizenship was receiving sympathetic consideration.

He grew even angrier and regarded me the way policemen do in the Karoo when they spy our donkey carts traversing a farmer's fence. Such a glance is usually the prelude to searching our bags for stolen meat or firewood.

But I had no bags, except the leather satchel, and that was empty.

Determined to put him in his place, I said that I expected to be made a knight shortly. If not a baron. I was awaiting the call.

The wretch returned that had he known I was connected to nobility when I checked into his hotel, he would have demanded his money in advance. And, without more ado, he ejected me into the street.

Chapter Eleven

A dark and stormy night in a Royal Park;
back to basics; the genius of the English, yet again revealed;
Her Majesty — her story; the last safari

Nightfall found me, seated on a bench in the Royal Park called Green, watching a crowd of ducks squabble gently. I had been there for hours. My hunger was growing and something more than hunger — impatience. I had come to this place because it was perfectly placed for my final assault.

The gates of the park were closing. One by one the last of the loiterers slipped away. A group of youths I had watched earlier, as they removed their shirts and stretched out on the grass in the watery sun, were now pulling them over their maggoty-pale bodies. I noticed that the sun had caught only the vulnerable part of them, the national nakedness, and turned it to the mottled pink of the fleshy pods of the clapper bush; each young man flew the familiar flag of the English when they visit the Countries of the Sun, a red neck.

Last to leave the park were several gentlemen in long coats who had spent their time strolling up and down with their hands in their pockets. I had taken them for philosophers. Until a woman approached and I saw them, suddenly and expertly, open their coats. To my astonishment I spied that they were quite undone. One had the strong impression that this was an age-old custom. Red necks and exposure; these rites had probably been taking place in English parks for centuries. The woman on the receiving end of the unexpected manoeuvre screamed and hurried from the park. But no one seemed (or cared) to notice.

The park emptied. The gates were locked, leaving the world to darkness and to me. Beside the lake I built a shelter of willow branches; with fire sticks from my quiver I started a small, discreet blaze. I consulted my hunger. I studied the ducks. My cardboard suitcase abandoned, my precious gifts for Her Majesty lost, reduced to nothing more than a few last coins from the Farebrother donation, I cut a very sorry figure for the ambassador of the Red People about to present his credentials to the Queen of England.

I found myself hungering for the land I had left behind me: for gemsbok cucumbers, salt yet sweet; brandybush berries; and the woody delights of the Kalahari truffle that grows when the rains have been fat.

The rain began falling, yet it did not break the drought in my heart. This may have been the weather the cuckoo likes, but I could not say the same. I thought bitterly, what good is a shower of blessings upon atheists?

Too much water is never good; it sends people mad. !Kwha gave his creatures dry seasons, deserts, thirsts, so that they should ache for the love of the All-High and pray for his gift, the sweet she-rain to fall and make all below grow fat and moist. For everything God loves is wet.

In my country when it rains all creatures pray, for then all the world is holy. The green succulents step closer to the edge of the old dam that has not seen water in living memory. After the rains the replenished dam sends streams of water down the cracked, weed-choked stone channels no one has cleaned in years into the peach orchard, where the fruit, heavy on the boughs, aches to be picked, as cows with swollen udders groan to be milked. The little half-frogs, with tails between their legs, that are also the rain's things, lie just beneath the surface of the water, eyeing water-spiders and flies that come for their first taste of life in a burning world. And, in the reeds, the black duck clears his throat. Once, twice. And coughs. Reeds that have had to live all their lives with their ankles in dust are suddenly up to their waists in water, and stand shaking their hair in delight, like girls bathing before weddings.

But in England their rain means nothing to them; they consider it merely water. What heresy! Windmills make water; clouds make water; man makes water. But only God makes rain. Blessed be the name of !Kwha.

If ever one of mine should read these lines, they should think this of me; there is a corner of some foreign field that is for ever Bushmanland.

A dinner of ducks roasted over a discreet fire. A shelter of willow branches. A hollow for my hips, lined with down. Then I laid me down to sleep. I turned to the east, as we do, at the very last; I watched as the moon began the nightly hunt through the dark fields of Heaven. Then I called on the High God by his seven holy names.

> Come to my help. See your child is hungry.
> Your child sets off into the bush.

> Help him to find an animal, even one dead,
> Which he can carry home to his hut,
> And live in your sun for another day.

I slept as I imagine one will sleep at the last, when the after-world awaits, a land – it is said – of locusts and honey. Those of my family, knowing that water and melons and meat cannot last, will build me a shelter against wind and sand and hyena and, leaving what little they can in the way of wild onions and brandybush berries, slip away for ever.

I awoke to find on my cheek the warm touch of a miracle. The sky was high, dry and blue; the sun blazed; it was the finest hunting weather I had known since arriving in England. The High God heard my prayer; he whispered in my ear the old truth: 'If the hunter does not go into the bush, how will Kaggen find him meat?'

And I knew shame. Was I not a Man of Men? A Red Man? A Man of the First People? The happy recipient of a culture so ancient it remembers the Early Times when animals were still people and all life slept together beneath the Great Tree?

I thought, yes, by George, now I will arise and go now. There is more than one way of frying a locust.

The perimeter wall of the Palace, I saw, was fortified. Barbed wire, and the metal spikes were sown upon the nape of the wall, and I could guess what lay beyond: trip wires and spy cameras. I recognized a system very much like that employed by most of our farmers, who do not move without their walkie-talkies and their Alsatians and their shotguns. Much the same security arrangements as are enjoyed by the Dominee in Lutherburg, who has ringed his

Pastorie with razor wire and searchlights and great notices proclaiming that he enjoys armed protection from the 'Make My Day!' 24-Hour Mobile Firepower Unit. 'Rooting For You! Shooting For You!' The difference, I suppose, being that the Minister in Lutherburg cowers behind his razor wire because he believes his parishioners plot to steal his milk, and tup his wife, and hobble his cattle, and poison his wells. Whereas the Queen of England only protects herself from the love her subjects bear her.

It would be child's play to enter the Palace grounds. But, once inside, would I ever emerge to tell the tale? First of the hunter's rules teaches that however luscious the game, good the spoor, sure the poison and certain the knowledge that the quarry will soon succumb, he must still assess the height of the sun, the strength of his legs, the time elapsed since his last meal, the distance home to his campsite before moon rise and lion roar. A wise hunter will therefore forgo the loveliest eland, the most succulent giraffe's child he has stalked for days, even if at last within bow-shot, and turn for home, knowing that another step is one too far, that to continue the hunt may see him well fed by nightfall but dead by the following noon.

Another way must be found.

Before the Palace lies a little island around which the traffic prowls day and night, often striking down those who attempt the crossing. The island is sanctified, it seems, by its proximity to the Palace and the great gates and the soldiers in their black hats and red coats. In this sacred place the devotees assemble, hoping for a glimpse of the Sovereign.

On the island I saw something that signified the gods were with me. For there was a golden statue of the Empress, none other than the Old Auntie with Diamonds in Her Hair, and she lifted her hand to me as if to say, 'Come,

David Mungo Booi, and all my children of the Far Karoo. Clamber, as these visitors do, into my lap.'

Without hesitating, I flung myself into the traffic and ran for the island.

I was received amongst the pilgrims gathered there without surprise. That a short, semi-naked man, wearing not much more than a big brown hat, bow and quiver, should be so easily accepted was as happy as it was unexpected. The dress and bearing of these people, each in its own way, was as individual as mine. Silken sheaths and conical hats; sandals and bangles and painted foreheads; a rainbow of robes, shift, smocks and pantaloons; a feast of bright eyes; a fluttering of excited hands; a stew of tongues; a warm humming hive of visitors. Mostly Children of the Sun, with here and there a foreigner from one of the mainland tribes, but not a single native to be seen in all that chirruping, excited island population.

Suddenly a fever swept the pilgrims on our island, a vision, a dream, a wild belief that they were permitted to enter the Palace, that now was the hour! Before I could advise them that the Palace was, and would be, barred to the likes of us, these enthusiasts produced tiny paper Union flags and, waving them like talismans to protect them from the killer traffic stalking their island, they flung themselves into the thick of it, carrying me in their mad stampede. I felt sure, if not of death in the traffic, then of certain disappointment.

Yet we made the Royal Pavement safely. We turned to the left and ran along the Royal Iron Railings that front the Palace yard. We came to a Royal Gate in the railings, and behold the gate was wide! My wonder grew with every step. And beyond the gate, lo, a Royal Door opened into the very Palace itself. My heart was sounding as loudly as the rattles tied to the knees of those who celebrate the Trance Dance. Surely, now, I thought, we will be stopped and turned away? And there stepped into our path an officer of the Crown, raising his hand and bringing our charge to a halt.

So near and yet so far! My companions, however, paid no attention to my sorrow. Quickly they formed an orderly line, and the officer walked along the line, taking money from each, and I assumed that we were being fined for trespassing on Royal Property.

But when I saw my friends being ushered into the Palace, the scales fell from my eyes. This was not a fine they were paying; it was a fee!

What pains I might have saved myself had I begun at the Palace with a pocket full of money! I had endured the most exhausting trials; been detained at Her Majesty's Pleasure; dropped on my head; saved by a flying Bishop; assailed in the Mother of All Parliaments; collected by the Lord of Goodlove Castle; experimented upon by his wife-lings. I had nearly been knighted; assaulted by football fans; and locked up with lunatics.

Yet the answer I sought had been, all along, as plain as the duiker's footprint in river sand, as obvious as the perfume of the lynx, as simple as snaring the bustard – I had merely to pay a fee at the Palace door.

Simple. Straightforward. Common sense. Like everything from Tiny Alma to putting a question in Parliament. The spirit of the grocer prevailed. There was nothing that was not on the market.

Let those who look askance at this sublime pragmatism consider the magnificent old public washrooms in Luther-burg. When we come to town on pension day and wish to avail ourselves of the facilities, we must first put a coin in the slot. Do those who obtain relief, at a price, feel any worse for doing so? And are the Lutherburg washrooms, with their majestic sea-green tiles, their gleaming copper pipes and their genuine neon lamps, any less grand for being supported in this fashion? Well, then, why should the principle of individual contributions to public works not serve kings as well as commoners?

So it was, at last, that I stepped into the Palace. All it took were the coins I carried in my apron pocket, the last of ex-Bishop Farebrother's donation to the developing world. Giving them up brought me double pleasure. Both entrance and relief — for how heavily they had thudded against my tender parts with every step I took.

On entering the Royal Apartments among the excited herd, the first thing to strike me was that the Sovereign had adapted our method of game control. But whereas we preferred a line of wooden stakes, each flagged with a fluttering ostrich plume, between which the herd of buck moved in docile lines towards the buried pitfalls, dug deep and covered with grass to conceal the long drop on to the sharpened stakes, the Monarch operated a system of guide ropes to direct her visitors and ensure they did not stray.

In the first of the apartments we gazed in wonder, expecting, I suppose, some early signs of Royalty, if only an equerry, a chamberlain, a beefeater a knight or a lady-in-waiting. But it was quite empty except for large plush chairs and sofas, and white-face clocks that muttered to themselves like women chipping eggshell for bracelets. Here and there, on polished tables, stood bowls of fruit, carved from wood cunningly painted and very beautiful (for they had been great carvers until they laid low their forests).

In general I would say that the Royal Furnishings were every bit as opulent as those of the 'Best Price' Burial

Society, whose showrooms I have visited in Zwingli – without, of course, the plastic floral wreathes of pink roses and Namaqualand daisies.

The only sign of human habitation were a number of mannequins standing in dark corners, whom I took at first to be pages. On closer inspection they proved to be statues of little black boys, barefoot, with red lips and wide white eyes, half-naked, holding candles or bowls of fruit. No doubt they were intended, these little frozen pages, to remind the Sovereign of her extended family, the Children of the Sun, across the seas.

I turned my eyes this way and that, sure that the gracious Sovereign would be with us at any moment. Great stiff portraits, by which their painters signified the sitters to be both Royal and dead, looked down their waxen noses at our party as we moved from apartment to apartment. It must be soon, I thought. A roll of drums, a flourish of trumpets. Suddenly we would be urged to prostrate ourselves for the arrival of the Queen of England.

But she did not come. Under flowering lights branching from high ceilings, whose leaves were chips of glass, through caverns measureless to man, we moved in silence.

Like the dreamers who see again in their sleep the long-vanished herds of buck that once thronged the plains, and rise from their beds to try to follow them, so we moved like sleepers ever closer to the pitfall. My brain was beating out the refrain: will it be soon? Will it be now? Will it be she?

But my heart now glimpsed another spoor entirely. What the others did not see I saw, what the others seemed quite unafraid of terrified me; for, with every step, we grew nearer our departure point. If she did not come soon, we would be shepherded out of the back door and into the wilderness.

Still she did not come.

I hung back. I could not do so for long without detection, I knew, but I had suddenly one of those revelations which the gods send their favoured hunters when, sick with hunger, they must decide whether to move on to the next stony, empty, heat-struck hill on a day when not so much as a locust has passed their nose. When the hunter risks all and sees not with his eyes but feels in his heart, in his side, in his hooves, the signals of approaching game, long before it appears, feels its breath in his lungs, its fur on his nape. I knew in my heart that *she* was close! At any moment she might appear.

Once again, I was mistaken. I had assumed a welcoming presence. I had believed that in buying a ticket to the Palace I was assured of a Royal meeting, or at least a greeting. And so did the other foreign pilgrims. For otherwise it seemed that our money had been taken under false pretences. But I began to see that this was to confuse our ideas of honour with those of a very different culture, for which the idea that you got what you paid for was lacking in grace and subtlety. The Sovereign existed, for most of her subjects, in rare sightings and distant glimpses; many had never seen her at all. Her corporeal presence was not at issue. She was more a form of faith. A foreigner might object, saying, 'But she's not there!' Yet that would be to miss the point. In her very absence she was present. And the English, quite properly, felt that if it was good enough for them, it was good enough for everyone else.

It was no longer good enough for me. As so often in the past, my hunting skills came to my aid. From each bowl of fruit we passed I removed a single item, a pear, an apple, a toothsome peach, and hid them beneath the crown of my tawny hat. The ostrich-hunter who plans to catch that sober bird will disguise himself in her plumage; he will wait for the brooding mother to leave her eggs and take a little walk in the veld. Sitting very still on her eggs beneath his cap of becreeping feathers, he is indistinguishable from the true bird. His arrow at the ready, he waits for her return.

Just so. As the departing herd wound slowly between the guide ropes towards the exit, I slipped under the ropes and melted into a darkened corner, where I took off my hat and extended my right arm. Then I grew very still. They have very poor eyesight, and virtually no sense of smell; my ruse, I felt sure, would not be noted. As I stiffened into immobility, in the shadowy corner, I had become just another little black pageboy, arm outstretched, proffering a bowl of fruit. Bowing – and I think Beth would have approved – but not scraping.

How long did I wait? I cannot be sure. All day long troops of visitors, the greater and the lesser deceived, migrated through the royal apartments, along tightly controlled game trials, eyes searching for a glimpse of their desired quarry, gasped at the chilly, empty magnificence and departed – disappointed. So lifelike was my camouflage that no one paid any particular attention to me, except a mother who reminded her child to be grateful, for there stood a member of some tribe so poor they used their hats for plates.

Evening fell slowly, in the unwilling English manner, and I heard the Palace doors begin closing, one by one. This was just as I had suspected; after all, I knew that the public washrooms in Zwingli close their doors at sunset, and great ventures resemble each other. Keys turned in locks; visitors came no more. Silence returned abruptly, just as it does when the swallows, those creatures of the rain, who dance on their tails in the evening air, feeding on insects we cannot see, suddenly at sunset vanish with the dying light.

Grateful for a chance, at last, to relieve the cramp that had built up in my forearm after hours of motionless hat-bearing, I was rubbing my muscles when I became aware of footsteps approaching, and there entered the room a chambermaid, carrying a kind of flywhisk, being a short stick surmounted with feathers, which she used for dispersing dust. With many a sigh, she busied herself tidying away the litter left by the departing visitors, stooping to retrieve sweet wrappers, wiping fingerprints from picture-frames, plumping up the pillows on gilded chairs where I knew none had sat, since across each seat stretched a length of twine to discourage such liberties.

This busy cleaner now crossed to me and, to my alarm, began vigorously dabbing her feather stick into every crack of me: my nose, my mouth, my armpits. The vexatious plumes descended lower and lower until I thought my composure should shatter when suddenly my blood froze, I felt no more the feathers' furious fingers. Her face! Perhaps in years it was a little more advanced, and a trifle more careworn, but the features were unmistakably those painted on the Coronation mug I had been shown at the inaugural meeting of the Society for Promoting the Exploration of the Interior Parts of England, in what now seemed several lifetimes before.

She wore a Royal-blue housecoat. Emblazoned on the breast pocket was a golden lion and unicorn fighting for the crown. Her hair was tied up in a headscarf, and when she spoke the tail of the scarf lifted as a wagtail's feathers do when it sprints across the grass.

Perhaps I started? Who can say? At any rate she abruptly

stopped dabbing at me with the infuriating feathers, pressed her ear to my chest for a moment, leapt back a step or two, very slowly retreated to the window and then, in a moment I shall savour for the rest of my life, the Queen of England addressed her loyal servant, David Mungo Booi.

Her voice, I should say, was regal; being high, small and taut like fencing wire, bending under the pressure of her queenly enunciation, it resembled the cry of the fish-eagle.

If I had come about taxes – Her Majesty declared – I was wasting my time. She had paid what she could. I would not get blood from a stone.

I said I had not come about taxes.

She put down her duster. Had I come to tell her that another of her Palaces was on fire? Well, she had this to say. Let it burn! She had only recently effected for repairs to a burnt Palace;* every tapestry, suit of armour, picture, she had paid to have restored without a penny from the public purse and precious little sympathy from her subjects. Despite appearances to the contrary, she was not made of money.

I expressed the hope that her Palaces would endure for a thousand years.

In that case, said the Monarch wearily, there could be only one explanation for my visit. What had her children done now? Hanky-panky? Kiss-and-tell? Secret phone calls? Bare-breasted shenanigans? Well, she was just not, repeat *not*, interested. And I would not have a penny from her. The royal offspring were old enough and ugly enough to look after themselves. Enough was enough!

I said I wished her family nothing but long life and many children.

---

* Presumably Windsor Palace.

I thought she rather flinched at this and I hastened to reassure her that my embassy had nothing to do with the matters she had been kind enough to mention; rather, it was my privilege to come to her as the first ambassador of her loyal Red People.

Her manner changed remarkably now. Declaring this to be fascinating news, and taking a little pair of silver scissors from her handbag, she snipped the white tape that protected the chairs and, patting a seat, pink as sunset and deep as an elephant's yawn, she invited me to sit beside her and tell her where in her former empire her Red People resided.

Back in the ages when my people *were*, I replied, we lived in the north-western reaches of the Cape Province of South Africa.

Cries of delighted recognition greeted my reply. She too had been to the Cape. And it was in the Cape that her great-great-grandmother had fought the 'Bores'. (Her tongue had difficulty – as ours does – in saying the names of our enemies, the Boers.) Her family had happy memories of these fellows, as they did of all the peoples they had fought and crushed. She had met several Bores while on her visit to my country as a young princess. Sadly, she had not met any of my Red People, who, she was sure, were absolutely fascinating.

She had a great gift for making one feel oneself to be the centre of her undivided attention. Her comments, warm and flowing, effortlessly relieved one of the responsibility of saying anything in reply. She pronounced herself absolutely delighted to meet a Red Man who could tell her more about the tremendous advances in my country. The black chaps and the Bores had hated one another, had they not? Yet now they were the best of chums. Wasn't that tremendously encouraging? And soon, she heard, everyone would be living in houses with four bedrooms and free telephones. Wouldn't that be tremendous encouragement to the rest of the world? She could not imagine how I had managed to tear myself away. How very, very touched she was by my gift of a hatful of fruit.

Did I plan to stay long in England? And had I brought other gifts, for her royal collections?

My answer dried in my mouth; the memory, still so raw, of my lost suitcase, and its treasures, assembled with such devotion by my trusting people, cut me to the quick.

What I had brought, I said, was a great gift of her great-great-grandmother to my people. What I had lost, alas, were the gifts of my people to Her Majesty.

I listed the treasures I had hoped to lay at her feet: a bow of the finest *gharree* wood, strung with sinew cut from the eland's hide; reed arrows, beautifully light, their heads of flint and iron bound with grass; a pair of ceremonial firesticks, so ancient it is said they were made in the First Times, when animals were still people, and had belonged to Kaggen himself; and the chief of music; the singing string, the Bushman fiddle, called the *gorah*, whose song is as sweet as she-rain after long drought; a rich necklace of ostrich-shell beads, threaded with ant-bear hair, fit for a royal throat; and two dozen copper leg-bangles that women prize: three of the choicest poisons in the world; as well as hides, honey and cups of tortoise shell.

Lowering her voice, she urged me to think no more of my loss. What she was about to confide was not to go beyond the palace walls – but my lack of native gifts came as a relief.

Mr Booi, murmured the Sovereign, we own more mummies, bottled infants, golden death masks, pickled hearts, Attic marbles, sacred phalluses from a dozen extinct tribes than we know what to do with. Not to mention axeheads, arrowheads, maidenheads, shrunken heads, assegais, wampum belts, *khukris*, feathered headdresses, jade daggers and assorted yellow idols, saved from their owners' ignorance and brought home for safekeeping, often at great expense, in our Royal Museums.

It had been the enlightened policy of her missionaries, she graciously explained, and her explorers, soldiers and traders, to remove native artefacts to England, where they might properly be appreciated. That policy had been all very well at the time. But unscrupulous peoples, she feared, had taken advantage of this enlightened policy by encouraging her missionaries, explorers, soldiers and traders to take entire temples and tombs home with them.

Such objects were all tremendously interesting, of course, but those who had forced on her representatives tomb and temple, and seen them crated home to England, had not thought about costs. Now, had they? Frankly, if she saw another shrunken head, she'd scream. And who was expected to pay for it? In reply she tapped the Royal Breast with her wand of feathers.

Her collection of flora and fauna, arrows and earrings, from distant, darker parts of the globe were the envy of the civilized world, but the wretched things were frightfully delicate, and (between herself, myself and the gatepost) not always very well put together. They travelled so badly. Then the mist and the damp ravaged them, and they fell apart as soon as one looked at them.

Since – blessedly, then – I had not added to her Royal Collections, what had I brought her?

Opening my quiver, I took from it the Paper Promise of the Old Auntie with Diamonds in Her Hair, and read it aloud:

'We, Victoria, by the Grace of God, of the United
Kingdom of Great Britain and Ireland, Queen, Defender
of the Faith, Empress of India, to Our Trusty and well-
beloved San People, of the Cape Karoo, Greetings. We,
reposing special Trust and Confidence in your Loyalty,
Courage and Good Conduct, do by these Presents
Constitute and Appoint you to be a Favoured Nation and
send you Our Sign of Friendship – wherever you are.
From the Snow Mountains to the Sourveld. From the
Cape even to the Kalahari. Assuring you of Our Patronage
and Protection in Perpetuity. Like a Lioness her whelps,
so do We, Queen and Empress, draw Our Red People
to Our Bosom. Let no one molest or scatter them.'

Her Majesty listened intently, nodding her head from time
to time when she recognized a phrase. At the end she
said, yes, that was Great-Great-Granny's Promise. Make no
mistake.

My heart was glad to hear it. Dropping to one knee, I
beseeched her to make good her great ancestor's promise
to her well-beloved San people. For indeed we had been
molested. We had been scattered. My people were crying.
They cried to the Great She-Elephant for help. Either to
ride to their rescue or to let them come to her, where they
might crouch like ants beneath her generous ears, guarded
by her tusks. And let her stamp to death our enemies
beneath her great feet.

She gave a wan smile. The Old She-Elephant was no
longer what she had been. She took her tusks out at night;
her great ears were torn; and she stood on her feet, all day
long, and they were in no condition to stamp anyone to
death. More was the pity!

As for the Promises passed out by the Queen Empress,

well, she would like to show me something. With that she rose to her feet and crossed to a cupboard, opened it and there spilled on to the carpet roll after roll of parchment bound in ribbon, emblazoned with great red wax seals. All of them, every last one, cried Her Majesty, another promise to another far-flung people. Picking up one at random, she settled a pair of glasses on her nose and read aloud:

'As we looked after you then, I beseech you, please look after your subjects now. Show us you are prepared to spill your blood for us – your Maori people.'

What could one expect, after one's relatives had dished out Paper Promises all over the world, as if there were no tomorrow? Well, today *was* tomorrow. And the sooner far-flung nations in the back of beyond recognized it, the better. Some recipients of dear Great-Great-Grandmama's Promises often made very unreasonable demands. One of her ancestors had dispatched a sea captain to discover these very supplicants, and they had repaid the Royal Kindness by killing and eating the Royal Ambassador. If they were not eating visitors, then they were eating each other. And now they were calling on her to spill blood!

Children! For all their war paint and the funny faces they pulled. When they did not get their own way, they were quite impossible! A great fuss followed by a sad case of the sulks; and then they thought nothing of lifting grass skirts and presenting their naked BTMs to all and sundry. On her last royal visit, posteriors had dominated every walk-about. It did not strengthen a relationship if you began by eating the Queen's representative and ended by mooning at her when she took the trouble to visit you.

And, anyway, the shedding of blood was no longer in

her gift. Normally one would have sent soldiers to do that. But now English custom demanded that the shedding of blood, wherever possible, should be left to others.

She was terribly sorry to hear that all was not well between the Red People and the Bores – particularly since they had seemed to be patching things up. But sending troops was just not on. Peace talks would be the most sensible thing. Perhaps one of her officials might act as intermediary and coax us to the peace table?

I said I was sorry, but that was not possible. Did the wild hare converse with the iron hook that rips out its throat?

The Monarch considered this and then munificently suggested that Her Government send a plane to drop food parcels on our remote villages and hamlets. She understood that this was increasingly the popular way of lending assistance in foreign conflicts in which one had no desire to become involved.

Alas, said I, my people did not live in villages; we moved continually in search of chance employment as fence-menders, hunters, tinkers, sheep-shearers, trappers.

Her Majesty now began to show small signs of vexation. If people could not be relied on to remain in one place but went walkabout at the drop of a hat, then they should not be surprised if the major powers did not shower food parcels on them. Aircraft cost the earth. Her own Royal Flight was seldom in the skies these days. Did I know that even her Royal Yacht was to be taken away? An elderly craft which rolled badly in heavy swells but had given sterling service as well as providing less fortunate people in far-flung places with a glimpse of luxury they might otherwise never have seen. If those who planned this destruction could have seen the pleasure on the faces of simple people, as we steamed into some foreign port, they would think twice about scuttling our yacht.

But then her own people, she feared, had a positive genius for wrecking the very things they did best. Under pressure from impudent upstarts from distant lands, her deluded subjects were turning their backs on the sacred trinity that had made England great: Queen, Church, Currency.

Had I seen the paying guests traipsing through her Palace? Did I imagine she liked strangers in her home? And the mess they left behind?

But we ask you, Mr Booi, she said, gazing at me over her spectacles, what option does one have? How else are we to earn funds for our horribly depleted Treasury? We sweep and scrub and clear up after the visitors. Who else is going to do it for us?

Now she offered a gracious apology for mistaking me for a tax inspector. They had made her life a misery, sneaking in and totting up her riches and demanding she cough up, as they put it, her share of taxes. What riches? Had I any idea how much she spent repairing gutted Palaces, plus the hideous costs of maintaining her children, plus free housing for dozens of staff who had ideas not just above their stations but above hers as well? Had I any idea what a decent page cost? Or a brace of heralds? How hard she had tried to cut back on staff? Yet even now people complained and carped. The lowliest page threatened to go to the tax people. The very soldiers in their sentry boxes demanded that she pay their fox-hunting fees – it drove her into a slough of despond, a *vita horribilis*!

And now there was talk of evicting her from her home and sending her to live in a ghastly modern barn, resembling, no doubt, some hideous municipal public outhouse known as a People's Palace.

As springs bubble up out of sandy riverbeds where a moment before there has been no sign of water, two majestic globules rose somewhere in the deep wells of the Royal Eyes and ran down the proud cheeks in two straight lines, passing on either side of her thin nose and rather pinched lips. What discipline they showed! As if they knew – those regal tears – that they were coursing down the face of the Queen of England, two soldiers on parade, determined to put their best feet forward.

And then, with an offer which melted my heart, she dried her tears with the quiet observation that she would do her duty, however sharp the serpent's tooth of ingratitude. She insisted I join her in a cup of tea. She slipped off into the silent, darkened palace, apologizing for the gloom, but electricity was simply too expensive; I heard her fumbling down shadowy corridors, stumbling every so often as she collided with an escritoire, a commode or some other item of priceless furniture.

She was back, a few minutes later, carrying two steaming mugs of tea. All her fine china had been sold off, along with the royal silver. Even this line of royal merchandise, destined for the gift shop, where paying visitors snapped up souvenirs of their visit, had proved quite useless. The royal offspring, she explained, were given to separating or remarrying so unexpectedly that nuptial mugs were no sooner painted than they were out of date. The royal cellars were crammed with discontinued marital lines she could not sell for love or money.

Did the Red People, she wondered, also have large families?

Only when food supplies permitted, I explained. We had children in order to provide hunters as well as for the love and comfort they gave, especially when we grew old.

But when food was scarce and a baby was born, the mother might disappear into the bush with her new-born infant and return alone. Everyone understood what had happened; the child had been, as we said, 'thrown down'.

She allowed that this seemed to her a jolly sensible arrangement, and sighed so that I thought her heart must break.

Now it was that !Kwha opened my eyes. When we hunt the eland, its trail grows weary after a few days, and we know then the poison had begun its deadly work; the blood shows thicker on the grass and soon we come across the beast, lying on its side, its great dewlap quivering, trembling and sweating in the throes of death as the poison works its way from its hooves to its brain, and the power goes out from the creature, and we say that his N!ow is deserting him. That power which is found in the giraffe and the gemsbok, in the *kudu*, in the wildebeest and harte-beest, and all the creatures. They give up their N!ow and it goes to Heaven, to the gods who send the rain. So the power of this once great Queen was assuredly going back to whatever gods, in their now long-forgotten past, had once smiled on this disconsolate race.

I saw before me an elderly lady in a headscarf, peering uncertainly at the world through a pair of thick spectacles, sipping a mug of cooling tea in a dark room. And I spoke in my heart this question: should the destruction of a Queen be any less tragic than the dying of the eland?

For what was Her Majesty but a member of a rare species? Whose natural habitat was being destroyed. Who faced prodigious odds in her struggle to preserve her ancient rites and customs. Royal numbers dwindled year by year, the few survivors of her line were harried from pillar to post. Her family band – attacked on all sides – faced a fate as cruel as anything we knew in the Karoo. After all, we had our donkeys at least. We had our zincs with which to build our overnight shelters. We had the sharp wind to lash us onward and a road that ran right into the horizon, along which we moved as we chose, when our blood was up and it was time to trek, asking nothing of anyone. Shearing done, fence poles sunk, goats slaughtered for a meal, and the five-man-can of sweet white wine, attended by its single cup, moving round the circle, pulling on black tobacco, we would dance until the white light came, and the dust itself sprang to its feet and danced beside us.

What had this poor woman to compare with that?

An idea took hold of me in the way the flames take hold of the candlebush on an inky night and it burns brighter than the evening star. For it took one to know one. But if our situation was bad, hers was infinitely worse.

I put down my mug; I doffed my hat, and, sinking now to both knees, I address her thus.

Having seen how she and her family band had been molested and scattered, I could not but ask: if this was the way people of England treated their Queen, did they deserve her? Therefore I, David Mungo Booi, appointed representative of the Red People, formally offered her safe refuge and asylum in our lands.

We would build for her a Royal Hut on the banks of the Riet River, where all the maps and all the missionaries agreed there has been since the beginning the place called Bushmanland. From the First Times, when the animals were still people, ages before the coming of the visitors who stole our land.

Installed in her great place, with her firesticks she would kindle the first fire outside the hut and it would burn in the hearts of her Red People. And then all the travelling bands, now so long dispersed into the hot country and the high country and the far places, would come to take embers from the royal fire with which to kindle their own. All the Red People: the wanderers of the Karoo, the people of the Kalahari, Caprivi, Okavango and Angola; the People of the Soft Sand, the People who follow the Eland; the People from the East; the River Bushmen; the Basarwa and the Remote-area Dwellers of the deserts of Botswana. Not forgetting the ≠Haba; the G//ana; the !Kung; the G/wi; the !Xo. And she would be our headwoman.

We would sit by her fire.

We would listen to her stories late into the night.

We would play the foot bow and the mouth bow, the thumb piano and the one-string Bushman fiddle.

We would fight to ensure she did not go the way of the quagga, the black-maned lion and the wild horse.

And at her royal camp, near the place called Canarvon, named for one who had been her relation, and not far from Calvinia, named for one who had been close to God, there would be singing and dancing until the dust danced with us and the world would know that, for the first time, the Bushmen had a Queen. And we would revere her until the end of time, even as her own people did not.

It was while still on my knees that I heard behind me hurrying footsteps, and into the room strode a quick fierce man carrying a riding crop. His hair had faded to the dull gleam of the golden double-daisy after cows have eaten it and their milk is already turning sour. He wore jodhpurs; he slapped the riding crop frequently against the side of his breeches with the flat retort of a rifle echoing across the veld when the Boers are shooting our springbuck.

The look of tender dismay that spread across the Sovereign's face told me at once that this person belonged to her family circle. It was also perfectly plain that she struggled to maintain her regal calm in the peppery presence of this quivery, irritable, sharp, barking man, who was now demanding, in a little voice, not unlike that of the jackal when it scents young lambs in the veld, to know if I was some sort of Chinese chappy.

Rising to my feet and replacing my hat, I replied that I was an ambassador of the Red People.

Was I not rather too yellow to claim that colour? came the response. And why the slitty eyes? Not another bloody foreign honour guard? He touched a flat hand to the bridge of his noble nose, saying he had had them 'up to here'. More odd-bods from the four corners than he'd had hot breakfasts; little nippy wallahs with wavy knives; also blokes who'd barely taken the bones out of their noses or stopped eating their cousins; not to mention painted chappies from unpronounceable places who sported the most disgusting engine cowlings over their primary bits and pieces. Queuing up to clatter around the Palace courtyard. Didn't matter much any more – if only the poor buggers had known. There would soon be no one left to guard. Her Majesty was surrounded by enemies. They picked off her relatives one by one. Attacked their hunting rites. Jeered at their marriages. The great panjandrums of the press, not to mention the weasels among her Ministers; all determined to sink the greatest Royal House in the world.

Addressing the Sovereign directly, he asked if it was any wonder that so many of their family had gone to pot. Made foolish marriages. Tried to pass themselves off as entertainers, architects, photographers, even – God help him – soldiers or sailors. Anything at all but heirs to the bloody throne! Descendants of the great George and his Dragon, of Arthur, of Harold, of Hengist, not to mention

Cnut. What good was I, then, ambassador of the Red People? Red, green or yellow – it was yet another damn honour-guard of slitty-eyed pygmies wearing funny hats and not much else getting ready to slam the stable door after the horse had bolted. Unless something was done, and done pretty bloody chop-chop, she could kiss her throne goodbye; and she had that from the horse's mouth.

She lifted her nose as though assailed by the rank perfume of that noxious shrub we call the dog-shit-and-piss-bush. When she replied, it was to introduce this individual as the Royal Consort; the Royal Upper Lip was as stiff as a bowstring.

David Mungo Booi, she informed her Consort, hailed from the far Northern Cape, where I had been cruelly oppressed by the Bores. She had found more wisdom in my little yellow person than in a number of people she could mention who had had far greater privileges. And enjoyed a far higher level of sophistication. In the first place, I understood entirely the threat posed to the survival of her family band. I was prepared to stand by her side and fight against the destruction of her natural habitat. I was amongst the few people in the world who did not wish to see her go the way of the quagga, or the wild horse, or the black-maned Lion. I had offered more than mere words; I had pledged an honour-guard of brave San hunters. And I had offered her asylum in far-away Bushmanland. A great place of her own, as well as music, dancing and esteem.

That was interesting, her Consort replied – and cracked his whip, several times – for the Monarch. But what of the children, for example? Would they have residence rights on her new estates between Calvinia and Canarvon? She knew how awkward they could be. What would they do all day? And what would he do?

I was happy to reassure him. Younger royal males would learn musical skills, the arts of hunting, the preparation of poisons, the carving of bows, the finding of honey. Females would study how to carry water in ostrich eggs, the science of roots and tubers, healing, dancing, how to shampoo themselves with sheep's fat and *buchu*, and the knowledge of where the tsama melons lay thickest. The Royal Consort would do, as he had always done: consort with the Sovereign, fish, ride and issue advice, offer opinions and give orders wherever he travelled.

This was satisfactory, Her Majesty declared. But before finally severing contacts with her ungrateful subjects and moving Crown, Consort and household to the banks of the Riet River, she would have to go through the proper channels. However, she anticipated little opposition.

At which her Consort nodded agreement – and laughed bitterly. I should make arrangements for their asylum in Bushmanland as soon as possible.

My impatience now was almost ungovernable. I longed to inform my people of the immense privilege about to descend upon them. But one thing remained.

Again I knelt. I had come to England, I told the Monarch, in search of a child: 'Little Boy' Ruyter, stolen from his family by her red-coat soldiers. His family had my solemn promise that I would return with the bones of the stolen child and we would lay them to rest under the Karoo stars.

Once upon a time – Her Majesty replied – there had come into the family possession an aboriginal child of very small stature. This manikin had served first as the great Queen Empress's hunting dog. Then as a chimney sweep. Finally as a nursery jockey. Mounted on one of the Royal Dogs, he raced around the garden to the great amusement of the Royal Children, who loved him almost as much as their favourite pets. When one day he tumbled from the back of a Great Dane, in a particularly exciting race, and broke his neck, the children had been inconsolable for days.

The manikin had been given a state funeral and laid to rest in one or other of her Palaces. Very few foreigners could be said to have risen so far, so fast, in Royal Esteem.

But in which of the Royal Cemeteries did my country-man repose? I asked. Each of her Palaces might have such a graveyard for family pets. And she had many Palaces.

More than they knew what to do with, her Consort confirmed. And a lot of bloody good it did one.

Perhaps the best method, Her Majesty graciously suggested, was to move from Palace to Palace, taking pot luck.

Eeny, meeny, miny, mo, catch a red boy by the toe, sang her Consort, in a surprisingly clear tenor.

I needed only to mention her name, Her Majesty assured me, and to say I had come about the remains of 'Little Boy' Ruyter, the jockey. She would leave instructions that I be permitted to rummage in the gardens of rest to my heart's content. There was just one tiny point of law we should clear up, her Consort interposed. If it could be proved that the child had been stolen, well and good. His remains should then be returned to their rightful owners.

If, however, the Queen continued, her historians could show that her soldiers had paid for the child in beads, copper wire, cowrie shells, fish-hooks or tobacco, then there was no question of returning him: he remained the property of the Crown.

And with that, giving me a gracious smile, she closed her handbag and moved it to the left, as if signifying by this precise gesture that the audience was over. I should not worry about getting in touch with her, she smiled as she rose and offered her hand, because she would be getting in touch with me.

Her Consort, torch in hand, now led me through darkened corridors to a door at the rear of the palace. As I bade him farewell, without warning he shone the torch on to his face and asked me what I saw. Startled, I replied that I saw a fine English gentlemen. He shook his head. No, that was not true. He was, in fact, a foreigner. *Almost* as foreign as I was. Certainly as far from home. Probably a good deal unhappier.

But what then, I stammered in my astonishment, of his jodhpurs and his whip, the cut of his jib, his vowels, his enunciation, even his stiff upper lip? Surely all showed him to be authentically native.

Again, a quick, regretful shake of the high-domed head. He had adopted their colouring. Camouflage. After years of practice he had acquired this protective covering. He had studied their ways; he had learnt that if you would be truly indigenous, you must learn to pull finger, park your pint, get on your bike, call a spade a bloody spade, live for horses, have a bash at Johnny Foreigner. He had done his bit. Belonged to the right clubs, Colonel-in-Chief of a half a dozen bloody regiments, drunk and joshed in the mess, and thrown bread rolls at more regimental dinners than he could remember. Changed his name to something more acceptable, denied his ancestry, forgotten his country, given a lifetime's service to the family firm.

But where had it got him? Had the locals been deceived? Not a bloody bit of it. After years of parking his pint and getting on his bike and calling a spade a bloody spade, he had got precisely nowhere. To his face it was

'Your Royal Highness, this,' and, 'Yes, sir, that' – oh, they were a people for paying lip-service. For bowing and scraping and gongs and ribbons and lords and ladies – but the moment his back was turned, then he was just an out-of-work Johnny Foreigner with an unpronounceable name and disquieting personal habits.

It took one to know one. Precisely because I too was up the creek without a paddle, he offered a word of advice. On no account should I venture near any of his wife's Palaces dressed as I was. Better to forget the entire thing. Forget all about 'Little Boy' Ruyter. Go home to my own people – before it was too late. He foresaw a bad end to my expedition.

I was grateful for his advice, but I could not turn back. I had promised the Ruyter family, and honour required that I keep my promise.

The Queen's Consort sighed. He did understand. Entirely. Like him, I suffered from an exaggerated sense of honour – and a right bugger it was – though, after years of living amongst the natives, his sense of honour was now somewhat attenuated. But I should rest assured that honour would not help me if I ventured very near Windsor dressed in a skin apron and covered in salad oil. I would be taken for an arsonist, a lunatic or a mad dog. And he would not give two pins for my chances. Then, saying he sympathized, as one dago to another, he pressed a purse into my hands. I was to get myself a decent tailor and a decent set of wheels. He insisted on giving me, as well, his riding crop. He told me to keep my head down, and if the Great Unwashed got my scent, I had better pull finger and get the hell out of there, chop-bloody-chop.

I tried to thank him, but he would have none of it. Two oddbods, abroad in darkest England – God help us –

must show some solidarity. And with that he pushed me into the street, clutching his purse in one hand and his whip in the other.

Turning for one last look at the Palace, I saw him leaning against the kitchen door, an elderly, balding, irascible foreigner, far from home, at sea among strangers. I prayed again to the great god !Kwha to direct my footsteps to the grave of the missing child. And, looking up, I saw at an upstairs window a small figure in a headscarf carrying a feather duster, which she raised now, and waved me into the dark.

Postscript

At this point, the journals of David Mungo Booi break off.

The questions that haunted me were: how had the notebooks of David Mungo Booi been repatriated? And where was he now?

One evening I was sitting in the bar of the Hunter's Arms, watching Clara, the owner, being managerial with a couple of drunken farmers who leered happily every time she turned. I understood the interest. She was wearing a new hairpiece, a chestnut shank twisted into heavy, chain-like plaits which flew this way and that, like bell ropes, when she turned her back. In a tight Tyrolean tunic and skirt, embroidered with forget-me-nots, she looked a bit like Heidi. Except for the parabellum holstered at her waist, and the blue UN baseball cap. A present from Jean-Pierre from Geneva. That's why Clara was in Swiss mode; she wanted Jean-Pierre to stay.

But just as she'd failed to get the UN to declare the

Hunter's Arms a protected enclave, she'd got nowhere trying to persuade the UN to extend its mandate in South Africa. They had declared the elections free and fair, and they were pulling out.

The farmers examined her behind with clinical interest. Clara felt it; she spun around, and her blue baseball cap slipped over one eye.

That's when it came to me.

I remembered old Pa Blitzerlik by the fireside as he described to me the woman in the post office who had given him the notebooks. A white woman – in a blue hat. He had sketched with his hand what I taken to be a moon, an arc, a half-circle of air, a curve of such beauty he had never forgotten it.

I checked. It turned out that a certain Elizabeth Farebrother, an Englishwoman, had served as a voluntary electoral observer over in a place called, appropriately enough, Bushman's Fountain in the Murderer's Karoo. The pity was that she had been gone a fortnight. Where she had gone no one could tell me. Volunteers served a term and then signed off. Addresses were never disclosed. But the UN in Geneva would forward letters.

I wrote several times. No reply. I had more or less given up when I got this parcel from England. A plain brown, padded envelope into which had been stuffed, none too carefully, a big brown hat. I knew it at once, of course. A broad crown and three internal pockets, sewn with twine. I noticed a whitish ring around the crown, a kind of tide-mark, as if it had spent some time immersed in water.

In one of the secret pockets I found a note.

As far as she could 'ascertain', Beth Farebrother wrote (strange, that word, 'ascertain' – so apparently scientific, suggesting diligent research, but allowing enough leeway to cover a helpless, stumbling search in the dark), Booi had set off along the Thames. He had not got very far.

She'd seen a television report about an abandoned cart, no driver, found beside the river, near Richmond. Most alarming were the two donkeys, still in harness. The donkeys had not been fed or watered for some days. Several dozen people had offered to adopt them, children had collected money to buy these abandoned beasts an honourable retirement in some donkey refuge. Various animal welfare groups had demanded that the owner of the donkeys be found and prosecuted, not only for deserting the animals: a whip had been found in the cart.

Beth immediately went south and spent some days searching the towns and villages beside the Thames. She got nowhere. The donkeys had been saved, the story was forgotten. She was about to leave when she came across a group of children playing near the river. A small boy was wearing a tawny hat, far too large for him. The children told her they'd had the hat 'from another boy'. They had played a game for it – the game appeared to involve jumping in the water. The 'other boy' had been bad at it, and he had lost his hat. They were vague about what happened next and said the other boy had 'gone away'.

But they had given her the hat. Indeed, they had seemed quite relieved to be rid of it.

One might speculate about his fate, Beth Farebrother wrote, but what good would it do?

But I would like to speculate. What would have happened had things been other? For if you compare the lives of the great explorers, David Mungo Booi does pretty well. He moves through England with just the right amount of ignorance, essential if you are to make headway, and he is relatively kindly and enlightened in his views of the natives.

But compare the deaths of the great explorers, and a crucial difference is revealed. When Booi's namesake, Mungo Park, perished in West Africa nearly two centuries before, his country mounted an expedition to find out what happened to him and to repatriate any relics which might have remained when their man drowned in a river while being attacked by natives. The expedition found his hat, which floated, and his journal which they published.

However, when David Mungo Booi perished at the hands of little savages in England, it was noted only by a woman who had once taken part in the Eland Dance with him; when she returned his notebooks, they were used to make cigarettes, and now she posted back his hat, which, if also returned to his own people, would most likely be used to make a fire.

When his other great namesake, David Livingstone, died in Africa, his heart was buried in the savannah and his body in Westminster Abbey. From what Beth had written, one could speculate that David Mungo Booi had drowned in the Thames. Or, perhaps more accurately, in his own misconceptions of England. His inability to comprehend the true nature of the country through which he passed was no greater than that of his brother explorers in Africa; he shows scant sign of recognizing how bitterly divided it was, given to increasingly irrational and violent hatred, and he seems at the end to have parted company from reality (how else could you explain why a man who knew the tale of Dicky the Donkey harnessed his expedition to a donkey cart!).

There was going to be no great ceremonial laying to rest of his body or his heart. But I did bury his hat. On the road to Zwingli, under an open sky. And I raised a cairn of stones beside it and left this monument with an inscription borrowed from Livingstone's monument in Westminster Abbey, to which holy harbour he was returned by his faithful African servants who pickled his body and sailed home with it.

Above the buried hat I set the inscription:

BROUGHT BY FRIENDLY HANDS
OVER LAND AND SEA
HERE LIES
DAVID MUNGO BOOI
EXPLORER
MISSIONARY
WARRIOR

Khoisan click sounds

The five basic clicks in this (Standard Khoisan) system are given below, together with their traditional labels and descriptions of their method of articulation and their sound.

⊙   Bilabial. A bilabial stop or affricate. Produced by realeasing air between the lips, often as in a kiss. Found only in !Xõ and Southern Bushman languages.

/   Dental. A dental or alveolar affricate (sometimes described as a fricative). Produced by a sucking motion with the tip of the tongue on the teeth, as in English expression of annoyance written 'Tisk, tisk', phonetically [//]. Found in all Khoisan languages.

≠   Alveolar. An Alveolar stop, produced by pulling the blade of the tongue sharply away from the alveolar ridge, immediately behind the teeth. A difficult sound for many people, rather in between / and ! in sound. Found in all Khoisan languages.

//   Lateral. A lateral affricate (sometimes described as a fricative). Produced by placing the tip of tongue on the roof of the mouth (the exact position varies) and releasing air on one side of the mouth between the side of the tongue and the cheek. More simply, the clicking sound film cowboys use, [// //], to make their horses go. Found in all Khoisan languages.

!   Palatal, sometimes called cerebral or retroflex. An alveo-palatal or palatal stop, produced by pulling the tip of the tongue sharply away from the front of the hard palate. When made with lips rounded, it sounds rather like a cork popping from a wine bottle. Found in all Khoisan languages.

From: *Hunters and Herders of Southern Africa*
Alan Barnard
(C.U.P. 1992)

My Mother's Lovers
Christopher Hope

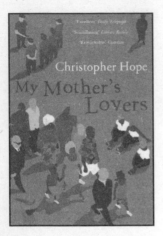

Once it seemed to Kathleen Healey that Africa was empty and all of it belonged to her. An aviator, big game hunter and knitting devotee, she would land her plane wherever and whenever she chose. She was free with her favours too, and her multitude of lovers came from all over the continent.

When Kathleen dies, her only son Alexander returns to Johannesburg to carry out her last wishes. But then he meets Cindy September, and Alexander must confront the final part of his mother's legacy – his capacity for love.

'Hope writes with extraordinary exuberance and invention. His narrative is like one of the great rivers of Africa, carrying everything before it, and dazzling the eyes with its glitter... This powerful, disturbing, scintillating novel confirms me in my view that Hope is one of the dozen best novelists in this country today.' Francis King, *Literary Review*

'Remarkable... Grave and tender, savage and subtle.' Giles Foden, *Guardian*

'Biting, outrageously inventive and peopled with memorable characters.' Paul Hopkins, *Irish Independent*

'Exceptionally funny... Hope's novel is an addictive read.' Brian Martin, *Sunday Telegraph*

'This is a big novel, funny, sad, rumbustious, bitter... just like Africa.' Allan Massie, *Scotsman*

 Atlantic Books
£7.99
ISBN 978 184354 383 1
www.atlantic-books.co.uk